Stonyford Submission III

Also by Bennie Ray Murdock

Stonyford Submission
Stonyford Submission II

Stonyford Submission III

Bennie Ray Murdock

Wagoner Oklahoma

Published by Word Out Books An imprint of AZ Entertainment Group LLC

cover design by AZ Designs

ISBN: 978-1-947035-68-3

For inquiries, including bulk orders of 100 or more, please contact:
AZ Entertainment Group LLC
PO BOX 854
Wagoner, OK 74477-0854

Email: info@az-entertainmentllc.com
Website: www.az-entertainmentllc.com

Printed in the United States of America

Dedicated to Ms. Tracy Powell
one of a kind

CHAPTER ONE

BEFORE OPENING THE DOOR, I once again found myself peering out the front window. I then did the same from both side windows.

I was hoping to see a few staff officials or some other authority from the boys ranch coming to our aid. This was something they normally would have done by now under such conditions.

But, to my surprise, I could see no one coming in our direction from the boys ranch. Not even a car or utility truck in motion. There wasn't a single sign of movement. No vehicles transporting goods or passengers, not even farm equipment traveling along the narrow, winding road that led to the boys ranch from the town of Stonyford.

I could see no movement coming from either direction.

That's when a very strange feeling set in, causing what could only be described as an astonishing amount of paranoia, along with its intense delusions concerning a nonexistent reality.

It felt as though this strange sensation was taking control of the crew's intended destination.

As I stared with my eyes set firmly to my left, I could see a slightly glossy section of the boys ranch off in the distance.

I could also see some of the other helicopters, with a partial view of the pilots and co-pilots. They seemed to be trying to figure out what to do while making sure all the power was turned off in their craft.

I then once again attempted to make contact with everyone I could using the transmitter.

"Pee-wee, Cat, Midwest, MacDonald, Knucklehead and Commander," I called out. "You guys copy?"

At first, the only thing that could be heard was the usual electrical charging sounds and the same high-pitched static that had earlier been occurring nonstop, obstructing any form of communication. But now, the radio receiver and transmitter seemed to be changing to a clearer pitch. It was as though the interference had faded, creating less noise and finally allowing our voices to be heard over the transmission.

Click! Click! Click!

Click! Click! Click!

At first, all I could hear was the clicking. But now, the voices of the crew came through. The electrical elements that had once prevented us from communicating with each other on the transmitter had apparently subsided. Even the instrument panel itself seemed to recover from whatever had caused the failure and was returning to normal.

"Pee-wee, Cat, Midwest, MacDonald, Knucklehead and Commander," I again called out. "Do you guys copy?"

"Pee-wee, copy!" he finally said.

"Cat, copy," he said with a chuckle.

"Midwest, copy!"

"MacDonald, copy!"

"Knucklehead, copy!" he added with a slight giggle.

"Commander here, sir. I copy, loud and clear."

"All right, then. Welcome back, everybody," I said. "I'm sure you're just as curious as I am about whatever that situation was all about. But now it's time to check everything out and find out what's really going on at this junction. And before I forget to remind you guys, make sure you continue to keep a close watch on each other from this point forward.

"And another thing. However we landed, I'm just as lost and confused as you are, but as I was saying, it's time to find out what's really going on around here."

Before opening the door, I realized I needed to tell everyone to check the air quality and how important it was for them to take full advantage of the emergency respirators already onboard each of the helicopters.

The respirators were there for emergencies like the one we were about to venture into at the boys ranch.

I said, "Guys, use the emergency respirators onboard your craft to protect against any type of virus around here. There could also be some poisonous air pockets around here. There could even be something far more dangerous than the coronavirus. So please, you guys, don't be acting foolish when it comes to your health."

I cautiously unlocked the captain's door on the helicopter. To my surprise, I found the same quietness outside the craft that could oddly be felt inside.

I could see nothing on the surface of the craft that showed any sign of damage. The only thing I noticed was a small amount of liquid that had formed on the body surface of the helicopter and its blades.

It really wasn't all that uncommon to see this kind of substance on the blades, especially during the early morning hours when everything is subjected to atmospheric moisture in the air. This kind of moisture can form on any craft, both during landing and takeoff.

There was also quite a bit of bird matter spattered across the blades. This also often appeared on the craft's body surface. It wasn't unusual and happened even while in flight.

In the distance, I could partially see through a clearing in the fog-like cloud that had been obscuring our visibility. The cloud-like substance seemed intentional in the way it hindered our progress, like a discourteous obstacle placed in our path. I couldn't help but think that it had played a major role in creating the tense confusion that had bewildered the entire crew.

Although it was early evening, not early morning as I had first thought, it was still surprising to see the liquid substance forming not only on the blades of each of our crafts, but across the entire surface. Whatever the substance was, I couldn't consider it normal under the present circumstances.

The substance had formed so heavily across the body of each craft that it looked as though every helicopter had been completely drenched in some kind of sediment-like liquid material.

"Hey, Scare Crow. You copy?" a voice said on the transmitter.

"Copy," Tony responded.

"Hey, this is the Cat."

"Oh yeah, Cat. What's happening, man?" Tony asked.

"Hey, you know something? I could've sworn not too long ago I heard something like a foghorn blowing from somewhere around here, man," Cat said.

"What?" Tony asked. "A foghorn? Where?"

"Cat, you heard what?" someone asked, laughing. "Man, you need to leave that shit you smokin' alone. That stuff got your ass all fucked up."

"I ain't been smokin' nothin'," Cat said. "I'm telling the truth. It's somebody out there blowing a freakin' foghorn. And I heard it!"

"Okay, maybe you did hear a foghorn blowing," Tony said with a chuckle. "But just where did you hear it coming from?"

"Man, it was somewhere out there in that fog and all that

darkness," Cat said. "I heard it. And I ain't been smokin' shit since we been here."

"Hey, you guys," someone said, trying to get their attention. "Anybody copy?"

"Yeah. Copy you loud and clear," Tony responded. "What's happening with you?"

"I just wanted to let you guys know I think I, too, heard something like a foghorn blowing," the person said, sounding certain of what he had heard. "And to be quite frank about it, the horn sounded almost like a warning, telling us not to come any closer. In other words, it sounded like a warning of impending danger."

"Hey! Just who the hell is that speaking?" someone else suddenly asked.

"And just who wants to know?"

"I think I asked the question first, smartass."

"Just who the fuck you callin' smartass? You repugnant, filthy bastard."

Indistinct chattering continued over the transmitter.

"Hey, Scare Crow. This is a crew member from the Commander," a voice said. "You copy?"

"Copy you, member from the Commander," Tony responded again. "What is it I can do for you, other than what was just heard?"

"For one thing, whoever was talking about hearing a foghorn? I think he's gone off the deep end with that crap, you feel me?" the Commander crew member said. "I think he's another one of them weirdos trying to get some attention with that bizarre superstitious bullshit, if you ask me."

"Yeah?" I said. "Despite his beliefs, we're all presently experiencing the same weird results from whatever's happening around here. And these things are going to continue."

"Man, Doc. I thought you were out there searching to see if you could find something," Tony said, surprised to see that I hadn't gone anywhere and was still inside the craft. "That's why I was still answering the calls."

"It's cool, man, I know," I told him, smiling. "That's exactly why I didn't actually go anywhere and hurried back here. I didn't want these guys' imaginations running wild with all this weird stuff happening around here, the foghorn blowing and no telling what else. I'm sure everybody heard it."

"Where'd you think it came from? Because I think I heard it, too," Tony said while rubbing the side of his face.

"I really don't know. But it sounded like it came from somewhere in that direction," I told him, pointing toward Snow Mountain. "I think what I'm going to do is have everyone check their craft and gather up their equipment so we can prepare to move out on foot. We gotta find out what's happening around here."

"You serious, Doc?"

"Journalist or not, this mission in itself is serious. None like any other I've ever experienced," I told him.

"And what about us ladies up in here?" Regina quickly asked. "What're we gonna be doin' out there?"

"Oh yeah, that's right," I said with a slight grin. "I sincerely believe we're all, in one way or another, taking this journey personally. I'm doing everything I can to make sure we all use the skills necessary for this mission. It's important that we, as a group, show compassion and look out for one another. You can rest assured, Regina, you too, Sandra, and Karen, that this entire crew you're with in this strange situation are tremendously good people to be working with under these circumstances. This group has your back and is ready to prevent any unnecessary trouble."

"Bumps!" Regina said.

"I know I'm a very skilled journalist," Sandra said, smiling. "But I think I'm getting scared being here and it still dark outside. Why it still dark in Snow Mountain when it light everywhere in other area?"

"Girl, you don't have nothin' to worry about," Regina said to Sandra. "All of us are up here to do this job, and then after that we is outta here in a freakin' hurry. You feel me? Tell her what I'm talking about, Murdock. Am I telling the truth?"

"Anyway," was the only word I said.

Click! Click! Click!

Click! Click! Click!

"Hey, Scare Crow. You copy?"

"Copy," I answered. "Whassup?"

"Hey, dude, this is the Knucklehead waiting on you to give the OK for us to conquer this shit up here. You feel me? My crazy ass crew is ready to go out and subdue these motherfuckers right here and now and take over anything in these mountains, whether it be in the dark or in the light. We're ready and going mad to do this. We're restless, Doc. My guys are craving it, like some contagious killing disease in their heads prompting them to wanna do this shit right now. Man, the Knucklehead and his crew got the force and some heavy power. And believe me, Doc, we're armed with a little bit of everything just waiting to be released."

"I feel you, Knucklehead," I quickly told him. "That's just what I needed to hear from you, potna. Thank you much. But what about everyone else out there? Gotta see if they're ready to do this, too."

"Ain't nothin' but a word you speakin'," a voice said loud and clear on the transmitter. "Y'all just talkin' about doin' this shit. But we been ready to fuck some of this shit up since childbirth. You know what I'm sayin'? Hey, no offense on you guys' conversation, but check this out, homies. Midwest and the crew is ready to fuck something up—terribly."

"Uh, yeah. Excuse me, young'uns," another voice said on the transmitter with an obnoxious chuckle. "This here is the Commander and his crew, ready to treat you guys like the stepkids you truly are. And we mean that statement literally. Man, the Commander is ready to rock and roll like a freakin' wild, uncivilized tidal wave. Better yet, we comin' like the Tasmanian Devil. Now can any of y'all feel that?"

"Man, y'all ain't sayin' shit," another voice said over the transmitter, unfamiliar to everyone on the mission.

"Oh yeah?" someone replied. "Identify yourself."

"They call me the Earthquake, cuz," the voice said.

"The Earthquake?" someone asked.

"Uh-huh. Yeah. The Earthquake."

"Any explanation for that name?" he was asked.

"Yeah!" he snapped. "Cause when I move, you move!"

More indistinct chattering followed.

"All right. Now hold up, you guys. Time out," I said. "Just hold up. It sounds like we might have something like an impostor on this mission."

"Somebody get a rope," someone said jokingly.

"Yeah, 'cause this ain't no New York City," another voice added.

"Gotta do some investigating," Tony said, grinning.

"Earthquake? Seriously?" I asked. "Who are you, really?"

"I'm widespread throughout every ocean and every seashore," the Earthquake said, laughing. "And I'm strong just like the wind, and at any given time I can tickle your little fancy with my sensational touch."

"Sounds just like some goddamn gangster rapper trying to put down a few rhymes, you ask me," one of the crew members said. "I think what should happen is we wait until it gets really busy around here. Then we'll see just what this Earthquake person is made of."

"Whatcha sayin', old man? I'm a coward or something?" the Earthquake asked.

"Hey, Earthquake," I called out on the transmitter. "This is the Scare Crow. Unless you've been invited on this mission, it's best that you start shaking your ass away from here. You feel me?"

"What makes you even think I'm here with you guys?" the Earthquake said with a grunt. "I could be your imagination."

"Yeah, well. Wherever you are, we're really in no mood for your distraction," I told him.

"Hey, Scare Crow. This is MacDonald on the Lodi. You copy?"

"Copy you, MacDonald," I responded. "Whassup?"

"You want me to find him?" He sounded determined to track down the Earthquake. "It's all up to you, Doc."

"Check this out, MacDonald," I said, knowing his ability to track someone down. "I'm aware of your qualifications, and I know the grades you earned during training. You proved yourself a very dedicated marksman when it comes to firing tactical weapons as part of a well-planned strategy to gain the upper hand over your opponent. I appreciate that kind of skill.

"But right now you're on this mission as both a journalist and a pilot, and also a highly skilled marksman. And although there are times when you can be strange, weird, and unique, I wouldn't have you any different from who you really are. You are among the best and have come from the very best.

"The individual calling himself the Earthquake apparently doesn't have a clue what he's up against.

"But we'll find him in due time, MacDonald.

"And when we do, you'll have my permission to do to him whatever you please."

"Copy that, Scare Crow," MacDonald replied respectfully.

*

The purpose of this mission was not about taking someone out just because you knew you could. And it certainly wasn't about going after someone for running his mouth or playing childish games over the transmitter. The mission to Stonyford was about a group of dedicated journalists and media personnel working together to uncover the truth behind the terrible situation unfolding in Stonyford, California.

Everyone on this journey had stepped forward for a reason. Many of them brought strong skills in photography and video. Their assignment was to record this mission step by step with accuracy. They were not here because they were friends. Most had earned their place because of their experience.

Their job was simple in principle—document everything.

Every step of this venture would have to be carried out with patience and careful attention. Some members of the group might find parts of the mission exciting, but others, including the Earthquake, would soon find themselves caught in events they did not fully understand. Many would ignore the danger waiting ahead of them, which was exactly the situation Satan had already set in motion.

Everything Margaret had warned me about was revealing itself.

It was no accident that each of our crafts had landed perfectly and in formation, exactly in the direction we had planned to take off again. I already knew that this trip to Stonyford would mark the beginning of a final confrontation between the forces of good and evil.

Margaret had spoken openly about the town and about Lucifer's plan to destroy it. According to her, the devastation would not stop with Stonyford alone. The destruction would spread outward into nearby towns throughout the region.

This was the beginning of Lucifer's prophecy being fulfilled.

Margaret had described how his influence would move across the entire region. She reminded me of the ancient story of how God cast Satan and his fallen angels out of heaven after their rebellion. These immortal spirits had followed Satan and were thrown into the bottomless pit.

And now the pieces were beginning to fall into place.

From the sound of his voice, just as Margaret had warned, I realized the Earthquake was none other than Ethan, the same young child Margaret had spoken about.

She said he would eventually be found hiding beneath one of the sinks in the mess hall at the boys ranch, trying to conceal himself from danger.

According to the report I had read, Ethan was believed to be connected to the strange creatures capable of transforming themselves into human form. These creatures could duplicate the exact appearance and likeness of the children living at the boys ranch.

Originally, they were said to belong to the fairy-tale chimera family. The chimera was a monstrous creature described as having the head of a lion, the body of a goat, and the tail of a serpent. Most stories about these creatures were dismissed as ancient tales meant only to stir the imagination.

But in reality, and at this present moment in the Stonyford, California region, we were dealing with facts tied to unfolding events.

As Margaret had told me, Ethan would be the same young child later rescued by Flight Commander Taylor. And who do you think would bring about both Chad's and Taylor's deaths only minutes later while they were trying to rescue the two men operating the ranger station in Stonyford?

The young child.

Ethan.

*

"All right, everybody. Listen up," I said over the transmitter. "I think I know what's happening here. Believe me, it's going to sound a bit spooky. This person you guys keep hearing, the Earthquake, it's my guess he's trying to pull the wool over our eyes. He'll try just about anything to pull you into his death grip so he can take your life."

Indistinct clicking sounds followed my statement.

"Hey, Murdock!" a very familiar voice called out to me on the transmitter. "This is Big Lazy. You copy?"

"Copy, Big Lazy," I responded. "Whassup?"

"Hey, man. Pee-wee and I was wondering if you was really serious about this Ethan guy?"

"Yeah, Doc," Pee-wee cut in. "Man, are you really serious?"

"Damn!" someone else shouted, sounding much like the Cat. "You got me trippin', too, after that statement. I know I'm supposed to be tough like a real cat, but man, Doc, after hearing what you just said about this Ethan person, I'm really confused right about now. It's like I don't know if I wanna just kick back on my backside in my kitty box and relax with a purr or what. You feel me?"

"Hey, you guys. Check this out. Are we really on some more of that weird voodoo crap again, or what?" a voice that sounded like Manny said. "Next thing we'll be doing is sprinkling garlic powder over our shoulders and everywhere around us. Then we'll be trying to protect everybody from the coronavirus and the Big Bad Wolf."

"Well, you guys can call him whatever you want," I said, referring to the many names of the Devil. "What I'm trying to do is bring to your attention that he's real. And according to the conversation I had with Margaret, the Devil is the one in authority here. He's determined to prove himself to all of us. It's like he's trying to fulfill the prophecy he believes he's forewarning us about. Lucifer is doing this in advance. He's forewarning the entire region about what he claims is his divinely inspired message, trying to present himself in the likeness of a prophet."

"Uh, please excuse me, Murdock," a female voice suddenly came on the transmitter. "But I just happen to be standing here listening to y'all's conversation about the Big Bad Wolf and the

Devil and everything else. And it was really impossible for me to stand here and keep quiet any longer."

"Well, what's the problem?" I asked. "And who are you, if you don't mind me asking?"

"Oh, no," the lady said with a slight giggle. "That'll be no problem letting you guys know about my crew and where we come from. My gals and I all come from the Highline country of the state of Montana."

"Oh, okay," I said, remembering. "And what part was that?"

"Sweetgrass and Shelby, to be exact," she said with another country-like giggle.

"All right then, Ms. Montana," I said. "Then tell me, whassup?"

"Oh, I just love to hear you say it like that," she said, sounding cheerful. "But I'm pretty sure y'all already know what's happening, don't you? Anyway, I just happened to be keeping myself busy with my craft's radio. And with y'all boys continuously bringing up the Devil and all, I thought maybe you could shed a little light on all them horrible tragedies that've been taking place in the Stonyford region."

"Damn! And here we go again," Cat said. "Just what the heck are you talking about, lady? What tragedies are you referring to?"

Before I could say anything, Pee-wee came on the transmitter.

"Excuse me, Ms. Montana, but this here talking is Pee-wee, ma'am," he said. "And I think you already know who I am. I'm the navigator of the Sacro, from Sacramento, California. And the person you were just listening to before, that was the Cat. He's the navigator of Lodi, from Lodi, California. You still there?"

"Copy that, Pee-wee," she said with another giggle. "It's really nice meeting you. All of you."

"So now, and not to be rude or overlook what you were saying about the situation in Stonyford, I was wondering if you wouldn't mind repeating it so everyone can hear you," Pee-wee asked.

"Oh, that wouldn't be any problem at all," she said, beginning to speak in her soft Montana accent. "They were saying something about people being found in various stages of decomposition, and that most of the bodies had been scattered about. Some were hacked to bits or cut into little pieces so they couldn't even be identified.

"They were also saying that some killings looked like the work of gang members, and that it wouldn't be surprising if the murders turned out to be gang related.

"But that was just a theory and the opinion of an official working a gang unit from out of town. Those officials weren't aware of the facts that this part of the region is known for strange phenomena taking place.

"But they did say that in each case, most of the victims had suffered violent deaths, and all of them had been murdered.

"And for some of the women and children, they're saying it might have been the work of a serial killer. They said the killer spread the remains all over the place. Some of those remains were found from Maxwell to Garberville, and even up toward Eureka and around the Mount Shasta area.

"They were also saying it reminded them of serial killers from the East Coast. Like Vincent Johnson and David Berkowitz. And also Joel Rifkin and Jack the Ripper. They even mentioned sexual predators like Gary Ridgway up in Washington State, who confessed to killing at least seventy-one women.

"These killings, even though they happened in different towns throughout the Stonyford region, look connected. Some of California's top law enforcement officials described it like a giant octopus. They said its tentacles stretch out in every direction, reaching for victims like the Tasmanian Devil.

"They said those tentacles were like rows of suction cups, pulling the life out of just about every goddamn thing they touched."

*

Listening to this sweet lady from Montana describe what she had heard on the radio made everyone think twice about the mission. Her description had a way of reminding you just how precious life really is, especially in those moments when everything you've done in life seems to flash before your eyes.

I have to admit I found myself thinking about Margaret Johnson and how much she reminded me of the grandmother I had spent most of my life wishing I had known.

For reasons I couldn't fully explain, I felt a certain sense of guilt. It was my responsibility to make sure every member of this mission made it home safely. I knew the trip wouldn't be easy. And knowing that, I couldn't ignore the possibility that some members might become victims of whatever it was we were about to face.

But I kept finding my thoughts returning to that strange young boy with the mysterious power, Ethan.

I thought about how he had already tried to slip quietly among us like a slimy, slithering snake, calling himself by a name like Earthquake.

Now, we were already exposed to his danger.

My thoughts turned again to Margaret and the warning she had given me about Ethan. She had said that eventually I would meet him.

But she never said whether that meeting would happen in the town of Stonyford, or somewhere else entirely, like a jail cell.

But as I already knew, it was now time for this meeting with Ethan to begin. It was time for me to bring this dangerous spectacle out front on a much larger scale and expose him like never before.

It was time to bring Ethan to everyone's attention.

But unfortunately, it was already too late for the town of

Stonyford and much of the surrounding region. Everything was about to become turned upside down, like a corrupted conviction. That kind of manipulation was exactly what Lucifer used against those followers who blindly accepted his demonic teachings into their lives.

"Okay, everybody, listen up," I said over the transmitter. "As each of you should know, I'm aware that most of you are wondering what we're up against. So check this out, and hopefully what I'm about to say will give you a better understanding of the situation.

"First thing is this: the individual you've come to know identifying himself as the Earthquake is none other than the Devil. The only thing I can ask of you guys is to be careful, because Ethan is on a very vindictive mission to deceive you. He'll come at you pretending to be part of the team.

"But you'll notice something isn't right when you realize he's using the same cunning tricks he used on the people in Stonyford to capture their attention and persuade them into believing him through deception.

"I can only ask that you not fall for his deceptive appearance, his unsupported claims, or the show he puts on to gain your trust.

"Ethan will continue using this kind of manipulation to keep your interest in him. That is exactly why he hasn't simply disappeared from this region.

"He has already captured many souls, and his behavior will continue.

"But one thing is certain. It would be very foolish for any of you to allow yourselves to fall under his influence or become confused about what I'm trying to do here by warning you.

"His mission is to invade your thoughts. Once he does that, you'll find him speaking to you directly. That's how he builds a relationship with you. He will make you feel like you share something in common.

"Again, I can only ask each of you not to allow yourselves to become caught up in this dramatic performance by Ethan.

"Remember, we're dealing with the Devil himself. He's the same spirit who once was cast out of heaven after his failed rebellion against the kingdom.

"And now, after his fall, he roams the earth portraying himself as the god of the universe. His spirit moves freely, filled with anger, hatred, and violence.

"Every living being is his enemy.

"He carries deep resentment toward those he cannot claim as his possession. That hatred becomes even stronger toward those who reject him.

"As Margaret told me, his punishment for this region will be violent and swift for some, but slow for others. Those who oppose him will suffer the most.

"And as she explained it, Lucifer believes he holds the ultimate authority in deciding how his game is played. He places everyone on a leash, like animals.

"She also said his spirit's presence alone would create confusion throughout Stonyford. Many people would no longer be able to tell the difference between good and evil. Everything would become distorted, like a jumble of angry voices echoing through the darkness.

"His spirit will cause the people of this region to growl angrily at each other, bare their teeth and speak in furious tones. This kind of behavior will happen, in many situations, without warning.

"He's going to be snatching residents of Stonyford, California, and people from the surrounding communities right out of their beds and off the streets like never before. He'll grab them violently and tear at them in his effort to destroy them, leaving only pieces of them behind.

"But Margaret also told me that for some, Lucifer will use a much gentler approach, recognizing the condition of their health.

"He's going to use their weakness to torture them deeply, inflicting severe physical pain on those who cannot move quickly to safety, or even fully comprehend the punishment he is bringing upon them."

"Hey, Doc!" someone abruptly called out my name. "You copy?"

"Copy," I responded. "Who is that?"

"Man, this is Bucketmouth," he said.

"What's happening, Bucketmouth?"

"Are you talking about the elderly?" he asked.

"The elderly, those in infancy, and anyone else he can snatch," I responded.

"Wouldn't you say that would be really cruel for something like that to happen to people already suffering?" someone asked. "I mean, what good is it to inflict pain on people who can't defend themselves?"

"Well, to be quite honest about it, I've never met anyone who said the Devil had any mercy on them," I said. "And when you think about it in biblical terms, Satan is out to destroy all of us. If you take the time to read the Scriptures, you'll find plenty of evidence that supports that truth, including the warnings about the Four Horsemen."

"The beasts!" someone suddenly yelled out over the transmitter.

"Yeah, and let's not forget Riders of the Storm," another voice shouted. "All you gotta do is read the book of Daniel."

"And don't forget Death and Hell," someone else added.

"Yeah, well," I said with a chuckle, "it's obvious some of you guys already know what I'm referring to. That's all right."

"Okay. So just what are we going to do about that fella, calling himself a member of this team?" Eddie Gillespie asked. "I'm talking about that sonofabitch running his mouth about his name being some fuckin' Earthquake or something. Like somebody's supposed to give a fuck."

"Damn, potna," someone said. "Didn't you just hear what Murdock was saying about that bitch-ass motherfucker? He's the Devil."

"But wait a minute, you guys. Hold up," I said. "Whoever's asking what we're going to do about the Earthquake might actually have a good point.

"So check this out. What I want everyone to start doing is identifying yourselves. From this point forward, wear your microphone headsets and keep them on. And I need you guys wearing whatever military gear most appropriate for this mission.

"The Devil planned this so-called ceremonious inauguration. So I guess it's our turn to spoil the fun by showing up uninvited.

"Locked, loaded, and ready."

*

Click! Click! Click!

Click! Click! Click!

"Who the heck is that clicking?" someone asked the crew.

"Sacro, negative!"

"Lodi, negative!"

"Commander, that's a negative!"

"Midwest, I second that negative."

"Montana, that is a negative."

"Bucketmouth, negative!"

"Wolfman ain't doing no clicking. That's a negative."

"Scare Crow, negative!"

"This is Knucklehead of Sacro," he said. "You sure that isn't that thing calling himself the Earthquake making those clicking sounds? Maybe he's imitating one of us? Trying to draw somebody into a trap."

"I'd say that's a negative, Sacro," Tony responded. "Whoever it is, it's coming from somewhere behind us."

"This is the Commander. I got 'em locked in on my scope. And whoever it is, they're flying something like an Osprey."

"This is Lodi," another voice said. "I see it moving slowly in behind you. It's one of those MV-22 Ospreys. Now he's acting like he's trying to catch up."

"I got 'em on the radar, Doc," Tony said with a chuckle. "Damn! That mother's really on the move and gaining."

"Now, Tony. I hope you realize that radar can also detect every position, size, velocity, and the exact distance, don't you?" I asked him. "Just keep watching the radarscope's screen. You'll see the object as it is analyzed by multiple electromagnetic waves."

"And what is that behind it moving around like that?" Karen asked, pointing at a strange object on the radar screen following a short distance behind the Osprey.

"Mmm," I mumbled. "Now that's strange. Any of you guys out there see what that is trailing behind the Osprey?"

"Whatever it is, it's holding its distance and altitude," a voice came over the transmitter.

"MV-22 Osprey, this is the Commander and Reinforcer with the team in flight with the Scare Crow. Do you copy?" the Commander asked.

Indistinct chatter and static followed.

"MV-22 Osprey, this is the Commander and Reinforcer with the team in flight with the Scare Crow. Do you copy?" the Commander asked again.

"Roger that, Commander," someone from the Osprey responded.

"What's your purpose for coming in behind us, Osprey?" the Commander asked.

"Well, for one thing, the Osprey is fully equipped for cargo and support," the person said. "It's considered one of the most efficient aircraft for missions like this. I thought maybe you guys could use the assistance."

"Wait a minute. Hold up," I quickly said. "Just what are you talking about? What assistance are you referring to?"

"It's the Osprey," the person replied firmly. "And you sound like someone other than the Commander."

"And eventually, you would expect that to happen."

"Ultimately," the person said. "And might I ask who I'm speaking with?"

"This is Murdock," I answered. "I'm in charge of this mission and the communications with my crew."

"Well, it's a pleasure to finally have the opportunity to meet you, Mr. Murdock," the person from the Osprey said respectfully. "I've heard a lot about the Scare Crow and the rest of your squadron of journalists. Just watching your crew flying their helicopters in this direction at a time like this, I couldn't wait to see if there was some way I could offer assistance."

"What do you know about this mission?" the Commander asked.

"Well, I know the town of Stonyford has something that's holding it captive—forcibly," the person said. "The people presently living in that part of the region have become something like prisoners. And word is that it's the Devil himself acting as the gatekeeper."

"And how did you say you could assist?" I asked.

"It's the Osprey, Mr. Murdock," the person said. "My craft is fully ready and equipped with a whole lot of this and a whole lot of that. It's loaded with just about every type of ammunition you might need for this mission, including explosives and multiple projectiles that can be discharged from a distance and strike their intended targets accurately."

"Well, all right then, Osprey," I said over the transmitter. "Can't think of anything else except to say welcome aboard this mission."

"I'd second that motion," the Commander said.

"Ain't got no problems here on Lodi," someone else added.

"We be jammin' the same from Midwest," another voice said in agreement.

"What's your distance, Osprey?" someone asked.

"I would say, judging from the navigation instruments," the person replied after checking, "we're somewhere around four-point-eight kilometers behind you guys."

"Damn!" I uttered. "Okay then, Osprey. I honestly feel you folks in flight need to start taking extra precaution while advancing. And remember to stay vigilant of everything around you and your craft."

"Why's that?" the person on the Osprey asked. "Could it be because of that thing back there on my tail following us?"

"Thought you knew," I responded.

"What the heck are those things called?" he asked.

"Well, from the looks of it, I'd say it's most likely a chimera creature."

"Bullshit!" he shouted. "Them freakin' things, from my understanding, are made-up creatures from people's imaginations."

"That's what they say, my friend. But not around here in this neck of the woods," I told him firmly. "They're everywhere. And I do mean everywhere. And I believe we all know just who the hell that one is following close behind the Osprey."

"What's that, Murdock? Hold up, man," the person on the Osprey suddenly said, sounding bewildered. "What the heck are you talking about? Knowing who that is behind the Osprey? What, you know the names of these things or something?"

"Just let me put it this way, Osprey," I said. "Not long ago we had an intruder interrupting our conversations over the transmitters. He was an uninvited entity trying to come aboard our craft. That intruder is what prompted me and my crew to make some quick decisions to keep that thing from getting access to any of the helicopters.

"You see, before this mission even started, I had a very unusual conversation with a gentle elderly lady named Margaret Johnson. During that conversation, she told me I would end up in this part of the region, and that I would meet someone named Ethan.

"And to be frank, I believe that same individual is the entity we're dealing with right now. The same evil spirit of the Devil that's trying to disguise himself somewhere behind the Osprey. And he's capable of approaching each one of these crafts while wearing different appearances.

"Ethan is the one calling himself the Earthquake. That's his way of trying to get on board these crafts while hiding who he really is.

"And right now we're seeing him again, trailing behind the Osprey and disguising himself as a chimera. Only this time he's got wings, and claws big enough to tear something apart, shaped almost like the claws of lobsters, with a segmented body and jointed limbs."

"Hey, Murdock. The Osprey should be coming near our location," Tony said while watching the object on the radar. "He seems to have slowed down quite a bit from what I can see and should be within a few miles from here."

"That thing on the screen behind the Osprey is particularly large," Karen said, pointing at the display. "That thing is enormous for something that's supposed to be a chimera. Wouldn't you think? At least according to what the computer is showing."

"Hey, Pee-wee. You still out there, potna?" I called on the transmitter.

"Roger that, Scare Crow. I know that's you," he said with a chuckle. "What's up, Doc?"

"You got a visual on the object trailing behind the Osprey?"

"Roger that, Doc. One hundred percent."

"Tell that there Knucklehead to take 'em out to the ball game."

"Copy!"

"MacDonald, you copy?" I said.

"MacDonald, copy!" he answered.

"That object behind the Osprey, you see it?"

"That's a really big object trailing behind the Osprey, Scare Crow," he said. "Got it in sight."

"Have your way with 'em," I told him.

"Thank you much," he said, giggling. "About time."

"Osprey, you copy?" I said.

"Copy!" the Osprey answered.

"You see that wide open gap up ahead of you between our crafts?"

"Copy!"

"Well, it's there for your convenience. You feel me, Osprey?"

"My convenience? That's like asking me if I like cotton candy. I can dig it, Scare Crow," the Osprey said with a chuckle. "Thank you much for the love for the Osprey."

Within seconds the Osprey was touching down, its engines rotating upward toward the dark sky. Bright lights shone from the aircraft, making it a remarkable sight, especially the engines. There was one mounted on each of the V-22 Osprey's wings. During flight they rotated horizontally, and at the flip of a switch they turned upward into a vertical position. Each engine vibrated heavily, full of raw power.

The V-22 Osprey reminded me of the AV-8B Harrier I once saw landing on the USS Kearsarge to refuel and load what looked like more weapons and ammunition. I assumed the extra artillery was meant for additional air strikes.

But the Osprey was here for us, bringing its strength to help bring down an enemy so ruthless and merciless that only the combined effort of everyone on this mission could hope to defeat it.

Engineering the systems that shut down the Osprey's engines was an impressive sight to watch. One moment the huge propellers were spinning, and the next they slowed and stopped completely. The aircraft's bright identification lights quickly shut off as well, preventing unwanted attention and hiding the Osprey's location.

Watching it settle there, I thought about the craft's speed and versatility. The Osprey had come in fast and now rested exactly where it had been meant to land.

From where I stood, I could see the pilots becoming visible as they began climbing out of their seats.

Although the Osprey isn't as massive as the MH-53, it is still an aircraft known for getting in and out of almost any situation, often with the same reliability you'd expect from aircraft like the C-130 or even the B-2 Spirit.

The Osprey was also used during the airstrikes in Libya, when crews from the 26th Marine Expeditionary Unit reportedly rescued the pilot of a downed U.S. Air Force F-15E Strike Eagle after the aircraft malfunctioned. Both the pilot and the weapons systems officer ejected safely before the crash.

If you remember, the mission was to protect Libyan citizens from the forces of Muammar Gaddafi.

Shortly after the Osprey landed and its engines shut down, I made an announcement over the transmitter advising everyone to take extra precautions and remain onboard their craft.

I reminded everyone again to wear the clothing appropriate for this mission.

Straining my eyes for a better view of the team, something caught my attention. These were some of the proudest and most responsible journalists I had ever worked with, now operating as part of a coordinated mission with authority granted from higher command.

What surprised me most were the weapons. Several of the crafts, including my own MH-53 J Pave Low, had AIM-9 Sidewinder missiles mounted along their sides.

The Osprey, as expected, carried the majority of them, clearly visible along its underbelly.

Located near the right front side door of the Osprey, just behind the pilot's seat, I could barely make out through the darkness and fog one of the flight crew gripping what looked like a fifty-caliber machine gun. From the way he held it, I was sure it was ready to fire at a moment's notice.

Just as I was about to say something over the transmitter, I was interrupted by a hail of gunfire. Explosions followed, sounding as though they were coming from the direction of MacDonald and Knucklehead.

The crew reported the chimera had made a threatening move behind the Osprey. The firing was their attempt to take the thing out.

Hundreds of flashes and bolts that looked like lightning filled the dark sky as the gunners on the Osprey joined the assault.

As the sky lit up over the boys ranch during the violent attack on the chimera, an anguished cry suddenly tore through the air. It was an agonizing scream unlike anything I could properly describe, the sound of something suffering from extreme physical torture.

Though I would like to think that the scream came from Ethan, something in me was telling me otherwise. Still, we were under entirely different circumstances now, and because of the situation at hand, this moment could officially be described as the beginning of our human incarnation into this deadly belligerent conflict.

The loud scream continued. Everyone covered their ears to protect their eardrums. I could see the members of my crew doing everything they could to shield themselves from the sound. The howling carried on like a loud, furious objection that refused to end.

"Hey, Murdock," Tony suddenly said, calling my name in an uneasy tone.

"Yeah. What's happening?" I responded.

"Man, I know for a fact that thing had to be one of them chimera," he said, still staring into the distance. "I mean, just look at that thing. It's way out there, burning up, and we can still hear it like it was right here. You know what I mean?"

"What you talking about, Tony, that thing way over there?" Karen asked, pointing toward a fiery object tumbling from the dark sky.

"Yeah, that's it," Tony said, watching the burning object as it slammed into the side of a hill.

"That's a different one," Karen said. "The other one following that airplane with the propellers that looked like a helicopter. That thing got shot down way back there. Don't you remember?"

"Oh, yeah. That's right, it did, didn't it?" Tony said.

"Uh-huh," Karen replied, still watching the burning object on the ground.

"All right, you guys. Everybody listen up," I said loudly over the transmitter. "Whoever or whatever that thing was, this is only the beginning of what's to come. From my estimation, and I regret having to say it, these things are most likely headed toward Stonyford. And from what I can figure, these freakin' things could very well be duplications made in the exact likeness of Ethan, AKA the Earthquake."

"Hey, Scare Crow," a voice called over the transmitter. "This is a member of the Midwest team. You copy?"

"Copy," I responded. "Whassup?"

"I got a 60-power XPS waterproof spotting scope with a 78mm objective mounted on the side of our craft, and the damn thing was bouncing off some big rocks on the side of a hill. Then all of a sudden that goddamn bitch just took off flying."

"Okay. But isn't that what it's supposed to do?" I asked with a slight chuckle. "It did have wings, didn't it?"

"Oh, hell yeah. That bitch had wings," he said. "But it started flying on its own. I didn't do a damn thing, Doc."

"So where'd it go?" I asked.

"Yeah, where is it now?" someone else asked.

"That nasty, filthy bitch out there burning up," the Midwest member said. "That bitch is on fire."

"Okay. Those of you with night-vision binoculars to spare, lend a pair to anyone who doesn't," I said. "And those of you skilled with bow and arrows, step forward."

"Hey, Scare Crow. You copy?" another voice called over the transmitter.

"Copy," I responded. "Identify yourself."

"This is Carl Mitchell, sir. Navigator of the Osprey here with my co-pilot Robert E. Coppage," he said. "You copy, Scare Crow?"

"Roger that, Carl Mitchell of the Osprey," I responded. "This is Murdock, the one in charge of the mission. We spoke earlier."

"Are you a pilot as well?" Mitchell asked.

"That's affirmative, Carl Mitchell," I told him. "Navigator of the Scare Crow with my co-pilot Tony and the rest of the crew."

"Just so you know, the Osprey is here for your advantage under the circumstances. It's fully loaded with just about everything you'll need," Mitchell said.

"Sounds good to me," I told him. "Anything else?"

"Yeah. What's the air quality like around here?"

"That all depends on where you guys are from originally," I said.

"Why's that?" he asked.

"Because this is, although mountain terrain, still country," someone said over the transmitter.

"By the way, Mitchell, where did the Osprey crew come from?"

"We're all from the East Coast," Mitchell said. "Philadelphia, to be exact."

"Damn. No wonder you're concerned about the air quality. None of y'all know anything about the country," a woman's voice said, giggling.

"In other words, prepare to be smellin' a bunch of bullshit," another voice added with a chuckle.

"The air is nice and clear so you can get a good sense of who that thing following you was," Karen shouted into her headset.

"Oh, no you didn't," I said after hearing Karen respond so quickly.

"I don't know about this anymore," Regina suddenly exclaimed, sounding exhausted and emotionally upset. She was sweating profusely while everyone listened over the transmitter. "This place isn't safe for us. Something's not right about this. My intuition and my laptop messages are jumping all over the screen like they're trying to warn me about something. It's giving out very bad vibes."

"I agree," someone said on the transmitter. "I'm here with the Commander, and I thought it was just our craft having equipment problems. But after hearing what that lady was talking about, I suspect there is something about this place causing everything on our radar to malfunction."

"Yeah. Ain't nothin' workin' properly on the Lodi either," another voice said.

"Same situation onboard the Sacro," another voice added. "We're picking up quite a bit of really strange movement and eerie activity at 0315, about three hundred feet out."

"And just why is that?" a voice, sounding like a lady, asked.

"Well, that's only if you don't want your baby coming out looking like one of these chimera creatures," I said. "That's really up to you."

"Not onboard this craft, sister," another lady's voice added.

"Fuckin' idiot," someone said, sounding confused.

"Hey! You guys flying that UH-60 Black Hawk," I said, cutting off what I knew was about to become nonsense. I needed everyone to keep their cool. "Something tells me you gotta be from the 82nd Airborne Division's 1st Brigade Combat Team. Tell me if that's affirmative."

"That's affirmative there, big guy," a voice said over the transmitter.

"Thank you much for bringing that M119A2 105mm howitzer."

"You got that, Doc," the voice said. "This Bud's for you."

"Hey, Mitchell of the Osprey. You copy?" I called out.

"Copy," he responded. "What's up, Doc?"

"How many of those XM806 .50-caliber machine guns are onboard the Osprey?" I asked Mitchell. "I'm asking because I understand that particular .50-caliber allows quick barrel changing without adjustments for headspace and timing. Can you tell me if that statement is accurate?"

"Thought you knew," Mitchell said with a chuckle. "Doc, I even have a few attack-guided rocket missiles from one of those prototype JLTVs. These are definitely in the 'cool' category."

"Yeah, well. I really don't think any of my crew members are into trying to use anything as 'cool' as you're describing," I told him. "And surely none of us are as cool as the group Morris Day & The Time. We're 'cool' in our own way and style, just not that cool. We're a group of journalists who arrived in these mountains by a fleet of helicopters. We're not from some type of aviation regiment. Our operation primarily consists of documenting what we write on official paper so our findings can furnish evidence through informative resources. The information will then be presented as factual, though in an artistic form as a PBS documentary."

"Mmm," Mitchell mumbled over the transmitter. "PBS is one of my favorite programs. You think you guys can let me play a role in the documentary, like Samuel L. Jackson and Richard Roundtree when they played 'Shaft'? Can you dig it?"

"Yeah, right!" someone said sarcastically over the transmitter.

"Mitchell, check this out, man. Would the Osprey by chance be carrying any of those headlamps?" I asked him. "You know, like the ones miners wear?"

"More than enough," he said.

"What's the run time on them?" I asked.

"Somewhere around twenty-four hours," he said. "But that depends on the type of batteries you're using. And by the way, Doc, you can tell whoever made that sarcastic remark that I didn't appreciate their sarcasm. Matter of fact, my crew is here to assist you guys in disengaging the enemy."

"I feel you on that, Mitchell," I told him.

"Hey, Doc, it wasn't any of us who said that," one of the crew members said.

"My radar picked up the voice. It's an unidentified entity," another crew member said.

"That reminds me. You guys make sure you're wearing a watch so you can keep time," I said.

"And what about helmets?" Tony asked. "You know, some of those high-impact military types."

"Hey, Mitchell. Did you hear that question?"

"Uh-oh. I don't think he heard me," Tony said.

"Got 'em," Mitchell said surprisingly. "I heard you the first time, but I was thinking about what you were saying about an entity. Do you guys need anything else?"

"I've got a question or two for the Scare Crow before we move out," someone said.

"And might I ask just what that could be?" I asked.

"Don't you think it would be in our best interest if we started this mission with one of those quick airstrikes?"

There was a momentary silence.

"Why don't you let me address that question to the entire crew," I said. "Because, you see—"

"Damn!" someone exclaimed over the transmitter. "Sounds like that guy's itching for war."

"You're damn straight I am," the person said with a stern voice. "I came up here for some action."

"This is MacDonald," he said over the transmitter. "I'm ready to do this too. What's the delay? I can't wait to use my M203 grenade launcher."

"Hey, I got this Mk 19 grenade machine gun locked, loaded, and ready,"Ms. Montana said over the transmitter.

"And don't forget about the Wolfman," he said, laughing and howling like a wild wolf. "We got these AT4 rocket launchers locked, loaded, and ready."

"Same here," Bucketmouth said. "We're ready to do this with our SMAW rocket launchers, a few M4 carbines, and some M203 grenade launchers."

"This is Pee-wee," he suddenly said. "You guys can say you're ready if you want to, but that's really strange. I'd bet anything you don't have one iota of what it is you're really up against. So keep saying what you want, but the time is coming when we're all going to have to prove ourselves."

"Okay, everybody, listen up," I said over the transmitter. "Make sure you're fully equipped. Anything you're without, report straight to the location of the Osprey. But each pilot is to remain onboard their craft. Better yet, I need an extra body to remain on-board each craft to keep a watchful eye on our surroundings should Ethan try anything."

"But what about the air quality?" someone asked.

"All clear," a voice said on the transmitter.

After finding myself once again repeating my past behavior, and , anticipating someone might be coming to our aid, my perception about how paranoid I had become was astonishing. Still, I could see no staff officials en route to ensure our safety. Again, I could see no movement coming from either direction.

Then, I made a conscious decision, one perceived by the entire group as guided by honest moral principles.

By now the majority of the team had gathered nearby where the Osprey had landed and were being issued the necessities required for the mission. From what I could observe, Mitchell appeared to be a well-mannered gentleman of noble intelligence from a specific rank. Coppage seemed much the same. His mannerism and style showed class, a very refined trait under the circumstances.

But make no mistake about it. Onboard the Osprey were about seven crew members, known as an elite part of the squadron, ready to conduct a vigorous battle. In their possession was an astronomical amount of ordnance.

I then thought to myself, this bitch is loaded with just about every kind of real freakin' heavy gun, and what looked like thousands upon thousands of pounds of artillery and ammunition.

Military weapons, ammunition, and high-powered military equipment seemed to be everywhere.

I wondered how such a craft as the Osprey, carrying such a load, could even fly.

With the vast majority of the crew now having exited their craft, I found it feasible to question the Osprey team about the situation in Stonyford. While conducting this mission, I also wondered if this journey might end up becoming a recovery mission as well.

"Hey, Coppage. Check this out, man. What's the deal with the situation in Stonyford?" I asked him. "We've been hearing all kinds of weird stories."

"It's some terrible shit going on," he said, his head down while tightening the elastic band on his headlamp with one hand and sipping from a container of V8 juice with the other. "It's really terrible."

"I think some of your guys could use a few of these Red Rhapsody Odwalla Superfoods right about now," one of the Osprey crew members said, almost like a suggestion. "There's also a mixture of different sports drinks onboard."

"You guys hear that?" the Cat asked in a whisper. "All kinds of sports drinks onboard the Osprey if you want any."

"Also, you guys, we have plenty of radio headsets here that are a lot better than always listening to everything from the transmitter on your helicopters. We have enough of these headsets for everybody," one of the ladies onboard the Osprey said.

"What about gloves and sniper scopes for our rifles, and a few extra cases?" someone asked.

"Got 'em," the Osprey member said.

"By the way, you guys, please make sure you take the time to sign your name on this list," another Osprey crew member said. His name was Joshua P. Olga. "It's just so our records will show who the equipment was logged out to."

"Ah, shit! Hold up, you guys," a voice suddenly said frantically.

"What's the problem?" a lady's voice asked.

"Yeah, what's the problem?" another lady asked.

"I think I'm missing one of my crew members," he said.

"Just what in the hell are you talking about?" he was asked.

"I'm missing one of my crew members, just like I said."

"And how's that?" someone asked. "Who's missing?"

"One of my men," he said again, emotionally distraught. "It got 'em."

"It? Who?" another member asked. "Who the hell are you talking about?"

"What the fuck!" someone yelled. "Just how the heck did you lose one of your crew members? How'd that happen?"

"Everybody start looking around," I said. "See if you can find out who he's talking about. He could be somewhere out here passed out or something."

"He ain't sick, you bastard," a grumpy, irritable voice suddenly said from somewhere in the darkness. "His bitch ass is gone, just like the rest of you little bitches are going to be real soon."

"Man, just who the fuck are you?" one of the crew members asked. "Come on out here so we can see your punk bitch ass. Come out in the open so we can see you."

Suddenly, an awful scream came from somewhere we couldn't see. The early morning dawn was still in that period between nightfall and light. Although daybreak was upon us, which is what we thought when we landed, the sky was filled with a bright, fog-like substance. Our journey to Stonyford had been full of strange occurrences .

"Hey, somebody point a light out there in the direction where the scream came from," Cat said. "I thought I saw something moving around in the dark. It looked like it was coming this way. Might be the person we're looking for."

"No, I don't think so," one of the crew members said firmly. "What you might be seeing is somebody, or possibly something else, out there in the dark pretending to be the person we're searching for."

"What makes you so sure?" I asked.

"Because our guy was just standing right here beside me and got snatched right out from under our nose," he told me. "It was like something grabbed him before he could even say anything."

"And you didn't see who grabbed him?" I asked.

"Oh, hell no," he said, scratching his head. "It happened so fast. I only felt the wind circling around me."

"Man, are you serious?" Mitchell asked. "You really didn't see who snatched him?"

"I didn't see nothing," he told Mitchell. "We were standing right here when something just yanked him away."

"Just like that?" Cat asked. "Something just yanked him away?"

"Uh-huh," the person being questioned said.

"You guys weren't smoking any of that shit, were you?" Peewee asked.

"Man, all I know is Bearcat was standing right here next to me. We were talking about something when, out of the blue, it happened," the crew member said again. "The next thing I knew, he got yanked really hard backward. And that was that."

"Well, whatever's happening, we've got people out there in the dark searching all over the place," another crew member said.

"Where's Murdock?" Cat asked.

"I think he's still over there somewhere by that Osprey, getting a reading on a few things," someone said.

"MacDonald, this is Cat. You copy?"

"Copy," MacDonald responded from his helmet microphone.

"Keep vigil, buddy," Cat told him. "Shit's starting to come to life around here. I think it's that chimera thing again. You know what I mean?"

"I think you mean Ethan," Ms. Montana said surprisingly.

"Thought we destroyed that thing a long time ago," MacDonald said, pointing his M9 pistol in the direction where the scream had come from. "Didn't we see that thing burning up and fully engulfed in flames after being blasted into pieces all over the place?"

"Your guess is as good as mine," Cat said with a slight chuckle. "It's like the crew member we lost out there in the dark. One of the guys says he got yanked or snatched by something. I don't know what to think. But it's obvious our brother is missing, and our mission is to find him."

"Pee-wee, this is Murdock. You copy?"

"That's Murdock right there trying to make contact with Pee-wee," Cat said. "I'm heading over there to see what's happening, MacDonald."

"Copy!" MacDonald responded. "I got this over here."

"Roger that," Cat said, heading back toward the Osprey where some of the crew members gathered and talking with each other.

By this time Pee-wee had finally made his way back to where several crew members were standing and gathering information. This wasn't long after he had rushed out into the dark field where the search for the missing crew member was taking place.

"Hey, Pee-wee, any luck on our guy?" I asked him immediately, hoping to hear the complete opposite of what he was about to tell me.

"Negative," another member said before Pee-wee even had a chance to respond.

"Nothing out there that we could find," Pee-wee said, disappointed.

"Damn!" Cat shouted. "We all heard the scream. But now it's like, what the fuck! Dude just upped and vanished into thin air or something."

It wasn't hard for me to sense that what we were up against was weighing heavily on everyone's mind. It was like a devouring parasite eating at us with an overwhelming appetite.

But they knew the danger of this mission, and the only alternative was to keep moving forward. Our mission was to deal with whatever lay ahead of us, waiting somewhere in what we thought was the early morning dawn.

Yet the darkness of night still clung to us, surrounding us in an elusive manner. Our lives felt as though they were hanging in the balance, where temperament and character could easily turn irritable and hostile under the pressure.

I also sensed an inner awareness of the possibility of activating ballistic missiles. That course would mean the dreadful free-fall of an immense amount of deadly projectiles through clear trajectories, bombarding the entire Stonyford region with a heavy arsenal of weapons and military hardware.

"Check this out, Olga and Coppage. Since Mitchell put you guys in charge of the Osprey," I said, wanting to ask them again about the situation in Stonyford. "When I asked what the people were going through, the only thing I was told was that the situation was tragic or terrible. What I want to know is, just what is it that's so terrible?"

"That's it," Olga said while staring in the direction of Stonyford.

"It's something really bad happening down there, and I don't see you guys wanting anything to do with it," Coppage said. "It's really terrible. I'm trying my best not to even think about it."

"Hey, Doc," Tony said. "From what I've been told, shit's supposed to be really fucked up down there in Stonyford. It might be best if we wait up here at the boys' ranch. But with so much at stake, I'm sure everyone would agree. We're all ready to do this thing."

"You guys know something? I really wish you could hear yourselves. What the fuck is happening with you?" I asked them. "You sound like a bunch of sissies trying your best to come up with reasons why we should avert this mission. I was hoping you'd tell me something about Stonyford that would make my blood boil. Instead you're out here sounding like a bunch of cowardly, timorous faggots."

"I ain't afraid of the Big Bad Wolf," one of the Osprey crew members said. "Man, if I die tonight, so be it."

"All right then. Now check out what I'm about to say. It's just an example," I told them. "Like you were saying, 'if you die tonight, so be it.' The Wolf is out there, no doubt about it. But I'd rather die on my feet trying to destroy the Wolf than die on my knees while he devours me. Don't let the enemy catch you slippin'."

"It's like everything has gone haywire, if you ask me," another of the Osprey crew members said. "It's mad havoc and widespread confusion everywhere you look in that town. There's destruction and the smell of death not only in Stonyford, but in just about every surrounding community as well. Emergency alarms going off all over the place, but nobody is paying them any attention."

"Well, I'm through asking about the situation," I told them. "I see now it's all about actions speaking louder than words."

"Sounds like it's time to rumble," I heard someone say from somewhere off in the distance.

"Yeah, that's right. It's time to rumble just like the ass kickin' that went down in Manila," I said loud enough for everyone to hear. "Except this rumble is about survival and trying to save a region that's become susceptible to the influence and power of various entities."

Suddenly someone screamed in anguish. They were saying something about finding multiple remains inside an old, rundown house. Whoever it was yelling said the bodies appeared badly decomposed.

"Oh God, no!" a very familiar voice that sounded like Midwest said on the transmitter. "Please don't let it be her."

"Hey, somebody keep an eye on him," Pee-wee said, referring to Midwest. "I'm heading over there to find out what's happening."

"I'm going with you," another crew member said.

"It's all right, guys. I can handle this," Midwest said after hearing them on the transmitter. "I got this."

"Are you sure, Midwest?" I asked him. "Just because someone mentioned bodies being found doesn't mean it's your missing wife."

"I said I can do this, Doc," Midwest exclaimed. "So let me do it!"

I have to admit I was just as confused as he was. I found myself wondering whether some of the remains might actually be Midwest's wife. The crew she had apparently traveled with on this journey to Stonyford were said to have all vanished while en route. Word was that the group she was with had headed in a completely different direction.

It was also my understanding that the boys' ranch was still in full operation. But from what we could see, the place had not been in operation for quite some time. From the reflections of the lights flashing everywhere, even the once modern cafeteria, which had looked like a restaurant capable of serving at least seventy-five people at a time, had obviously been destroyed.

The destruction of the buildings was an awful sight, especially remembering how the boys' ranch had once operated. What had once been a beautiful structure had been reduced to almost nothing. The entire operation seemed to have fallen victim to something no one could quite understand.

I wondered how many others, like myself, had believed the boys' ranch was still in operation.

"Hey, you guys. Over here. Right there," one of the crew members said, pointing to a specific location in one of the demolished structures where what appeared to be human remains could be seen. "You see, that's nothing but ashes and skeletons of kids scattered everywhere."

He was absolutely right.

I could clearly see that a section of the structure had once been part of the framework and storage area connected to the cafeteria. What I couldn't understand was why all the skeletal remains were stockpiled in the cafeteria, unless they had been hiding there during the time of their deaths.

Suddenly everyone heard someone say, "Monkey see, monkey do. I got that bitch's ass, just like poppa gonna get you."

The voice was Ethan's, referring to Midwest's wife, following him to the Stonyford region.

"Man, fuck you, Ethan," someone yelled on the transmitter in an angry tone. "Punk-ass bitch! I'mma blast you just as soon as I see you."

"Yeah, fuck you, punk!" someone else said. "I'mma get you the first chance I get, and I ain't lettin' up. You talk all that shit. Come out in the open so we can see you."

"Just chill out, you guys," I said so they wouldn't get revved up prematurely. "Never let words show your emotions. Ethan knows he's in control if you let him upset you. His goal is to knock you off balance, and once that happens, he wins. Plain and simple."

After Midwest had taken a brief glance at everything, it wasn't hard to see the relief in his posture. I could see the tension leaving him as he inhaled deeply and began breathing with renewed ease. That relief came from realizing his wife's remains were not among those found.

"Hey, you guys. What about that house over there on the far side of this field?" I said so everyone could hear me. "Did anybody go over there and check it out yet? And what about those house trailers on the other side of that hill? There should also be a few Airstreams, maybe some Montana fifth-wheels, and possibly a few fishing boats. There should also be a speedboat and a pleasure boat somewhere around here. Make sure you check all of them out if any of those things are still around. But as you know, I'm a bit doubtful and cautiously optimistic."

"You sure do sound like you really are," a voice sounding like one of the sweet ladies from the Highline of Montana said with a chuckle.

"You know something, Doc? Come to think of it, I do remember reading an article in a report about this place," another of the Osprey crew members said. "If I'm correct, the article mentioned an expensive motor home that was once at a campground somewhere on the other side of that ridge up there. But that's only if I'm not mistaken about which ridge it was referring to."

"Well, you know something? I think you're right," I said. "But we should look into that later. In the meantime, let's go see what's in that building over there."

"Strange it's still standing," someone said. "What's that, a dormitory?"

"That's exactly what it is," I answered, hoping there wasn't anything ahead of us that we would regret seeing.

"Think there's someone still inside this place?" someone asked me. "I mean alive. Like a transient just passing through."

"Your guess is as good as mine. I'm just hoping we don't find any skeletal remains in there," I said, still doubtful. "But we'll never know until we find out for ourselves. Am I right?"

"Uh-huh," the crew member said.

That was when I made it known that if we ended up finding more remains, I would have to get Midwest involved immediately to check whether any of them belonged to—

"Check to see what?" a voice asked. "Why would—"

"What, don't tell me you forgot that quick," I said. "We're talking about Midwest."

"Oh, damn! I forgot just that quick, like you said," the man replied. "I'll head on inside and see if I can help the team already in there."

"Good idea, as far as I'm concerned," I said, wondering what, if anything, they would find. "And if anybody sees the Commander, let him know I'm trying to contact him. Please. Thank you."

"Last time I saw him, he was still over there somewhere near his helicopter," a crew member said, pointing in that direction.

"Commander, this is Murdock. You copy?"

Indistinct static.

"Commander, this is Murdock. Do you copy?" I asked again.

Loud, random noises came through the transmitters.

"I say again, Commander, this is Murdock. Do you copy?"

Long periods of silence followed.

"Co-pilot of the Commander's craft, do you copy?" I said urgently into my personal radio. "Co-pilot of the Commander's craft, or anyone else onboard. Do you copy?"

More bursts of static and random noise.

"Hey, Murdock. That disturbance you're hearing might have something to do with that weird atmospheric cloud still hanging over this area. I think that thing is responsible for all the static on our radios and transmitters," one of the crew members said.

"Why don't you get a few of the guys together and go over there. Try to find out what's happening, will you? And get back to me ASAP," I told them.

"On it, Doc," he said. "I'll have the Commander contact you immediately."

"Make sure he does it right away," I said.

"Yeah! I finally found your location," another crew member came rushing up to me, somewhat short of breath. "Doc, it's big-time problems down in Stonyford. And I'm talking serious problems."

"That's some of what a few of Mitchell's crew members were saying. The only thing was they couldn't really elaborate in detail to tell me what I wanted to know," I told him. "So hopefully you can provide some helpful insight."

Just as he was about to start describing the tragic events taking place in Stonyford, a burst of rapid gunfire and loud explosions shook the region like an earthquake. Dark dust clouds erupted upward into the sky like giant mushrooms. This was followed by what sounded like thousands of rounds of ammunition and other explosives.

Various tactical weapons could be heard echoing throughout the area.

Looking around, I could see crew members in the distance

wearing military-style body armor. I could also see side holsters carrying weapons such as Glocks, Kel-Tecs, M9 pistols, KA-BAR knives, M1911 pistols, and other various weapons.

Each of them also carried high-powered tactical assault rifles with sniper scopes mounted on them.

Some crew members were carrying what looked like enormous amounts of explosives, ammunition, and high-powered projectiles that could be launched, with additional ammunition stored onboard the Osprey as reserve.

Onboard one of the CH-47 Chinooks there was also another arsenal of AR-15 tactical rifles at our disposal.

I could see that everyone was wearing different assortments of camouflage pants, shirts, and jackets, along with military boots and fully equipped tactical modular backpacks.

The sudden firing grew far more intense than anyone had anticipated. Massive explosions lit up the sky. Everything was happening fast and without warning. Each blast thundered through the air, filling the atmosphere with powerful projectiles streaking across the darkness and striking their targets.

"Move! Get out the way! Get out the way! Move!" someone suddenly shouted, warning the crew to clear the path of fast-moving projectiles such as rockets, ballistic missiles, and harpoon missiles.

"Move! Get out the way! Get out the way! Move!"

CHAPTER TWO

LOUD SCREAMS COULD BE HEARD throughout the area as each projectile hit its target, obliterating it instantly.

Crew members could also be heard shouting about the danger they faced as they tried to eliminate the threat to the region.

As Margaret said, the only way to win the battle was to exterminate Lucifer's army of fallen angels. They were said to carry every deadly disease imaginable to mankind. They had become dissimilar to everything God created in heaven and on earth.

"This is what's happening in Stonyford," Coppage shouted over the explosions and gunfire. "It's one hell of a battle going on down there. All that light you see in the distance is coming from Stonyford. Everything is really fucked up down there."

While we were talking, explosions continued all around us as gunfire and rocket-propelled missiles struck giant creatures of an unknown species.

Could these things really be part of the interbreeding of the fallen angels? I thought to myself. Don't look like any freakin' chimera to me.

Whatever they were, these creatures appeared to be twenty

to thirty feet tall. Some of them had huge wings, each with a span of roughly eight to twelve feet.

"Murdock, this is a member of the Midwest crew," a voice called over the radio. "You copy?"

"Hear you loud and clear," I replied. "Go ahead."

"Man, Murdock, we've got remains up here in this house. They've been here for quite some time. Too badly decomposed to tell if they're male or female. One of the team members is checking the clothing for possible identification."

"Hey, Murdock," someone else yelled over the radio. "From all the light flaring up around us near what looks like an old picnic area, I can see what might be the remains of a helicopter not far from where a projectile exploded. You copy?"

"Copy," I responded. "Are you sure it might be a helicopter?"

"Roger that," he said firmly. "Think we should move closer?"

"Hey, Murdock," a member of the Osprey crew said. "I've got an idea, since you already have a few of your crew members in place."

"Yeah, and what's that?" I asked.

"I was thinking about whatever those things are that we're up against," he said.

"Yeah, and what?" I asked, waiting for him to finish.

"Well," he began, "those things, whatever they are, are mainly out there near the area where your guy said he spotted the possible remains of a downed helicopter. Am I right?" he asked.

"Go ahead," I told him.

"What I was thinking is this. During our showcase of the Osprey down in Stonyford, we demonstrated a test dummy and some controversial devices to show the kind of damage they can cause."

"And just what are these things you're talking about?" I asked.

"They're called Bouncing Betties," he said. "Landmines made in China."

"Bouncing Betties," I repeated, letting him know I understood. These were the kind once buried a few inches underground during the Cambodia era. Pressure from a footstep would trigger the device, causing it to leap upward before exploding and spraying deadly shrapnel in every direction, shearing the legs off anyone within range. "What's your point?"

"Well," he said, "since you already have some of your guys out there, I was thinking they could assist a few of the Osprey crew members. Then we could place some of those old Cambodian landmines out there in the area where those creatures seem to be coming from."

"Wait a minute," I told him quickly. "Let me check something. That might actually be a good idea."

"Crew members out there on the picnic ground, you copy?"

A burst of static answered.

"Crew members out there on the picnic ground, do you copy?" I called again.

"Copy!" someone replied. "Can barely hear you. Lots of static."

"Roger that, Picnic," I said. "Stand by for a few minutes."

"Copy!" he responded.

"How many of you are there?" I asked.

"All together, four," he replied.

"Copy that, Picnic. Stand down for now and hold your position. You've got company coming to join you."

"Copy!" he said.

"Everybody stand down," I shouted over the radio. "Everybody stand down. I repeat, stand down."

The firing stopped almost as quickly as it had started.

"Cease fire!" someone yelled from somewhere in the darkness to my right, helping suspend the gunfire and the hostility, at least for the moment.

In general, I had to keep reminding myself that most of the

crew members, regardless of their profession as experienced journalists, were also trained killers. Under the circumstances, I wasn't sure how the stand-down would affect them, or whether it was even possible for them to stop firing and adapt to a temporary cease-fire.

I made the decision to postpone the action because we needed time to move into another part of this already deadly mission and lay an unknown number of land mines.

The Bouncing Betty was no joke. This was the Type 69 Bouncing Betty, a nickname Americans gave to a bounding fragmentation land mine.

These mines were once said to have been defused by a Cambodian named Aki Ra. In the mid-1970s, when he was only five, he was separated from his parents by Cambodia's Khmer Rouge and taken deep into the jungle with other orphans. At the time, Pol Pot and the Khmer Rouge had plunged the country into chaos. Schools, hospitals, factories, banks, and monasteries were closed. Teachers and businessmen were executed. Millions of city dwellers were forced into labor camps.

It was my understanding that the small hands of children like Aki Ra became invaluable tools. They trained him to lay mines, defuse them, and dismantle enemy mines they found. Then they reused the TNT to make improvised explosive devices.

"About how many of these things do you think we'll need?" I asked the Osprey crew member. "Or maybe I should be asking how many you have."

"Well," he began, "from the looks of things, somewhere around fifty to a hundred. And I believe I left about two hundred onboard the Osprey."

"Fifty to a hundred?" I asked. "We'll be here all night planting those things, don't you think?"

"Not if we get started right now," he said, grinning in the dark. "How many crew members did you say you already have over there in the picnic area?"

"About four," I told him. "Why?"

"Because I'll be sending the six I have to get the job done," he said. "My experts in land mining. Three of them are from Cambodia, and the others are from right here in the U.S."

"And these particular mines are the Bouncing Betties?" I asked.

"Well, not all of them," he said. "We also have a few in the stockpile like the Frog, the Drum, the Betel Leaf, and the Corncob. Most of them were manufactured in China, Russia, Vietnam, and a few in the United States."

"That figured," I uttered. "I just knew we had some part in the product's manufacturing."

"Ready?" he asked.

"Do it," I told him, giving the go-ahead. "But first, let me let the crew know what's happening."

I got on my radio and informed everyone about the mission to lay the mines near one of the entrances to the boys' ranch.

"I need everyone to continue to stand down for now, at least until these mines are in place. It'll be roughly fifty to a hundred on the outer edge of our perimeter. Through your binoculars, you should be able to see signs of activity from these creatures. You should also be able to see the remains of what appear to be one, maybe two, small helicopters."

Behind us there was an old barn. From what I had been told, somewhere behind that barn were also the remains of people who had fallen victim to whatever it was out here preying on others.

Something was deliberately seizing people with precise timing, quietly and with intense premeditation, snatching its victims without making any sound of its presence, ambushing them as it moved through the area and carrying them off.

"Okay, let's do this."

"Murdock," a voice said over the radio in a whisper. "This is

Cat. You copy?"

"Copy," I responded. "What's up?"

"We just found the remains of the Commander and a few of his crew out here behind that barn you were talking about."

"Damn," I said. "Hate to hear that. Hurry up and get back on this side of the perimeter."

"What about the remains?" he asked. "You want us to bring them with us?"

"What's the condition?"

"Pretty mangled," he said. "I can't understand why anyone would do something like this. All of them seem badly disfigured around the face, though still somewhat recognizable."

"You guys hurry up and get out of there," I told him again. "Whatever did that, I'm sure it's watching you. Most likely getting ready to snatch its next victim."

"Murdock, you copy?"

"Copy," I responded.

"The 'Picnic' is in motion," a voice said. "Any suggestions?"

"How many attending?" I asked.

"Ten to the event," the voice said. "Four here, and six will serve the host."

"Make sure the four cover those serving the lost," I told him.

"Roger that."

"Pee-wee, you copy?" I called on the radio.

"Copy," Pee-wee answered.

"What's your status?"

"At the house," he said. "Remains are everywhere."

"What about the mobile homes?" I asked. "Has anyone checked them?"

"It's all bad," he said. "Nothing but remains. Looks like the people who were staying in them."

"About how many per trailer?" I asked.

"From what we could see, ten to fifteen per trailer."

"That's impossible," I whispered into the radio. "How could that be? Unless those trailers are where these things are storing the remains."

"Think that could be it?" Pee-wee asked, wondering if I might be right.

"Think about it," I said. "It's like these things are snatching people the way a farmer gathers his crop."

"Gotta interrupt," another voice came over the radio. "But I think you're right. As a result of whatever this is, human-like crops are springing up all over this place."

"Man, this is some of the same stuff happening down there in the Stonyford area," Coppage said. "But shit's really fucked up down there."

"Coppage," I said. "I keep hearing you guys say that, but you know what?"

"What's that?"

"Nobody's telling me anything," I said.

"Yeah, you're right," he said. "I know what you mean. It's like, damn. Everything was a celebration. It was off the chain. Then something strange started happening. Something from underground erupted and started shaking everything. It was crazy. All those carnival rides started jumping off the tracks. People were flying everywhere. They were screaming and crying for help, but nobody could do anything except run in the opposite direction, because things really went crazy.

"All of a sudden—"

"Hold up for a minute, Coppage," I said. "I want everybody to hear this. I'm going to hook you up to the unit onboard the Osprey."

"Want me to start from the beginning?" Coppage asked. "Or from where I am?"

"Hey," I said to one of the Osprey crew members, "mind plugging this jack into your transmitter so everyone can hear what's happening down in Stonyford?"

"Got you," the crew member said, taking the jack and plugging it in.

"Appreciate that," I told him.

"No problem," he said. "How high do you want the volume?"

"Just turn it up enough so everyone can still control their own radios," I said. "I just want them to hear what's being said."

"That should do it," the crew member said.

"Good looking out," I told him, reaching for the mic. "Testing, one, two, three. Can you guys hear me?"

"Loud and clear," Coppage said.

"Okay, everybody," I began quietly. "As you know, we have an important mission underway. I'm here at the Osprey with the co-pilot, and he has information I think you need to hear about what's happening in Stonyford. I'll be speaking with him as he explains the situation.

"For those of you who haven't met them, the co-pilot is Coppage and the pilot is Olga. They're the ones navigating the Osprey.

"Go ahead, Coppage."

"Yeah. Like I was telling Murdock, something really crazy is happening in Stonyford. Everything was a celebration at first. Everything was cool. But then something started happening, and the ground began shaking like crazy. It was like something deep underground erupted. People started screaming and yelling for help. The ground began exploding, and steam started shooting up from everywhere."

"I saw all of this with my own eyes. Dark, thick lava, like something from a volcano, started bubbling up from the ground, catching everything on fire, even people. It started burning just about everything. I couldn't believe it. People were burning right there in front of me.

"They screamed for help, but nobody could do anything. Everything was happening so fast, yet it felt like it was moving in slow motion."

Back where I come from, people consider me an scholar because of my education. I've had special operations aviation training, along with many hours in special combat operations during my early years in Iraq and Afghanistan. My training includes rigorous coordination and counterinsurgency operations.

I also served as a crew chief with the 25th Infantry Division's 2nd Battalion, 25th Combat Aviation Brigade, providing security while flying Black Hawk helicopter missions with Commander Olga over large sections of Afghanistan's Kandahar Province.

However the situation in Stonyford began, I can only describe what's happening there as horrible. People are being slaughtered like cattle. Some are being snatched from right under the noses of others while simply attending the festivities.

These snatchings were happening repeatedly during the festival celebrations.

Festivities like these are often emotional, high-energy gatherings, much like community celebrations across Montana's Hi-Line. Places like Cut Bank, Sweetgrass, Sunburst, Shelby, Dunkirk, Devon, and even Glasgow all hold events where people gather in the same way.

But what was the connection?

The events in Stonyford had become something far more disturbing.

Reports connected them to other incidents across Montana's Free Homestead region. In Great Falls and nearby areas, residents had reportedly been found killed and eaten by wolves and other scavengers. There were even disturbing rumors about giant rodents and blood-drinking human vampires emerging from corpses buried in cemeteries across northern Montana, then attacking people in their homes during the night.

According to *The New Midwest Post*, missing-person reports were being filed regularly by the families of these victims.

Throughout the region, authorities began discovering the remains of possibly hundreds of bodies stretching from California through Oregon and Idaho, and into remote areas of Montana's northern Hi-Line. Each of these corpses bore the same traits and patterns as those found in the Stonyford region.

Although we are presently in the Stonyford mountains, the results of this investigation have already drawn heavy media attention. The story has spread from Stonyford as far as Montana and has yet to reach its peak.

Small towns throughout the Stonyford region have had their share of trouble dealing with what appears to be a serial killer, or killers. Yet according to the investigative team assigned to stop this monster, nearly every place that could serve as a hiding spot has been found completely deserted.

And now here we are with the Osprey, hoping to assist you in bringing this monster down.

Shortly after midnight, the town of Stonyford began experiencing something strange and terrifying. Many of the people killed were visitors attending the celebration. Nearly every carnival ride malfunctioned, taking the lives of those onboard.

The Timber Wolf, the Momba, the Thunder Hawk, the Zamba Zinger, the Boomer Rang, and the Rip Cord all failed, sending riders off track. Many of the victims still cannot be found, especially in the darkness.

But the most devastating incident involved the Magic Mega Water Slide.

Earlier that evening, countless children had lined up to climb the steps leading to the top of the massive multi-lane slide. Guided by attendants, they prepared for the thrill of racing friends down the lanes before splashing into Stonyford Lake below, where lifeguards waited.

What no one knew was that sometime earlier that evening, someone had embedded thousands of extremely sharp box-cutter blades along the surface of the slide. The blades appeared to have been welded into place.

Anyone who went down the slide had no way to stop.

As they descended, the blades tore into them, slicing limbs, fingers, ears, and other parts of the body. Some victims were nearly decapitated. Many reached the water screaming and struggling. Others never surfaced at all.

Believe me, it was a horrible sight.

It was during that chaos that some of us noticed helicopters flying in the distance, which turned out to be you.

By then, we had already received orders to evacuate the area. Our request was to assist you in this mission, because there was little else we could do in Stonyford except destroy the place with the ammunition we had onboard the Osprey.

The Osprey itself is practically a mass of TNT.

CHAPTER THREE

SUDDENLY, THE ALL CLEAR SIGNAL WAS GIVEN.

"All right, everybody," I said over the radio. "It's time to do this. Everything is in place."

"Hey, Murdock," a voice came over the radio. "I think we're missing some more of our guys."

"Are you sure?" someone asked. "Check and make sure."

"That's a positive," another voice said firmly. "Only a few of my guys made it back from out there by the barn."

"Get ready to open up in that direction," I told him. "Get ready."

"What about up here where the house and trailers are?" Peewee asked.

"Get ready," I told him. "I want everybody ready. Picnic crew and Osprey crew, fall back to the picnic area. Form a deep, invisible trench-type perimeter around us and protect the helicopters. I want everybody armed and fully loaded. Anything comes your way, take it down."

"We've got something moving around out there," somebody said over the radio. "From what I'm seeing on my GPS and iPhone , it looks small. Could be a child or something."

"You sure it isn't a small animal like a dog or cat?" someone asked.

"I don't think so," the crew member said. "From the way it looks, it's walking upright like a human."

Hold up, I thought to myself.

"Tony, you copy?"

"Copy," Tony answered.

"Check this out," I said. "Karen or Regina got their headset on?"

"Which ones?" he asked.

"The ones behind my chair," I told him. "The helicopter Model H10-13XL."

"Both of them?" he asked. "Because there are two pairs behind where I'm sitting too."

"Yeah," I said. "Have Karen, Regina, and Sandra put on a pair. That way they'll hear everything we're doing. In fact, if any of you have those Model H10-13XLs, put them on immediately for this part of the mission. The construction and quality of those headsets are excellent."

"What about the GPS?" a voice asked. "Shouldn't we all have them?"

"Thought you knew," I responded. "Roger that. As well as the MX20 and Garmin's GPSMap 295, 400, 420, and 430, and GPS, Comm, VOR/ILS with glideslope and moving-map graphics on a large color display."

"Hey," the voice said again. "That target is getting closer."

"Damn," someone muttered over the radio. "Why aren't any of those Bouncing Betties going off?"

"Don't ask me," another crew member said. "But I've got the target on my scope. All I need is the go-ahead and it'll be history. Bye-bye, señores."

"Or señorita," another voice added.

"Whoever or whatever it is doesn't look like it's coming straight toward us," one of the crew members at the picnic area said over the transmitter. "Looks like it's coming this way along the creek by Snow Mountain."

"Yeah, I see it too," Pee-wee said over the radio. "Looks small from what I'm picking up up here."

"Can anybody get a good look at it?" I asked.

"It's a kid all right," a voice said. "Boy or girl, I can't tell yet."

"What's the movement like?" I asked.

"Doesn't seem to be in any hurry," someone said. "Just taking its time, but it's definitely coming this way."

"Murdock, wait a minute," Karen suddenly said, sounding concerned. "According to a report I was reading from the initial investigation here years ago, the black box with the recorded conversations mentioned finding a little boy hiding inside one of the buildings. There was also something about sightings of a mysterious dog. It was first spotted during the drive to the Johnson residence by the older Sheriff Blake—not the son who's in charge today. They said the dog was sitting on the front lawn of the Johnson estate, just staring at everything and everyone."

"What are you talking about, Karen?" Tony asked.

"She's talking about something strange connected to that little boy coming up the creek by Snow Mountain," Regina said. "That might be the same boy."

"But check this out," Karen said, suggesting they listen to another part of the report. "They're also saying this might be the same little boy in all of these findings."

"How could that be?" Tony asked. "You sure—"

"No, hold up, Tony," a voice whispered over the radios. "Let her finish reading the report."

"I agree," I told him. "That little boy might even turn out to be the Earthquake. Could possibly be Ethan as well."

"Oh, it's him," Regina said. "I bet anything it's him."

"Pee-wee," I called over the radio. "What's the status on the object?"

"Still moving like it doesn't have a worry in the world," he answered. "We all have a pretty good look at it, whatever it is. But it's still moving up the creek toward Snow Mountain."

"Cat, what's happening out there?" I asked.

"We've got all kinds of weird things going on out here," he said. "But you know what I think? I think whatever those things are, they're taking on appearances like us, making us think they're human."

"You must be reading my mind," Karen said anxiously. "That's exactly what this report is talking about. It says there was some kind of transformation when the Sheriff and the others came up here to investigate people screaming for help. According to the report, remains were found somewhere near that barn. Others were found in a storage room in the back section of the mess hall. I believe that's where the kitchen used to be."

"Looks like it's blown to bits now," I told her. "But some of the crew did find skeletal remains where I think the back section of the kitchen once stood."

"Yeah," Karen said. "It was in that kitchen building where they had a bloody confrontation with what they thought were those giant thirty-foot-tall chimeras and other creatures crawling around everywhere."

"Coppage, you copy?" I said over the radio.

"Copy," he replied.

"Hey, man. Check this out."

"Okay, what's happening?"

"We need to get everything we can off the Osprey. You feel me?"

"I copy."

"I'm going to get a few of the crew members together."

"Think they can handle it? That's a lot of equipment, Doc."

"What's the smallest load we can move first?"

"Why don't I just come over there? Or better yet, you meet me back over here."

"Damn. I really didn't want to be going back and forth out in plain sight. But what the hell. I'm on my way."

"Want me to go?" Tony asked.

"Nah," I told him. "I need you here in case—"

"I mean, if you want to," he said again.

"What, and leave Sandra, Regina, and Karen here by themselves?"

"Oh, like it's been some help leaving him here," Karen said, nodding toward Tony. "He ain't no protection. Look at him."

"Yeah," Tony shot back. "Look at me, then look at you. We'll see which one that giant chimera grabs first. That's why I need to get away from the chimera we've got onboard this helicopter. We've got our own monster."

"Anyway," I interrupted, "I'm going to take a few people and move most of that equipment off the Osprey and onto these helicopters. I really need you here, Tony. But on second thought, maybe it wouldn't be a bad idea if you helped them."

"Hurry up and get his ass out of here, Murdock," Karen said. "Or better yet, let me go help them and keep his butt here."

"You really want to go, Tony?" I asked.

"That's the Osprey right over there, isn't it?" he said, squinting into the darkness.

"Yeah, that's it," I answered.

"Man, that thing is really big in the dark," he said.

"Believe it or not," I said, "that's what everyone says about what we're flying in. They say this MH-53 is big and ugly."

"Yeah, but wait till they see what's going to be getting out of it. Now, you really want to talk about something being ugly? That's going to be it. Just wait," Karen said, snickering. "Just wait till a chimera sees this thing."

"Ha! Ha! Really funny, Karen," Tony told her. "Really funny coming from you."

"You guys just don't quit, do you?" Regina said, staring at both Tony and Karen. "Just think. Before this is over, the chimera is going to have both of you."

"Okay everybody, listen up," I said over the radio. "I need you to keep extra watch while artillery is being moved from the Osprey onto our helicopters. Some equipment, like the large-caliber mounted weapons, certain machine guns, high-powered guided missiles, and a few other ballistic missiles, are too dangerous to have onboard our helicopters. These weapons will most likely be used in the beginning phase of the operation as part of the plan to eliminate the aggressor.

"This will be done in stages, hopefully."

"What about when it comes time to get out of here?" a crew member asked. "How and at what stage are we going to do that?"

"Good question," I told him. "But first things first. Some of you will continue doing what you have been doing. Document this entire event. Others will be using just about every weapon available in combat to bring down the enemy. Do it forcefully and with everything you've got."

"What about the ammo?" someone else asked. "What if we start to run out?"

"With the ammunition we are being supplied from the Osprey, it's highly unlikely that will happen anytime soon. You will have more than enough for whatever it is we are up against."

"Hey, Doc," another crew member called over the radio. "You copy?"

"Copy," I responded. "What's up?"

"I'm not sure what's happening, but I think the object is now moving in our direction," he said in a low whisper. "From what I can see on my radar, it's moving really slow, almost like a crawl. Like a snake creeping up on its prey."

"Murdock. This is Knucklehead. You copy?"

"Copy that, Knucklehead," I answered. "What's up, man?"

"Uh, I got the motherfucker on my radar too," he said in a low, rough, gravely voice. "I'll have it on my scope in a few. Want me to go ahead and take it down?"

Click! Click! Click!

Click! Click! Click!

"Clicker," I said quickly over the radio. "We copy you. What's up?"

"Hey, you guys," the person clicking said. "Why don't you hold up for a minute before you do anything."

"Yeah, well," Knucklehead responded. "What's the reason?"

"Yeah, and who are you?" I asked.

"Man, this is Charlie Hart over here with Michael Clifton," he said, sounding uneasy. "You guys, that thing you're calling the target, I really think it's a small kid coming our way. So don't fire. Let me find out what it really is first."

"Okay, everybody," I said over the radio. "Continue to stand down for now until somebody confirms what this thing is. Karen, Regina, Sandra. What can you give me about the target?"

"Thought you'd never ask," Regina said. "From this report, there's something difficult to explain about a little boy and a dog. The people who wrote this report kept mentioning them throughout the investigation. They appear and disappear, then show up somewhere else again."

"Just so you know, Regina," I said, "you're on mic. Be as specific as you can so everyone understands what you're describing."

"I understand," she said. "Everything about the boy and the dog is a mystery to everyone."

"But who are they?" Tony asked. "Where did they come from? Did the report say anything about that?"

"At this point, everything is still a mystery," she told him.

"I mean, did the dog belong to the boy or what?" Tony asked.

"Doc, this is Coppage again," he said over the radio. "You copy?"

"Copy," I answered. "What's up, Coppage?"

"From the report I remember reading, I think it came from those people who burned up inside that motor home earlier while camping up here. It said they were yelling about a dog that was trapped or tied underneath a trailer. When they freed it, the dog ran away and never came back."

"Yeah, I remember that part too," Karen said. "The report said that after they finally identified those individuals, they turned out to be the teenagers who had come up here in their jeeps. How they ended up burning inside that motor-home camper is still a mystery.

"And that dog?

"It's supposed to still be out here somewhere."

"Well, what about the little boy?" someone asked over the radio. "Whatever happened to him?"

"That's the mystery surrounding this whole situation," Regina said. "No one really knows what happened to the boy or that dog. Well, not until now."

"Now here you go, Regina," Tony said while scanning the helicopter's transmitter, which picked up a strange signal. "Hold up. You hear that, Murdock?"

"What?" I asked.

"Hey, you guys," a voice came over the radio. "I think we've got something else moving out there in the dark. Something predatory. Keep your eyes open."

"What's the radius on what you're picking up?" another voice asked.

"It's coming toward this location fast. About ten miles out and closing by the minute."

"Murdock," another voice called. "This is one of Midwest's crew. Whatever it is on the radar, it's moving in a wide circular motion."

"Damn thing is all over the place," another voice added.

"Hey, Doc. This is Olga," he said. "You copy?"

"Copy that, Olga. What's up?"

"I bet that's those two crazy guys from earlier down in Stonyford. The ones flying that German BO-105 helicopter and doing all those aerial tricks."

"Aerial tricks?" I asked. "Like what?"

"You know. Loops and rolls. The kind they do in those aerobatic helicopters."

"Excuse me for interrupting," another voice said over the radio, "but what does that have to do with our target? That thing is still crawling along like a snake and starting to pick up speed."

Suddenly a loud scream cut through the radios. It was someone yelling for help.

Then another scream. Then another.

"Jesus fucking Christ!" one of the crew members shouted. "Somebody help us!"

"Where are you?" another voice yelled into the darkness. "Where the fuck are you guys? Answer me! Where the fuck are you?"

A moment later, massive explosions erupted as the landmines detonated almost simultaneously. The blasts echoed nonstop.

The sky lit up around us from gunfire and attack missiles firing at anything that moved in the distance. The ground shook violently with every explosion. Each blast tore through the terrain, ripping apart sections of the mountains as if the earth itself had no defense against the force tearing through it.

*

This was the beginning of what Margaret had described. It was the beginning of Satan's deadly scenario, one he would brutally use to destroy this entire region from northern California to Oregon, into Idaho and Wyoming, and across the homestead Montana Hi-Line.

This was the beginning of what man receives not from God, but from the devil himself. For such things are foolishness to man. Neither can he know them, for they are spiritually discerned.

This was the beginning of both death and hell, as described by Margaret.

The people celebrating their joyful festivities in the small town community of Stonyford had unknowingly become part of a mystical phenomenon connected to Satan and his fallen angels. The nature of this unfolding drama would reveal the immortal beings attendant upon Satan. No longer subject to death, they would appear once more, just as they had when attempting to overthrow the kingdom of heaven, celebrating their victory over the entire Stonyford region and claiming the residents of these communities.

Satan, for example, would deliver from the bottomless pit his entire squadron of vexatious demons. These spirits, eager to take their place among the living, would rise forth. Some would remain as subordinate and wicked spirits.

The salvation of this region would instead reveal the selfish works of Satan. His deception would appear elegant and clever, just as it always had. His charm would delight many, much like the wearing of a gold chain or bracelet believed to possess magical powers. What appears as an amulet of blessing would instead bring harm, injury, and suffering.

That suffering would be undeniable and repeated again and again.

This entire region would embrace a misleading relationship crafted by none other than Satan himself. Like a skilled craftsman, he would present his work with careful precision. Like a chairman presiding over his enterprise, his goal would be to gain this region for his own purpose.

To Almighty God, it would appear as if Satan had spread his wicked influence like a sweet fragrance among the people, establishing a new regime to reign with terror across the land.

The residents of Stonyford had allowed their community to become like the lake of fire, representing death itself.

The resurrection, as it now appeared, seemed to grant victory to Satan's fallen angels, allowing them to emerge from the bottomless pit with dreadful power.

Lucifer's intended goal was now at hand with great expectation.

*

"Man, what the hell is going on?" a crew member cried out. "It's just like the Book of Revelation has come to life."

"Hey, keep the Good Book out of this," another voice yelled. "This is between us and them. Whatever they are."

"What the hell are you talking about?" someone else shouted. "All of this is part of the Tribulation. A tale of our redemption and a freakin' celebration of whatever it is that's about to happen around here."

"Redemption for what?" another voice asked.

"The Devil," someone added. "The Devil is about to appear."

Firing and heavy explosions continued. Everyone kept shooting at large creatures attacking the crew throughout the region.

Cries of agony echoed from every direction from people trapped in unbearable suffering.

This was the beginning of what some believed to be Satan's new covenant for the region as the terror continued to unfold. At that moment, the destruction felt like something dreadful and deliberate. Something that promised suffering for those caught within it.

"Hey, Doc," Olga shouted. "We're out of here. I think your crew got everything they need off the Osprey. Anything left, we'll be using it on the way up."

"What the hell are those BO-105 helicopter guys trying to prove at a time like this?" Coppage asked. "They're flying around like they've lost their minds."

"Damn stupid idiots, fooling around like that," one of the Osprey crew members muttered. "Crazy bastards."

"Isn't that the same helicopter crew that was in Stonyford doing those aerobatic flights?" I asked Olga over the radio.

"That's them," he said. "I told you they were crazy."

"They act like they can't see all this firing going on down here," another crew member said over the radio. "They're headed in the wrong direction and don't seem to give a damn."

"We're out of here, you guys," said Olga as he and Coppage began starting the Osprey's engines. Each engine stood upright and the rotaries began to spin. Once in flight and at the proper altitude, the engines would swing downward into their horizontal position.

Watching the Osprey lift off, I began thinking about the situation. In the distance I could see bright, shifting silhouettes of human figures moving in combat across the ground. Their helmet lights flashed through the darkness, reflecting off the chaos below. The lights revealed members of my entire crew, devoted professionals loyal to the mission, fighting as thunderbolt streaks of machine-gun fire ripped violently across the night sky while huge creatures waited in the darkness to slaughter us.

It sounded like thousands of rounds were being fired. M240G machine guns, tactical rifles, and landmines erupted almost nonstop.

Then, to my surprise, I saw the German BO-105 helicopter explode in the distance near Snow Mountain. A blazing fireball burst into the sky before the wreckage crashed near the creek running through the lower basin of the mountain.

Deep down, I knew they were dead.

Moments later another explosion ripped across the darkness. The Osprey itself erupted into a fatal fireball and dropped from sight between the huge hills and mountains surrounding the region.

"Olga! Coppage!" I yelled into the transmitter. "Do you copy?"

There was no response.

"Olga! Coppage!" I shouted again. "Do you copy?"

Still nothing.

Everywhere I looked, the world seemed to burn out of control. We were battling an enemy that simply would not die. Crew members were sprinting across the field, engaging the creatures in desperate combat.

"Pee-wee," I called over the radio. "Do you copy?"

At first, there was only static.

"Copy," Pee-wee finally answered.

"Are you all right?" I asked.

"Affirmative."

"What about the target?" I asked. "Is it still moving?"

"Target boarded the Osprey five minutes before takeoff," he said.

"What?" I shouted. "Boarded the Osprey?"

"Yeah," he said. "Thought you knew. That's why Olga seemed so happy to get out of here. He wanted to help save the kid. But—"

"Oh man," I muttered. "I don't believe this. That kid—"

"That was the kid," Karen said quietly. "Or whatever it was."

"What's happening?" Pee-wee asked.

"Man, that kid wasn't a kid," I told him. "He's the same one those other people thought they were saving before we got here."

"The Earthquake!" Pee-wee shouted into his mic. "That was really him."

"Yeah," I said, not wanting to believe the Osprey crew fell victim to his cunning ways, pretending to be a child in need of help. "That was that son of a bitch. He just killed our friends. He took 'em out, Pee-wee. He fooled them after all the warnings I gave about his skillfulness. Damn it, the Osprey crew still fell prey to him, and he destroyed them."

"Better warn everybody else about what happened," Tony said. "You know he's coming back."

"Yeah, but in what form?" I said, wondering who Ethan would try to portray when he returned. But it was what Margaret said that had me most concerned. She didn't clarify whether I would end up meeting him in Stonyford, or in jail. Maybe it was the possibility of something happening one way or another that bothered me most, especially after the hell my crew had already gone through.

"Incoming!" somebody yelled as a huge explosion made a violently loud sound like a volcano, within a short distance from the landing strip.

"Everybody take cover," I yelled over my radio.

"Man, that was close," Tony said, stunned that an explosion had happened that near. "My ears are ringing big time."

"Charlie Hart or Clifton, you guys copy?" I called out on the radio.

Static.

"Charlie Hart or Clifton, you guys copy?" I called again.

Nothing but static.

"Incoming!" another voice screamed in the distance as another explosion violently shook the ground. Random screaming came from the direction of the picnic area, where huge flashes from the planted landmines discharged and sent debris high into the air, lighting up the dark sky.

"Pee-wee, Knucklehead, Cat, MacDonald, Midwest, and the remainder of the Commander's crew," I called out over the radio.

"Do you guys copy? I repeat, do you copy?"

"Pee-wee and Knucklehead, Sacro, copy!" they responded.

"Cat and MacDonald, Lodi, copy!" a voice yelled.

"Those of us remaining from the Commander's crew, copy!" another voice said.

"Midwest, do you copy?" I asked again.

"Midwest was last seen over there in that trailer park after finding a few items belonging to the Mrs.," a voice came over the radio. "Haven't seen him since."

"Pee-wee, you got that?" I asked.

"Heard it," he said. "Want me to check it out?"

"Roger that," I told him. "Take a few with you, and take down anything offensive."

"Ten-four," he responded.

"Anybody in the vicinity of the picnic area? Come back at me," I said on the radio.

"Hey, Doc," a voice whispered. "We got serious problems down here. We need help, man."

"Without me questioning, you got that coming," I told him. "You got that coming, buddy."

"Hurry up, Doc," the voice said. "These things are tearing him apart right here in front of me. All these explosions ain't doing a goddamn thing to scare them off. It's like it's what they want or something. You know what I mean?"

"Tell me what you're talking about," I said. "What are you talking about, buddy?"

"These goddamn freakin' giant vultures, Doc," he said, panting and taking short breaths as if he couldn't get enough air. "They're right here in front of me, tearing and ripping him apart. These things must be at least fifteen feet tall, with wings I'm sure spread a good goddamn thirty feet across on both sides."

"Everybody's listening, buddy," I told him. "We're on you."

"Hey!" another voice cried out over the radio. "Better watch out for these giant vinegaroons too. There's a troop of them on the move. If I'm correct, I don't believe they're venomous."

"What the fuck do they look like?" someone asked.

"Giant scorpions," he said. "But wait a minute before you do anything. Oh, fuck, man. These things got huge tails with deadly stingers. What the fuck! They're deadly!"

Suddenly we could hear screaming coming through the radios.

"Oh God, help me!" the voice cried out. "Help me!"

"For Christ's sake, Doc," another voice said over the radio, "we got rattlesnakes all over the place attacking our guys. They're everywhere, and other kinds of venomous creatures running around."

"Where are you?" I asked. "What's your location?"

"I'm over here in the trailer park with some of the guys," he said. "I was watching Midwest when he disappeared down one of these hills. I couldn't stop him, man. None of us could stop him. He was in a hurry going down this hill leading to that creek. The only thing we could see in that direction from where we were standing was that helicopter burning."

As we talked, another huge explosion erupted, apparently from the Osprey. There were still plenty of explosives onboard when it was attacked by the chimera-like creatures. The blast could be seen for miles around the region, and we could see huge flashes of light coming from Stonyford.

As we scattered across the boys ranch, remains of the people who had ventured into this area before us were being discovered, as if they had huddled closely together before being slaughtered. From the evidence left behind, it appeared that most of them had been herded or forced into a narrow corridor of some kind and then slaughtered.

As the blasting from the land mines continued, loud plaintive howls could be heard from the direction of Snow Mountain. They sounded like wolves and other wild animals attacking crew members who could be heard fighting fiercely for their lives.

Assessing the situation, I could see that nearly everything in the immediate vicinity, including the boys ranch, was engulfed in flames.

Even with all the firing from our weapons striking their targets, loud screams of agony could still be heard from crew members in every direction.

The screaming echoed repeatedly, like a sound carried and thrown back by thousands of voices, rolling across the land like a tidal wave.

It was time to get everyone out of the situation and move on to Stonyford.

It wasn't my intention to leave anyone behind, but as in any battle there will always be serious injuries, some killed, some missing in action, and some taken by the enemy.

But the moral principle in this situation could easily become as misleading as it could be guided by the truth when fighting an unseen enemy. In retrospect, reviewing Stonyford's past and the events surrounding it, if Margaret's account contained no errors then this entire belligerent campaign by Satan will be brutal. Even when the natural man receiveth not the things of God, that which he has inherited from Satan is still by all means foolishness unto him.

"Okay everybody," I yelled over the radios and transmitters. "Time for us to get the hell out of here. Start pulling back and head for your helicopters. If any of you are wounded, don't try to make it back to your helicopter on your own. Yell out and let us know where you are. Worst case is that you stay quiet and get left behind. That would be an unnecessary tragedy."

"It's time to give it everything you've got. Fire those weapons like never before. Start blasting the fuck out of anything you believe isn't friendly. Take it down. Once you reach your helicopter, mount whatever weapon you want on it. Strap in and keep firing. You'll know when it's time to ease up."

"What about the Commander?" someone asked.

"What about him?" I said.

"I mean, are we going to circle back and see if we can find him?"

"You mean are you going to fly over there to see if you can find him," someone else said.

"Why not all of us?" the man asked.

"What about Midwest?" another voice said. "He's out there too."

"What about everybody that's still out there?" someone added. "Man, we can't just leave them."

"Listen to me," I said over the radio. "I know how all of you feel right now. But you can see what we're up against. I'm surprised you've held up as well as you have under the circumstances. We are under attack. All of us. Whatever we're fighting is trying to wipe us out. This isn't a joke. This is really happening."

Just as I was talking to the crew, a loud explosion erupted so violently that scattered debris and pieces of human remains littered the entire area around our helicopters.

"Man, what the fuck!" MacDonald shouted. "What's all this?"

"Hold up, you guys," Pee-wee yelled. "Doc, I think something just hit one of our helicopters."

"Man, are you sure?" I asked in disbelief.

"It did," Tony said, staring through his night-vision goggles. "All that muffled thumping noise we were hearing, we thought it was debris blowing up from the ground after that explosion and hitting this helicopter. But it wasn't. You won't believe it, man, but I think that's body parts everywhere. It's all over the place."

"Damn," I said. "Just what we needed."

"Hey, Murdock," a voice came over the radio. "You copy?"

"Copy," I answered. "What's up?"

"Man, this is Knucklehead. We got one of ours blown all to pieces out here. One of those things hit it with something really hard and heavy. From what I can see, there were no survivors. Nothing but casualties blown to bits all over the place."

"Knucklehead," I said, "make sure everybody around you has those guns mounted tight on their aircraft. Better yet, I'll tell them myself. Time to light this whole goddamn place up."

"Want me to do it?" Tony asked.

I knew he was just trying to help, and emotions were running high across the crew. But it was crucial that everyone stay in control. We had plenty of artillery and even more on the ground if we needed it. I could see crew members securing rocket launchers to the helicopters, along with antiaircraft guns and crates of powerful ammunition and equipment. The Osprey crew had supplied us with more than enough ammo for this operation. Now it was time to fight like hell to get out of this situation.

"Okay everybody, listen up," I said over the radio and transmitter. "Get ready. It's time to give it everything you've got again. Gunners, burn the hell out of those motherfuckers. And ladies, excuse my French, but you have heard nothing yet compared to what's about to happen on my count of one. Everybody get on your helicopters."

"What do you want us to do?" Karen asked, dressed in military fatigues.

"Damn," I said, staring at her. "Where did you come up with that? And why aren't Regina and Sandra wearing one?"

"They're back there," she said, looking ready for war. "They know where to find them."

"Is it enough for everybody?" Tony asked.

"Enough for us," she said. "But I don't know about you."

Just before Tony and Karen could start their usual attack on each other, a voice came over the radio yelling, "Incoming!" putting an abrupt end to their childish exchange.

Another explosion shook the ground violently, shattering the front windshield on one of the helicopters and injuring the pilot. One of the engine cylinders was forcefully ejected through the fuselage, disabling the helicopter and leaving it powerless. The crew immediately began removing its weaponry and stripping it of its electronic devices. They then placed highly explosive detonator devices inside its frame and set them on a timer to explode once they were clear of the area.

I could see weapons being loaded onto another helicopter while a few crew members mounted what looked like an M60 machine gun to the craft they planned to fly out of the area in. Each crew member wore night vision goggles and a metal helmet with a mic and heavy-duty plastic face shield.

Within what seemed like only a few seconds, the entire crew was ready for an all-out war. They mounted nearly every weapon that could be fitted to the helicopters while explosion after explosion slammed violently into the ground around us. Each blast sent tremendous clouds of dust and deadly fragments racing through the black sky above.

I couldn't help thinking about how proud I was to have such an elite group of people with me on this mission. Skilled journalists and media professionals who could look you straight in the face without fear and volunteer for something like this were more than I could have imagined when the trip first began. It felt as though I had my own military unit made up of people with many different skills, ready to fight without argument or hesitation.

They were ready at the drop of a hat to fire on the enemy at the slightest sign of aggression from whatever we were facing.

After what felt like hours of mounting and loading equipment onto every helicopter, I could see through my night vision goggles nothing had been left on the ground except for thousands of empty shells.

Everyone knew this was the moment for whatever was about

to happen. The anticipation could be sliced with a knife. Breathing could be heard over helmet mics as crew members secured extra weaponry onto the helicopters. Journalists and media people were moving with the coordination of military personnel, organizing themselves efficiently. Some were already manning machine guns and miniguns, hanging slightly outside their aircraft from secured seats while testing the stability of their firing positions.

The tragedy of the German BO-105 helicopter, the Osprey, and one of the UH-72A Lakotas, along with no telling who else, weighed heavily on everyone. We had lost some of the best crew members anyone could ask for. The loss had not been anticipated.

What was even more confusing was the fact that something mysterious and unexplainable had taken place during our approach to the boys ranch. During our struggle through the thick fog, something nearly impossible happened when our helicopters landed in what the FAA and any experienced pilot would consider a perfect landing formation.

Why, after all the difficulties we had gone through, would anyone then want to destroy us?

*

Could this be another part of Satan's religious work of doom revealing itself?

None of the crew practiced or believed in the mysticism of Satan through deep spiritual meditation in union with the devil.

The entire situation had become perplexing. The whole region of Stonyford seemed bewildered. The immediate area and its activities had forced everyone into an ultimate choice: surrender themselves to Satan, or die trying to resist his deadly grip.

He leaves no other options.

Under the circumstances, it was obvious that this was Satan's war and his intention was to win at all costs. His hostile belligerence, as we had seen, was brutally combative. It could be spiritually concealed, appearing smaller or less threatening than expected, as if diminished in order to distract a person from their focus.

His voice speaks to everyone firmly. At times it is intimidating, reaching into the depths of a person's being. Recognizing that voice can be like discovering a slithering snake or deadly lizard spreading its poison like a parasite feeding upon the soul.

Satan's intention is to infect the entire Stonyford region with his corrupt influence, spreading it thoroughly to prove his presence.

Everything during Stonyford's celebration had seemed prepared for the release and rebirth of Satan's fallen angels, creatures believed to have been imprisoned in the bottomless pit surrounded by the mountains and hills overlooking the region.

That pit had become their prison. Their defeat cast them out of heaven, tumbling to earth and buried deep within that abyss.

Nothing can be hidden from God.

Yet the question of their manifestation remains uncertain. Unless the trinity doctrine is false, disagreement with that doctrine could prove tragic for one's salvation.

If we attempt to interpret scripture carefully, to clarify its meaning or represent it artistically, we must sometimes insert explanation between the words of history itself.

Salvation throughout the Stonyford region has therefore become an issue of prophecy and doctrine. Scripture teaches that there is only one God. Yet within this new interpretation of events, some claim Satan himself now claims the power of blessing.

For it has even been written that Mary is the mother of both God and Satan, granting each authority through obedience to her.

Through such interpretations, some claim salvation through both God and Satan alike. These doctrines, once whispered quietly for generations, are now being spoken openly.

Stonyford and the surrounding regions, stretching as far north as Oregon and as far east as the Montana Hi-Line, had long been taught the doctrine of the pre-tribulation rapture.

Yet according to this new terror unfolding before us, everyone would stand condemned regardless of their beliefs or claims of salvation.

No one, it seemed, would make it to heaven.

CHAPTER FOUR

"OKAY YOU GUYS, let's give it everything we got," I said in a whisper on the radio. It was time for the crew to use the deadliest part of our artillery to fight what was trying to destroy us. "I want every large-caliber machine gun firing the fuck out of everything. Those of you specializing in the use of that freakin' AK-104 assault rifle, it's time to prove your skills.

"All right, get ready Tony, Regina, Sandra, and Karen.

Three... two... one!"

Explosions went off everywhere, only this time the barrage was far more intense.

"Pilots, start your engines and let's head down to Stonyford," I yelled over the radio.

Flipping every switch to power up the engine on this MH-53 felt like coming home again after a long vacation. The rising hum brought a feeling of pure delight, almost like hearing your favorite instrumental piece performed perfectly. The cockpit of this craft is designed so well for pilots and crew that it almost feels as if it surpasses its own limits.

The MH-53 is the Mercedes, the Benz, and the Rolls-Royce all in one powerful machine. Royal performance. The kind of authority you'd expect from a monarch ruling an entire kingdom of helicopters.

"Okay, maybe I'm going a little too far," I muttered to myself. "But the MH-53J Pave Low dominates. No doubt about it."

As for the crew, professionalism hardly seemed strong enough a word to describe them. There was no hesitation, no defect in their discipline. Throughout this mission they had operated with skill.

Watching the crew members still on the ground while the helicopters idled for takeoff, I saw them gripping high-powered machine guns mounted on tripods along the sides of the aircraft. Others were firing M203 40 mm grenade launchers, and a few were launching LAW 80 guided missiles whose blasts echoed across the region. Rocket launchers fired constantly while ammunition and artillery from the wrecked Osprey continued to detonate.

"Pee-wee, Knucklehead, Cat, MacDonald, members of the Commander's crew, Midwest crew members, anyone," I called over the radio. "Do you copy?"

"Pee-wee and Knucklehead, copy!"

"Cat and MacDonald, we copy!"

"Members of the Commander's crew, we copy!"

"This is the flight crew of Midwest. Rickey Bryant. We copy!"

"All right then, people," I said. "Take flight for Stonyford. Let's get the fuck out of this hellhole and take down every goddamn roadblock on the way. Fire on anything that isn't friendly with everything you've got."

"Hey, Rickey Bryant," someone said over the radio. "Where the hell did you come from, buddy?"

"The Special Operations Aviation Regiment out of Kansas," he answered. "A Special Airborne Division you probably wouldn't know much about, seeing as you've been up here in these hills all your life."

"Man, just who the fuck you think you're talking to?" the person asked Rickey Bryant. "Ain't nothing but crazy motherfuckin Green Berets and some bad-ass SEALs around here fucking shit up for the enemy. You feel me, Rickey?"

"Everybody use your gas masks," I told them. "You know, the JSGPM M50. And watch that muzzle flash when blasting those things."

"Incoming to the north," someone yelled over the radio.

"Hurry up and get that freakin' Chinook the fuck outta there," a voice rang out. "Things are aiming at you."

"Hey, MacDonald," I yelled. "Man, can you get a lock on that bitch?"

"Got 'em," he responded in a firm tone. "Come on to papa, baby. That's right."

"Incoming at twelve o'clock," somebody yelled. "Whoa! What the fuck! I'm hit. Somebody copy me? I'm hit!"

"Got you, buddy," another voice responded. "Just hang in there and try to bring it down carefully so we can rescue your dumb ass."

"Hey, man. Just don't let those things get us," the downed pilot said. "Hope we don't hit any rocks."

"Fuck the rocks, buddy," the rescuer said. "Bet you can't get away from this rocket."

"Rocket? What rocket?" the downed pilot screamed.

Suddenly, a huge explosion erupted from the direction of the downed chopper. It became apparent that the so-called rescuer was none other than Ethan, posing as the rescue team. By then other members of the crew realized what was happening and immediately opened fire on the helicopter Ethan was destroying it.

"Hey, Murdock. Man, would you by chance have any morphine or something I can take for this pain?" one of the crew members asked. "I need some medical attention quick, fast, and in a hurry."

"Identify yourself," one of the crew members told him. "Identify yourself."

"Ha, ha, ha," was all we could hear as the voice snickered over the radio in a deep tone. "You fuckin' bastards."

*

By this time I was more than sure everyone was flushed with intense anger toward the enemy. Another helicopter had been lost and more crew members' lives had been taken. Ethan had once again seized on everyone's mental focus, using it to gather information about this present enemy.

As the crew continued trying to examine the situation objectively, I found myself growing unsettled as well, drawn into a confrontation that seemed almost impossible to understand clearly. But it had become time to establish a different authority against the Devil.

The damage had already been done. Satan had used the chaos to illustrate his position, stirring hatred and as if preparing the ground for the creation of a new nation under his influence.

Stonyford had become vulnerable. His treatment of the region seemed designed to push his cause further, gathering followers willing to surrender their souls under conditions that were ugly, shaped by despair.

Everything happening throughout the Stonyford region could be described as unnatural. The facts themselves seemed so strange that they bordered on something imagined.

What the crew feared most was the possibility that whatever we were fighting might spread some deadly contamination across the region. It would destroy the population the way an invasion of serpents might overrun a land, allowing Satan's fallen angels to emerge victorious.

From what we could see, there appeared to be a protection shielding these creatures from the attacks we were launching against them. Our massive arsenal of weapons, even our poisonous gases capable of destroying entire communities, seemed to offer no real advantage against whatever we were fighting.

There seemed to be nothing available to us that could effectively block the process of their attacks. Still, our best guess was that these creatures were some grotesque combination of giant chimeras, overgrown varroa mites, monstrous serpents, and other poisonous horrors spreading devastation throughout the region.

There had also been reports of deadly wasps carrying crew members away into the hills. Scientists in earlier years had reportedly found thousands of eggs in that area before dying themselves from the stings of those creatures.

But the greater culprit seemed to be Satan himself, whose influence had settled over the entire region. From Stonyford's perspective, his presence was becoming increasingly dominant, and through constant pressure he was drawing people toward the belief that he alone was the true power governing their fate.

Such speculation is dangerous, especially when considering the supposed authority of the birth mother said to have given life to both God and Satan. The claims surrounding that belief seemed to demand explanations that stretched far beyond ordinary reason.

However unpleasant the thought may be, many people in the Stonyford region had come to accept these ideas as part of their beliefs. And although the consequences could be deadly, some communities had grown deeply enraged over what Stonyford had allowed to take root.

As predicted, many surrounding communities had refused to attend the celebration. Those opposing the inauguration claimed the entire event was nothing more than an anti-Semitic hate festival directed against anyone unwilling to accept Satan above God.

*

"Hey, Rickey," someone called out on the radio. "You still with us?"

"Copy that," Rickey responded. "I think it's getting ready to be foggy around here. Lots of fog moving in really fast."

"Hey, Cat," I called out on my radio. "You copy?"

"Copy," Cat answered, though static nearly drowned him out.

"You got anything on this fog Rickey's talking about?" I asked.

"MacDonald's already on top of it," Cat said, his reply breaking through bursts of electrical static.

"Hey, Rickey. You copy?" I called again.

"Yeah!" he answered at first. Then he corrected himself. "Uh, copy."

His first response barely registered in the moment's chaos. With all the explosions, artillery blasts, and the constant firing of large-caliber weapons, the radio chatter was almost lost in the noise. But the fog Rickey mentioned concerned me. I wondered if it might be another illusion created by Ethan meant to mislead us. We were already fighting an enemy we couldn't see, something determined to destroy us at any cost.

"Rickey, you copy?" I asked again.

"Copy," he answered.

"Where the hell are you? What's your altitude?"

"Ah, man, Doc," he said. "I'm high above you guys. Way up here."

"Excuse me, you guys," another voice interrupted. "But you know what? I thought I saw your craft climbing fast as hell. I bet you were climbing at at least nine hundred feet per minute."

"Yeah," Rickey said. "And after you saw what we saw, you'd be climbing that fast too. Just ask my co-pilot."

"Who's your co-pilot?" another voice asked.

"Hey, man. This is Pee-wee," he said. "That's just what I was about to ask you too, because we saw you climbing."

"It's John Dodge," Rickey answered. "He's a number one pilot from a bad-ass U.S. Military Delta Force. I think it's best you talk to him yourself."

"Hey, Dodge. You copy?" I asked quickly. "This is Murdock, though these guys call me Doc."

"Copy, Doc," Dodge responded.

"So Rickey's saying something about you being U.S. military. That true?"

"Copy," Dodge answered.

"What'd you fly?" I asked, wanting to know his unit.

"I work directly under Delta operator Major Morris McCoullum," Dodge said. "I piloted an MH-47E Chinook based out of Fort Campbell, Kentucky."

"Hot damn," someone yelled over the radio. "Did I just hear somebody say Kentucky?"

"Hey, mind your own business," Tony said with a laugh. "We're up here talking grown folks' business that you hillbillies know nothing about."

"Well, I'm a Kentuckian," the voice said. "And I love my bluegrass."

"Sounds like you're smoking it right now," another voice added.

"Hey, buddy," the voice from Kentucky shot back. "Just because I'm from Kentucky don't mean I've been smoking anything, you bastard."

"Anyway, Dodge, how the hell did you come across Rickey?" Cat asked.

"Me and Trickey Rickey go all the way back to the 160th Central Intelligence counterterrorism operations out of Washington during our Special Operations Regiment days," Dodge said.

"Ah, shit!" Knucklehead shouted over the radio. "Trickey

Rickey! Oh no you didn't just call him that."

"Trickey Rickey!" another voice added. "Man, what the fuck!"

Through the dark sky huge explosions could still be seen and heard as the remaining helicopters continued flying toward Stonyford. Flashes like lightning streaked across the sky around my craft from the constant gunfire and artillery shells exploding on impact as they struck their targets at full speed.

Weapons were firing from every aircraft. Each blast from our guided missiles briefly illuminated the creatures below as they scrambled for cover from the relentless barrage.

It was then we began to see the fog Trickey Rickey had been trying to describe. It appeared almost out of nowhere, spreading quickly through the air. The substance seemed strange, as if it were made of some unknown material capable of causing memory lapses like the one that struck the crew when we landed at the boys ranch.

Our helicopters had landed without anyone piloting them, something we still hadn't been able to explain.

But it was becoming obvious that even worse problems were waiting for us in Stonyford.

As I looked around to make sure everything was still intact, I saw no damage to my craft despite the heavy explosions around us. Sandra and Regina were busy on their Harris RF-3590 tablets, accessing a wideband network and sharing real-time information. Karen, however, sat quietly with her index finger brushing across her lips. I could tell something serious was on her mind.

I couldn't help wondering what things might have been like if I hadn't walked out of her life when she needed me most. That decision still haunts me. The memory is like a restless ghost that returns again and again, reminding me of what I did and of the beautiful thing I lost.

I have to admit I felt twisted up inside at that moment. The truth is, I'm still very much in love with her. But no matter what I feel, I have to stay cautious.

Then, suddenly, a voice shattered my thoughts.

"Incoming!" someone screamed over the transmitter.

A massive explosion erupted ahead of us. A huge red and yellow fireball burst in the air, bright enough to light the entire area like a nuclear blast above the boys ranch. In an instant we realized another one of our aircraft had been hit, killing everyone on board.

"Oxygen masks, everybody," I shouted into my mic while staring through my night vision lenses at the raging fire. "My guess is it's the fog. Or something in the fog."

"Ah, man," Cat shouted. "You guys see that?"

"Anybody know who that was?" Knucklehead asked angrily.

"Don't know yet," a voice responded sharply.

"What makes you think it's the fog?" Pee-wee asked.

"Man, Pee-wee," I said. "Look over there at Snow Mountain and tell me what you see. Isn't that the same fog we flew through just before we landed?"

"You mean before it landed us," Tony added.

"That's right," I said. "Before it landed us. Isn't that the same fog coming over the top of Snow Mountain?"

"I think it's coming back to get us," Karen said, staring out the left-side window through her night vision lenses.

"Hey, I think you're right," Pee-wee said. "I'm not doubting you, Murdock. Truthfully, I think we're all in agreement."

"Hell, got my vote," MacDonald said. "I'm just wondering what we're going to do about it."

"Well, whatever needs to be done, we better hurry," someone said over the transmitter. "I think I can feel a slight drag tugging on my chopper pretty hard."

"Hey, Doc. This is Trickey Rickey," he said. "You copy?"

"Copy, Trickey Rickey," I responded. "What's happening?"

"From what we can see up here, that fog is moving downward and heading in your direction. Thought you should know."

"Copy that, Trickey Rickey," I replied. "Good looking out."

"Wait a minute," Tony said quickly, switching his helmet microphone on. "Trickey Rickey, you copy?"

"Copy," Trickey Rickey answered. "Who is it?"

"Hey, man," Tony said. "This is Tony, the Doc's co-pilot. Were you able to see who that was that exploded from up there?"

"Ah, man. Hell yeah," Trickey Rickey said. "But that didn't come from no freakin helicopter."

"What!" Tony shouted.

"Hold up," another voice said in surprise. "It wasn't a helicopter?"

"Trickey Rickey," I said quickly. "You're saying that wasn't a helicopter that exploded? Then what the hell was it?"

"That was one of those things you guys were shooting at," he said. "From what we could see up here, it exploded after one of your rockets hit it."

"Man, that's bullshit!" Cat shouted over the radio. "You're crazy if you think anybody's going to believe that."

"Hey, man," John Dodge cut in. "Trickey Rickey ain't lying. I saw it too."

"And who the hell are you?" Cat asked.

"John Dodge," he answered. "Trickey Rickey's co-pilot. Now what?"

"Yeah, well," Cat said. "I think you guys been flying a little too close to that goddamn Kentuckian hillbilly smoking whatever crazy stuff he's been smoking."

"And this is your so-called crazy Kentuckian hillbilly," another voice said over the radio. "And you know what? I think you're the one who's nuts, buddy."

"Well, I'm not pointing out anybody's identity," John Dodge said over the radio. "But it was definitely one of those things that exploded. That was after it got hit by a rocket or something."

"I think you might be right," I said, stepping into the conversation. "From one of the reports years back, they mentioned something about a monster exploding and blowing up a large motor home or something like that."

"Hey, are you guys watching the way that fog is approaching you?"

"Murdock, you copy?"

"Copy," I responded.

"This is Knucklehead," he said. "Did you recognize that voice?"

"Uh, this is Dodge, you guys," he said over the radio. "We're getting nowhere up here. I think the fog must be putting out something like a magnetic pull.. We don't have the power to move forward."

"Hey, this is Pee-wee," another voice said, his words breaking through heavy static. "Whatever's happening, we're having problems with our throttle system. I can't seem to get any power."

"Jesus Christ," another voice yelled over the radio. "I was just about to call mayday. I'm about to find a place to land. I'm getting nowhere up here."

"Sounds like everybody's starting to have power problems," Tony said, staring out the front window. "You think it's him again?"

"Him who?" Karen asked, tightening her seat belt.

"You guys are talking about Ethan, aren't you?" Regina said. "Sandra and I already knew he was coming back. He won't stop until he kills all of us. You know that, don't you, Mr. Murdock?"

"Ah, man," Tony said suddenly, sounding startled by whatever he was seeing outside.

"What's happening?" I asked.

"Hey, you guys," a voice came over the radio. "You're not going to believe this, but just over there to the right is a car or something—"

"That's what I was about to mention," Tony said.

"What is it?" Regina asked. "What do you see?"

"I think it's a car or a truck coming this way," I told my crew. "But whoever it is, they're driving way too fast around those curves."

"Hey, Doc," a voice called over the radio. "You copy?"

"Copy," I responded. "What's happening?"

"Man, this is MacDonald," he said. "I think we got some crazy company down there off to the right. Looks like three or four vehicles following each other at a high rate of speed. Looks like they're heading toward the boys ranch. We need to find a way to stop them, if you know what I mean."

"Damn, that's right," Tony said. "Those things are going to get 'em."

"Ah, man. What the fuck?" somebody yelled over the radio. "You guys see that?"

"What's he talking about?" MacDonald asked. "What's he talking about?"

"Hey you guys, this is Trickey Rickey," he said. "Now that was really messed up."

"What, Trickey Rickey?" I asked quickly. "What's happening? What'd you see?"

"Man, the last car got slammed by something," he said. "Looked like it smashed into something on that road, and then something came out of those bushes along the side. I couldn't see what it was."

"It looked like some giant fuzzy, hairy torpedo," Dodge added. "Like something you'd see shot from a submarine. Except this thing came flying out of those bushes."

"Did anybody see what happened to that car?" Pee-wee asked.

"I don't know," a voice said over the radio. "But the other ones don't seem to be slowing down."

"What the fuck!" Trickey Rickey shouted. "You guys see

that?"

"Got it," MacDonald said.

"Hey, Doc," Cat called. "You copy?"

"Copy," I answered.

"I think I've got enough power to at least check for survivors after that hit," Cat said. "Any objections?"

As Cat carefully moved closer to assess what had happened to the damaged vehicle, a sudden cry of agony burst over the radio. Someone was screaming for help. According to the GPS readings, the signal was coming from the same area.

Then a second vehicle was struck violently, like the first.

The savage attack from these giant chimeras was far beyond anything science had ever explained. The entire Stonyford region was under assault.

At the same time, the thick fog began closing in again. It spread across the area and created another wave of uneasiness among the crew. Everyone sensed that the battle with the fog itself might become our deadliest engagement yet. Gunners began preparing their most powerful weapons, mounting heavier equipment in each craft.

"Hold up, Cat," I shouted. "The fog's moving in too fast for you to get lost out there. If you can't see any movement, then there aren't any survivors."

"Hell, not from that hit," someone said.

"And what about the other vehicle still heading toward the turn into the boys ranch?" Knucklehead asked. "Think we can at least try to help them or something?"

"Hey, a few of you guys from the Midwest crew," I said. "Fall back down to see if you can do anything. And anybody flying a 72X+, it's time to demonstrate your performance. Back them up. Any survivors, let's take them home."

"Man, looks like y'all got a bazooka mounted on that thing," the Kentucky hillbilly said as one helicopter dropped downward with a huge gun sticking out from its side.

"Yeah, is that right?" someone shot back. "Why don't you come down here and get a better view?"

"That's all right," he answered. "Thanks for the invitation, but I think I'll keep watch from up here. If the temptation gets strong enough, though, you can bet your ass I'll be on my way down there. Y'all just be careful and hurry back."

"Roger that, Kentucky hillbilly," the pilot of the 72X+ replied. "That's exactly what we intend to do. Who else I got with me?"

"Duce-Duce, motherfucker. Who you think?" Duce-Duce said with a laugh. "You got mail."

"Hot damn," the Kentucky hillbilly yelled over the radio. "Got another one of those ASS-72X+ machines tagging in right behind him like a fired-off guided missile. What the hell? Here comes another one."

We could sense that the Midwest crew intended to stay together in formation, just as Midwest had always required. Each of the ASS-72X+ helicopters began demonstrating its power, endurance, and survivability. Mounted along their sides were weapons specifically designed for that craft, equipment powerful enough to wipe out an entire community.

"Professionally, I strongly suggest that crew lead the way," I said, almost thinking out loud over the radio.

"I hear you," Tony said in agreement.

"I was thinking the same thing," another voice added.

By then the fog had crept even closer to our position. It had almost completely covered Snow Mountain. Considering the size of that mountain, watching the fog surround it as if it were swallowing the entire peak was an astonishing sight.

Then the reality of the situation began to sink in.

The fog had encircled Snow Mountain completely, wrapping around it like a ring on a finger. And the truth was becoming clear. We were its intended target. It was trying once again to draw the entire crew into its grip, just as it had done when we first entered this part of the region.

Huge flashes of explosions could still be seen all around us, coming from the journalist Marines who had become a vital part of both our crew and this mission. Over the transmitter we could hear reports of aircraft and personnel on the ground being rescued after being ejected from malfunctioning aircraft, the work of the best leatherneck force available for the job.

Entire sections of mountainside were being obliterated by the rapid firing of the weapons mounted on each helicopter, along with the aircraft circling closer to the ground. The scene below showed constant movement, every person either hunting or being hunted by some dangerous predator. Remains from both sides could be seen scattered across the ground like some violent scene staged for a public spectacle.

But unlike the scattered remains near the barn from years earlier, this scene would not be left behind for scavengers. There would be no scent of decaying bodies for vultures to follow. This mission would end with every fallen member returned to their proper place for honorable arrangements and recognition.

"Trickey Rickey, you copy up there?" I called over the radio.

"Copy, Doc. What's happening, man?" he answered.

"Anything we should know about?"

"Well, I think your next option is to get the hell out of there," he said. "All that firing isn't letting up. It's coming straight at you."

"Hey, Pee-wee. You copy?" I called.

"Copy, Doc," he answered. "What's happening?"

"You getting any drag on your chopper?" I asked. "Better yet, is everybody experiencing the same thing?"

"I think we're all feeling it," one voice responded.

"I know I am," another added.

"Hey, it's putting too much strain on my engine," Pee-wee said. "I've got the throttle at full power, but nothing's responding the way it should."

"Hey, you guys. This is Cat," he said, identifying himself. "Man, I'm having problems with my rudder pedals. I'm applying pressure, but nothing's happening. I can't get my craft out of this hellhole."

"Midwest crew, you guys copy?" I called.

"Copy," a voice answered, fading in and out through static.

"What's going on down there?" I asked. "Are you still reading me? Any problems?"

"Having trouble with the instrument gauges," the voice said. "Nothing's working right. My altimeters and directional gyro are going crazy down here."

"Damn," I said to the crew. "Everybody get ready to start preparing to land again before whatever's in that fog does it for us like it did before."

"What's up, Murdock?" Tony asked. "Thought we were headed to Stonyford."

"Those things got us again, don't they?" Karen said, a nervous grin spreading across her face.

"Everybody prepare to bring them down as quickly as possible," I said. "Just like when we landed earlier, try to keep the same spacing between us."

"Uh, this is the Midwest crew," a voice said over the radio. "We've made enough clearance and distance for you to proceed with your emergency descent."

"Roger that, Midwest," I replied. "Please continue keeping watch for possible chimeras coming out of the fog."

"Copy that, Doc," he answered.

"Thank you," I said as each helicopter began descending rapidly from less than one thousand feet, banking right or left into a lower level for landing among the debris and wreckage scattered across the area from missile strikes and exploding projectiles. "Be extremely careful. Avoid landing on any unexploded rockets. We don't want anyone going up in smoke."

"Hey, Murdock?" a voice called that sounded like Pee-wee. "Man, you copy?"

"Copy," I answered. "What's up?"

"I know you ain't going to believe this," he said. "But I gotta tell you anyway. You know that fog-looking stuff?"

"I copy," I said. "What about it?"

"Man, Murdock," he said, "from where we're seeing it down here, that thing looks like a huge ball of fusion energy."

"Fusion?" I repeated, stunned. "What in the world are you talking about?"

"Fusion?" Regina said as she began typing into her laptop.

"Man, I'm telling you," the voice continued. "Down here it looks like this huge, ugly, round ball of sparkling electricity. All kinds of different colors flashing out of it. Static everywhere. It looks almost stationary, but it's slowly moving in our direction."

At that point I no longer cared who the voice belonged to. All I knew was that he sounded excited about whatever it was he was seeing. From a scientific standpoint, though, fusion was something that existed mostly as theory or concept, often tied to ideas about remnants of life forms from ages long past.

But then I wondered how anyone could begin explaining something like that to a crew without sounding ridiculous, especially to a group of educated media professionals and respected journalists.

I started to feel that I lacked the authority or knowledge to explain what was happening. The situation was far beyond anything I understood. The strange fog clinging to the aircraft almost seemed like some reflection of the region's divided beliefs between God and Lucifer. Whatever the truth was, the entire crew was now witnessing something that felt supernatural and impossible to deny.

If what we were seeing truly was some kind of transformation, then perhaps the stage had been set for something far greater than any of us could imagine.

Still, whatever the substance of the fog was, it continued to cling stubbornly to each helicopter, holding tight as if determined not to let any of us escape.

"Has everybody landed?" I asked over the radio, frustrated by the realization that we were still trapped at the boys ranch. "Safely?"

The only response I heard was the word "copy," repeated over and over by what sounded like countless voices.

By now everyone could clearly see the enormous glowing sphere of fusion energy hanging in the distance. It looked like something out of a dream.

Was this some kind of punishment being inflicted upon us? I wondered. Was this what a loving father would allow to happen to his children?

"Man, Murdock," Tony said quietly. "I'd really like to have a chat with God."

"Yeah," I replied, still staring at the glowing sphere. "Me too."

"Hey, Murdock?" a voice called over the radio. "This is Cat," he said. "You copy?"

"Copy that, Cat," I answered. "What's up?"

"How far away would you say that thing is from us?" he asked, confused by what he was seeing.

"Tell him about a half mile," Regina said quickly.

"I'd say about a half mile or so, Cat," I told him. "You all right?"

"A half mile?" another voice shouted. "Man, that thing looks like it's just a few feet in front of my craft and getting closer."

"I think it's got some kind of illusion effect going on," someone said.

"Well, illusion or not," another voice said, "how long are we supposed to stay down here this time, Murdock?"

"Listen up, you guys," I began. "I'm just as confused about this thing as you are. But I'll tell you one thing. It's no illusion. I don't see anything false about that fusion happening right in front of us. This thing is real, and it's happening whether we understand it or not. For now all we can do is ride it out. It's not threatening us at the moment. The only real danger I see right now is some of you getting paranoid. Pull yourselves together so we don't lose anyone when it's time to make our move."

"You really think this thing's going to be that much of an obstacle when the time comes?" Tony asked.

"Truthfully, not unless people start losing their heads," I answered.

By then every craft had landed safely and shut down their engines, bringing the noise level down across the area. The helicopters had spaced themselves out carefully. When the moment came to move again, the roar of multiple engines starting at once would hopefully create enough confusion to mask our real position from whatever was controlling the fog.

"Hey, Doc. This is MacDonald," he said over the radio. "You copy?"

"Copy, MacDonald," I replied. "What's up?"

"I think I know what you're up to," he said quietly, letting out a low snicker. "But do you really think it's going to work?"

"Why not?" I said. "That is, if you really know what I'm up to."

"Oh, I know," he said again with that same quiet snicker. "Let the music play."

"What music you boys talking about?" another voice asked. "Mind if I get in on the action?"

"Yeah, well first identify yourself," Pee-wee said sharply. "Identify yourself."

"Fuck you, you clandestine incestuous son of a bitch," the voice shot back. "I'm your daddy, bitch."

"Who the hell is that?" someone asked, clearly alarmed.

"Who are you talking to?" another voice said. "Who are you?"

"No, you're the bitch, punk," a voice that sounded like MacDonald shouted over the radio. "Why don't you quit being a coward and show us who you really are?"

"I got your coward right here, MacDonald," the voice replied.

"Yeah, and I got yours too, Ethan," MacDonald shot back.

"Why don't you say my name, you freak?" one of the crew members yelled at Ethan. "Here it is. Yo mama, faggot. I know you got that, didn't you?"

"Everybody back off," I shouted over the radio. "Back off!"

Suddenly everything went silent.

A stillness settled over the area like nothing we had experienced before. It was as if the world itself had gone quiet. No voices. No engines. No weapons firing.

It felt like a strange secrecy had fallen over us, a refusal to reveal our presence. No one spoke. No one moved.

We remained there in silence, holding our positions, waiting.

CHAPTER FIVE

IT WAS LIKE REPEATING MYSELF. I was once again checking everything about my craft just as I had done after our arrival at the boys ranch.

"All right, you guys, I do believe break time is just about over. Let's get ready to do this once again," I said in a low voice on the radio. "Everybody copy?"

"Pee-wee and Knucklehead with our crew. We copy!"

"This is Cat and MacDonald with our crew. We copy!"

"Trickey Rickey and Dodge with our crew. We copy!"

"Duce Duce and my crew with the Commander's crew. We copy you."

"Midwest crew members. We copy you loud and clear."

"Yeah, this is Ethan and his crew. We copy you, sorry dead prick—"

I could sense the crew ignoring the attention Ethan was trying to draw. Was this what Margaret meant when she warned me that I would eventually encounter Ethan? She hadn't put it exactly that way, but that was how I interpreted her words.

It felt as though I had entered some strange competition with him while still trying to fulfill the obligation I had made to my supervisor when I accepted responsibility for this mission. I couldn't say Ethan's presence was unexpected. I had been warned about him beforehand. Margaret had told me to remain alert for Ethan's possible appearance. What she hadn't said was that he would become such a dangerous and determined part of the opposition.

*

The evidence and information the crew had collected so far seemed compelling and powerful. It suggested something resembling creation itself might unfold before us.

The gradual process of change no longer seemed like mere theory. It appeared increasingly possible that what we were witnessing reflected the same process scientists describe when explaining evolution.

This gradual transformation is something humanity often prefers to bury beneath eons of history. Yet it represents a common origin that links every living thing.

This process of physical existence extends far beyond simple theory. Over the years many researchers have described it through various means, and their conclusions have frequently been debated by those unwilling to accept such possibilities.

To dismiss such evidence entirely would be to ignore a complex and comprehensive body of knowledge that speaks not only through isolated facts but through broader patterns of understanding.

*

After checking my craft, nothing seemed damaged. Everything looked as though nothing strange had happened at all.

I checked my instrument gauges again.

"Could this really have been predestined?" I wondered.

Each craft was once again sitting in perfect formation just as before, except this time it was by our own doing rather than the mysterious force that had arranged us earlier.

Cautiously, I opened the door again.

Outside, I was met with the same unnatural silence that had greeted us when we first landed. It was strange, because I felt the same quiet inside the craft as well.

Then I noticed something on the outer surface of the helicopter.

The substance clinging to it could only be described as human matter, the remains of whatever had been destroyed during our battle with Lucifer's creatures.

"Uh, Doc. You copy?" a voice whispered over the radio.

"Copy," I answered. "What's up?"

"Man, this is Pee-wee," he said. "I got some really weird shit splattered all over my craft. Looks like blood or something."

"Hey," another voice whispered over the radio. "We got the same thing."

"Over here too," another voice added.

"Everybody just stay calm," I told them quietly. "MacDonald, I need samples of that material. Can you do that?"

"No problem," he said immediately. "Just give me a few minutes."

"Man, Doc," Tony said, "I don't remember us running into any birds."

"I don't think it's bird matter," I told him, staring out the open door.

"Then what?" he asked, reaching out through the sliding window, trying to wipe some of the substance off the front windshield.

"Some of our crew members," I said while watching the material slowly drip from the helicopter blades.

For a moment the air went completely silent.

Then Karen, Sandra, and Regina all gasped at the same time.

“What?” they said in hushed disbelief.

“I know you didn’t just say what I think you said,” Karen whispered. “Tell me you didn’t.”

“Yeah, we heard it too,” Sandra said, glancing around to make sure none of the substance had landed on her or Regina. “That’s not funny, Murdock.”

“It’s not a joke,” I said. “Come up here and look at it yourself. Touch it like Tony was about to do and you’ll see whether it’s a joke or not.”

“Man,” Tony said quietly, “how are we supposed to get this stuff off this thing?”

“We’re all going through the same thing,” I tried to explain. “All of us have this stuff on our crafts. It’s just something we have to deal with, especially in this situation. Just try not to get sick when I turn the windshield wipers on.”

“That’s when I’ll be closing my eyes,” Regina said. “I don’t want to be staring at dead body parts smearing across the windshield.”

“Girl, I feel you,” Karen said, watching Tony carefully inspect the tips of his fingers to make sure there wasn’t any blood on them.

“I don’t know why you’re doing that, Tony,” I said. “Just wait until we get to Stonyford. You guys haven’t seen anything yet. And remember what this mission is about. We are journalists. Our job is to get down and dirty, so the blood of our fallen comrades is going to end up all over us. There won’t be any room for sympathy out here. You’re journalists, and I expect you to get the job done. Do you copy?”

Suddenly voices began answering “copy” over the radio. Without realizing it, our microphones had remained open, allowing the entire crew to hear the conversation. One by one they responded to what they thought had been a command directed to everyone.

In a strange way it felt like an honor. Despite everything we had lost to Satan and his army of cruel demons, this crew still carried a sense of discipline and respect.

I noticed a faint clearing in the fog far off in the distance, approaching from behind one of the many mountains surrounding the region.

The boys ranch itself was in complete ruin. Everything had been destroyed. What remained looked like the aftermath of a disaster brought on by the chaos spreading outward from Stonyford, a destruction that had already scarred much of the surrounding countryside.

It was a strange feeling standing there again. Somehow we had been forced back to the ground by a power none of us could explain. And the last place anyone wanted to be was right here, in the dark, surrounded by the deadly creatures that crawled through the night.

Flying was one thing. Being on the ground in total darkness with predators hunting around us was something else entirely. After everything we had already endured, I don't think anyone in the crew intended to become another victim without fighting for a way out.

Nightfall in this part of the Stonyford region was never a comforting thing. Darkness here seemed to swallow every trace of light. From dusk until dawn the land turned black, deeper than any ordinary night.

Looking out the windows showed just how deserted the area had become. It almost seemed as if the state of California had abandoned the boys ranch entirely and moved its resources elsewhere. What struck me as strange, though, was the absence of any warning signs. No private property markers. No keep out notices. Nothing to warn people away from the decaying buildings that had once served as the kitchen, offices, and other parts of the facility.

The road that wound through the hills toward Stonyford lay completely silent. There was no traffic in either direction.

Whatever had happened to the vehicles we had seen racing along the road before the fog returned was anyone's guess. I could only imagine what they must have encountered.

From our position, we could see hundreds, maybe thousands, of deadly vinegaroons crawling across the hillsides.

Where they had come from was still a mystery. But from the remains of the boys ranch, we could see them clearly moving across the ridges above us.

I hadn't even seen or heard any wildlife. Not even a cricket. Just a silent stillness everywhere around us. The only movement I could see came from crew members shifting around inside their craft.

There were no insects on the ground. None flying in the air. Not a single bug moving anywhere around us. And not a single critter crawling in sight.

Then suddenly the power went out again. Everything died.

My master switches were dead, and the ADF (Automatic Direction Finder) had completely shut down, leaving us without power to the transmitters.

"Tony, check the circuit breakers," I quickly told him.

"Checking, but I can't see any problems," he said, staring at the panel.

"Hey, Doc," someone said over the radio. "You copy?"

"Copy," I answered, already knowing what he was going to say. "Whassup?"

"Man, it looks like everything just went dead," he said. "You copy?"

"Copy," I acknowledged. "Just hang tight. I'll get back with you."

"Hey, my laptop isn't working anymore," Sandra said.

"Neither is mine," Regina added, looking puzzled.

"Good thing I left this door open," Karen said, stepping out from the storage area of the helicopter. "Probably would've locked me in there."

"Yeah, good thing you did," Tony told her. "Not saying I would've missed you or anything. Though... probably would've had to use a GPS to find you."

"Fuck you, Tony," Karen shot back.

"Truthfully speaking, I really don't think this door is electric," I said, slowly sliding it back and forth to check whether any electrical system controlled it. "I don't think so, Karen."

"Damn," Tony muttered with a grin.

"Don't think I didn't hear that, Tony," Karen told him.

A few soft snickers moved through the crew.

I began thinking about how we had once again landed and were preparing for takeoff when suddenly the power in every helicopter abruptly stopped working. Here we were in the dead of night with thick black darkness closing in all around us.

I could see the weather beginning to change. The atmosphere was shifting rapidly, and the temperature began dropping at an unbelievable rate, not over minutes but within seconds.

Everything about the change caught us off guard. The cold deepened quickly, far beyond what anyone would expect in such a short time. The sudden drop reminded me of my visit with Margaret and how, within seconds, the temperature inside her apartment had changed from comfortable to a biting cold.

The transformation had been just as abrupt then. Bright, sparkling layers of frost formed along the window ledges, across the bookshelves, and along the frames of every picture hanging on the walls.

Small icicles began forming on the coat rack and even along the imitation rock surrounding the decorative fireplace. The dingy curtains that had been tied back with a dark piece of cloth seemed to stiffen and freeze together, thin layers of ice forming along the folds while moisture in the air condensed into a faint vapor that clung to the fabric.

"Looks like you boys are having some problems," a voice suddenly said over the transmitter in a deep bass tone. "Tell you what. Just submit to me. All will be forgiven, and I'll set you free."

No one answered.

There was no response over the radio or the transmitter. Not a single word. My guess was that the entire crew had heard the message loud and clear.

We all knew who it was.

This was Ethan speaking for the Devil himself.

The message was obvious. The deliverer of evil had declared himself king of this region, a kind of twisted messiah crowned not by any throne but by terror.

The idea of simply walking out of this place crossed my mind for a moment, but it was quickly dismissed. The grip Satan had on this situation was too strong. Every plan we had made to escape this nightmare seemed to collapse the moment we tried to act.

And even if we tried to leave on foot, the trip to Stonyford would be filled with dangers. Attempting to cross that terrain in the middle of the night with Ethan waiting somewhere ahead of us would be nothing more than walking straight into a trap.

For now our best option was to stay where we were, bunker down inside the helicopters, and secure everything inside each craft while we waited for the next move.

"Damn! Damn! Damn!" I couldn't help saying out loud. It was just my frustration showing. Satan was doing everything he could to keep us from reaching Stonyford.

That was when I remembered something that surprised me. On the way into this region, I had planned to make a quick landing at a certain location before reaching Stonyford. But somewhere along the way I must have gotten distracted. Between the music playing and everything else happening during the flight, the thought had slipped completely out of my mind.

"How long we gonna be here?" Karen asked, looking toward the door to the storage area of the helicopter. "Need something to cover this window with."

"Cover the window with?" I asked. "For what?"

"Yeah, for what?" Tony added.

"You don't know who might be out there trying to look inside," she said seriously. "Might be Bigfoot or somebody."

"Well he ain't gonna want your scary ass," Tony told her with a quiet laugh. "If anything, you'd probably scare him away."

"Who said I was scared?" she shot back. "Did you hear me say I was scared? No, you didn't. Yeah, that's what I thought."

"Check this out, Karen," I said, cutting in before the two of them kept going. "There might be something in one of the outside compartments that could cover the window. But after everything we've been through, I'm not about to go outside looking for it in this darkness."

"What about back there?" Regina said, pointing behind her with her thumb toward the storage area. "You might want to check there. If I remember right, I think I saw something back there that could cover it."

"See there, Karen?" Tony said in a wicked tone. "Something's in the storage area just waiting on you to come get it."

From what I could see out the front and side windows, there was nothing but solid blackness staring back at me.

That was when I thought to myself, hell no, I ain't going anywhere. No power. No lights. I definitely wasn't stepping outside.

It was so dark inside the helicopter we could barely see each other. The only thing visible was the slight movement of people shifting around while we searched for flashlights.

A few were found, along with some spare bulbs in one of the cabinets.

"There's gotta be more flashlights around here than that," I said. "Check all these cabinets. There has to be more than just this."

"Hell yeah," Regina yelled. "That's what I'm talking about. We got flashlights in just about every size down here in this cabinet, and some batteries and bulbs too."

I rushed over to where she was sitting. I couldn't see much inside the cabinet, but I knew what I was feeling around for. The moment one of the flashlights came on I shouted, "Let there be some motherfucking light up in here!"

A beam snapped on, and I yelled, "Yeah!" as light suddenly flashed across the inside of the craft.

"Hell yeah," Tony shouted. "Hell yeah."

"About time," Karen said. "Got some light up in here."

"Hold up, y'all," Regina said. "Me and my baby can see each other again. God done brought us out the darkness and into the light."

"Hey, Doc. You copy over there?" a voice asked over the radio.

"Copy," I answered. "Whassup?"

"You got it looking like some kind of spotlight show over there," the voice said. "You guys all right?"

"Everything is all right, my friend," I told him. "Just making sure these flashlights work. Glad you could see them."

"I'm sure everybody can see them as bright as they are," he said.

"Hey, you guys," another voice cut in. "Any chance you could spare a few?"

Hearing that made me realize it was time to pull everyone back together before we got carried away celebrating a box of flashlights.

"Check this out, you guys," I said quickly. "Only use the flashlights when needed. That means everybody. Check your compartments and see what's in them that you might be able to use."

"Bingo!" someone shouted over the radio. "One of my crew members just found a small refrigerator with plenty of water in it and a few sodas that still look good."

"We got another bingo over here," another voice called out. "Looks like a cabinet full of canned goods and some other items."

"Ah, hell no," I said out loud. "Hell no. I don't believe what I'm hearing. You guys aren't talking about finding food out here in all this mess, are you?"

"Hell no, Doc," a voice replied quickly. "I'm talking about the fridge aboard my troop carrier."

"Yeah," another voice said. "And I'm talking about the canned goods onboard my craft. I fly one of these UH-60 Black Hawk helicopters."

Suddenly, loud bumps came from underneath the body of our craft.

Then, after the bumping, we felt a strange jerking motion followed by a sudden violent jolt that left everyone momentarily frozen in place. For a second it felt like I had fallen into partial paralysis. I could barely move and had almost no sensation in my body.

But the bumping continued.

It sounded like it was coming directly from underneath the craft's body. We all stood still for a moment as if frozen in time. Something was happening on the outer structure of the helicopter, and I knew it was my responsibility to find out what was making those noises.

That was when I again thought about everything we had already gone through before ending up at this point in our journey. One thing we knew for certain: it wasn't me or Tony who had landed this craft earlier.

We could still feel something tugging beneath the helicopter, causing the occasional jerk.

The thought of the Invocation Benediction crossed my mind. At that moment it felt like the right time for prayer, asking for help against Satan and whatever power seemed to be working against us. I believed in the man up above, but I also couldn't ignore the feeling that the man down below seemed to have far more control over this situation.

Surrounded by darkness, I started thinking about the rest of the crew. I was sure everyone was afraid. This situation had shaken all of us.

My mind felt as if parts of the experience were being blotted out. Certain events and details seemed to slip away the moment I tried to hold onto them. Still, the memory of everything we had gone through kept returning again and again, haunting my thoughts.

I began wondering whether what we were experiencing was only the beginning. Maybe something even more sinister waited ahead of us.

We already knew the kind of wickedness Ethan was capable of with all his threatening tricks and deceptions. What troubled the crew was not knowing how long we could continue to endure this fight against him.

I found myself wondering whether something else was about to appear. Something that a religious person might call supernatural. Or maybe just some strange coincidence we didn't yet understand.

One thing was certain.

This entire experience felt as if it had been carefully planned by Lucifer himself.

The only thing I clearly remember was flying over a large mountain. Everything had been going according to plan, and the aircraft's instruments seemed to be operating normally under the circumstances. Then, in what felt like the blink of an eye, everything changed.

Everyone suddenly noticed a thick fog-like substance descending around us from seemingly nowhere, and things began to go completely wrong. The instrument panel in my MH-53J suddenly went haywire. Nothing was working the way it should.

Yet something must have been functioning correctly, because not only my big helicopter but every one of the other helicopters managed to land safely at the same time and in the exact place we had intended.

Who knew about that plan besides the crew?

Truthfully, I don't know how much time passed while I stood there thinking about what might have been happening outside the craft. I remember seeing my crew sitting motionless, listening and trying to hear the noise that had been coming from underneath the helicopter. But by then we couldn't hear anything anymore.

That was when I started telling myself the sound had probably just been the helicopter settling after everything it had gone through. Maybe it was simply easing back into stillness the way a person does after a rough trip.

I slowly moved toward the front window and reached for the dashboard, leaning forward to peer into the deep blackness outside.

The darkness was total. Deeper than anything I had ever seen before. It felt almost alive, as if something out there were staring back at me.

My mind began playing tricks on me as I continued staring into the night. For a moment I thought I saw a small flash of light coming from one of the old, dilapidated buildings nearby.

I kept watching, hoping the light would appear again.

But nothing happened. None of the crew said anything about seeing it either.

"All right now, Murdock," I told myself quietly. "You're just imagining things. You and the crew are stranded out here in the Stonyford mountain region. It's dark, and you can barely see anything. Yeah, it's scary, but you've got to get a grip before you drive yourself crazy out here."

That was when I realized there was no light in the distance after all.

That was when I told everyone to keep their flashlights off. If there really was something outside the craft, the last thing I wanted was for it to look back and see us staring out at it.

I began thinking about how strange the human brain really is. All those nerve cells and tissues packed inside the skull, interpreting every sensation and coordinating every movement in the body. Yet the same mind that controls us can also betray us, letting imagination take over until a person begins to lose control of their thoughts.

That was when I realized it was time to pull myself together and stop flirting with fear.

The only way I was going to figure out what was happening to my helicopter—or any of the others—was to quit overthinking and simply check things out myself. That meant opening the door and using a flashlight.

This was my craft, and I was the one in control. Fear had no place in my head.

Get the hell away from me*, Ethan,* I told myself, a bit of rough self-therapy to push the fear out of my mind.

Suddenly—

BAM! BAM!! BAM!

The noise exploded again from somewhere beneath the helicopter.

BAM! BAM! BAM!

"Man, what the—?" Tony said, looking around.

"That sounds like it's coming from the back," Regina said.

"No it didn't," Karen replied. "I've got this door open enough to see back there, and that's not where it came from. That was outside."

"Hey, Doc. You copy over there?" a voice came over the radio.

"Copy," I answered.

"You hearing any loud banging noises?" the man asked, apparently unaware the sounds were coming from near our craft.

"Affirmative," I said. "We're checking it now."

"Sounds like some pretty rough bumping going on if you ask me," a woman's voice said over the radio.

"Hey, anybody blasting a boom box?" another voice asked.

"Better not be," I said quickly, knowing the banging couldn't possibly be coming from a boom box.

BAM! BAM! BAM!

"Oh yeah, you freaking bitch!" someone yelled over the radio. "Just keep at it, you freak. We'll find you."

Something was definitely outside my craft, pounding away like crazy. And not only was it banging—the helicopter, heavy as it was, had begun to shake.

I'm sure more than one person in the crew was thinking about throwing open the doors, jumping out with weapons drawn, and firing at anything that moved. Fear and courage were blurring together.

The pounding kept going, loud and persistent, turning into a constant, nerve-grinding disturbance.

"Hey, you guys," someone called over the radio. "Something's moving out there."

"Where?" another voice asked.

"Yeah, where?" someone else demanded.

"Hey, Doc, we got movement all around us," another voice said, sounding certain.

"Don't nobody turn on any lights," I quickly told the crew. "Stay still for now. And keep the radio chatter down."

"What's happening?" Tony whispered.

"Hold up," I said quietly as I continued watching the darkness outside the perimeter of the boys ranch. "Listen up, everybody.

There are giant chimeras everywhere out there. But it looks like there's some kind of boundary they can't cross. Something's stopping them from coming inside this place. They're stuck on the other side."

"Well, I guess these ones have limits," I added. "They're not like the others that can go anywhere."

"I say we blast those sorry bastards," someone said over the radio.

"Hey, uh... you guys want to know something I forgot to tell you earlier?" another voice said quietly. "Back when we were trying to get out of here before, flying low over that creek... I swear I saw a big group of giant barracudas down there."

"Man, I'm telling you the truth," he continued. "Those things had the longest teeth I've ever seen. Long, narrow, sharp as hell. I wouldn't want to run into them. Some of them even looked like they were moving around on dry land."

"And you're saying these things were giant barracudas?" someone asked.

"That's right, my friend," the man replied. "Thousands of them crawling all over the place."

"And you saw them yourself?" I asked.

"Saw 'em acting like a bunch of goddamn piranhas," he said. "They were swarming all over the crew members who'd fallen into that creek."

"You saw that happening to our crew members?" I asked.

"That's right," he replied. "Saw everything. Even when some of those things you all call Chimeras attacked us. But the ones out here now are small. Hell, they're nothing but the babies. It's the others we need to worry about. Those are the parents of these young ones."

There was no doubt his words sent chills through everyone listening. Not only did he have a clear account of what had happened, but he had also recorded the entire incident. As a trained journalist and media professional, he had captured everything on camera, even while those deadly, stalking barracudas tore through the water.

And after witnessing all that, he had stayed focused and ready to keep moving forward with the mission.

"Everybody listen up," I said quietly over the radio. "Whatever you do, don't take off your helmet. Make sure your mic is working and that your helmet light is ready. Keep the lights off for now until I tell you otherwise."

"Pee-wee, Cat, and the pilots of the other crews, I need you to meet me in the center of this circle. Everyone else keep strict watch. We may be facing a very serious situation here."

"Uh, this is Pee-wee, Doc," he said. "You want us to bring anything? Like our rifles?"

"Bring whatever weapons you want," I answered. "But make sure they're the ones with the most firepower. Your lives may depend on it. And it's dark out here, so everyone should wear night vision lenses."

"Hey, you guys," another voice cut in over the radio. "My radar device just picked up something big moving around near the boundary line."

"Yeah, I'm getting the same thing on my radar," someone else added.

"Uh... I know you're not going to believe this," a member aboard one of the Lakotas said. "But these binoculars have me seeing something I'm almost afraid to say out loud. Man, this is crazy."

"Hey buddy, I don't know what's so crazy about it," another voice replied. "I'm seeing the same thing through my rifle scope."

"Yeah, well, that's nothing I can't vouch for," another voice said. It sounded like the kid from Sweetgrass up in the Montana Hi-Line.

"I think we're all seeing the same thing," the woman from

Shelby, Montana said. "My rangefinder's showing the same thing you all are seeing, and I've got to admit this is getting pretty creepy."

"Those of you outside your crafts," I said, "start moving cautiously toward my helicopter. Watch the ground for creatures crawling around you. Some of them may be waiting for a chance to grab one of us."

"Hey, Doc," another voice came over the radio in a low tone. "You copy?"

"Copy," I answered. "Whassup?"

"Man, you know, I've got this seismograph device here," a voice said over the radio. "You know, the kind that detects ground movement and vibrations. Earthquakes and things like that."

"Okay," I said, wondering where he was going with this. "And?"

"Well, from what I'm detecting," he said, sounding serious, "this thing is picking up vibrations that sound like huge footsteps. Deep, slow waves, like something massive walking around out there."

"What do you think it could be?" I asked.

"Man, from the sound of it," he replied, "it's like we're dealing with giants."

"Bullshit!" a worried voice shouted over the radio. "That's bullshit and you know it, Murdock. That crock and his seismograph machine. I spit on it. Nothing but a bunch of bullshit."

"Somebody help this guy calm down before he loses it," I said quickly over the radio. "He's about to blow a fuse."

"I'm not losing it," the man snapped back. "What I'm saying is that this seismograph doesn't make sense. That guy running that machine is turning this into some kind of mystical argument about giants and dragons. That's dangerous thinking. He's building theories from assumptions and trying to turn them into facts."

"I'm not talking about God or dragons, dummy," the man

with the seismograph replied. “I’m talking about measurable vibrations. Real signals. But whatever is causing them... it feels like something beyond anything we’ve encountered.”

“Well, whatever it is you two are arguing about,” Pee-wee broke in, “you better figure it out fast. That fog is coming back, and from what I’m seeing on radar it’s thicker than before.”

“Okay, everybody listen up,” I said over the radio. “Change of plans. Instead of meeting at my helicopter, we’re going to stay where we are. That fog is coming in again, and this time we’re going to fight our way out.”

“Arm yourselves with everything you’ve got,” I continued. “When it gets close, open fire on the fog and don’t stop until I tell you to stand down. Any questions?”

“What’s different about the fog this time?” someone asked.

“To be honest,” I said, “I think it’s alive.”

“How much time do we have?” another voice asked.

“None,” I answered.

“Hey, Doc,” someone else said, “can I ask something?”

“Depends on what it is,” I replied. “Make it quick.”

“How are we supposed to get out of here without power in the helicopters? What are we supposed to do, walk out of here?”

“That’s a fair question,” I said. “The moment the instrument panel lights back up, we’re taking off.”

“Well, we’re ready over here,” a voice said firmly. “We’re fully armed and ready to blast our way out if we have to.”

“Lakota crew seconds that,” someone else said.

“And we’re with you too,” another voice added.

“Hey, don’t forget about the Commander’s crew,” someone shouted. “Military style, baby. We’re armed with some badass motherfuckers and prepared to fight with fire.”

with the same emphasis," [illegible] replied. "I'm talking about measurable vibrations. Radio signals. But whatever is causing them, it seems like something beyond anything we've encountered."

"Well, whatever it is you two are arguing about," [illegible] broke in, "you better figure it out fast. That fog is coming back and from what I'm seeing on radar it's thicker than before."

"Okay, everybody listen up," I said over the radio. "Change of plans. Instead of [illegible] at my helicopter, we're going to stay where we are. That fog is coming in again, and this time [illegible] to [illegible] our way out."

"And [illegible] with everything you've got," I continued. "[illegible] when it gets close, [illegible] on the fog [illegible] and [illegible] small [illegible]. Any questions?"

"What's different about the fog this time?" [illegible] asked.

"The [illegible]," I said. "I think it's alive."

"How much time do we have?" another voice asked.

"None," I answered.

"Hey, Doc," said someone else. "Can I ask something?"

"Depends on what it is," I replied. "Make it quick."

"How are we supposed to [illegible] out of the [illegible] when [illegible] What are we supposed to [illegible] of it?"

"That's a fair question," I said. "The moment the instrument [illegible] backing up, we're [illegible] on."

"Well, we're ready over here," a voice said firmly. "We're fully armed and ready to blast our way out if we have to."

"Take [illegible] seconds [illegible]," someone else said.

"And we're with you too," another voice added.

They could [illegible] the Commander's crew [illegible] "We [illegible] smile [illegible]. We're armed with [illegible] and prepared to [illegible] with fire."

CHAPTER SIX

JUST AS I WAS ABOUT TO TELL THE CREW to get ready and that it was time for a full scale war against these deadly creatures, the entire instrument panel suddenly lit up like a goddamn Christmas tree. Everything began functioning just as if it were me or my crew members who had turned the power on in this heli-copter. This motherfucking MH-53J Pave Low had come to life.

We suddenly heard the humming from the electrical system, and the generator. The engine started and began to hum with a deep tone as the massive blades slowly moved. They turned through the slight foglike substance while the engine sound grew louder and louder with a deep pitch. The vibration spread through the entire craft, causing the helicopter to shake like an earthquake. It moved back and forth rapidly, full of life and energy.

The force of the engine sounded like a line of powerful loco-motives, grinding, and cranking sounds that had finally come alive.

As soon as I realized what was happening I dove for the pilot's seat and strapped myself in as fast as I could. I then noticed that my crew had done the same. From the expressions on their faces it was easy to see they were just as surprised as I was by what was happening and by all the strange phenomena taking place.

"Damn, every helicopter out here is lit up," Tony said. "Just look at that."

"Murdock, you copy?" a voice called out. "This is Cat."

"I copy you, Cat," I responded. "Tell me about it."

"What do you say?"

"Let's do this," I said on the radio.

The power from the engine felt like it was about to burst out of the craft. Even the ignition system was vibrating. I had almost forgotten what was happening outside my helicopter because I was paying so much attention to what was happening inside. It wasn't until I heard Tony's voice that I finally looked above the instrument panel.

That was when I noticed the massive blades spinning overhead, reflecting brightly in the outer lights mounted along the body of the craft.

Checking my gear, I could feel the vibration and harsh power of the engine as I took hold of the throttle and moved the rudders and stabilizer. The entire craft shuddered with strength as I looked out the side window and watched the reflection of the outboard lights on the dark ground around us.

I then stared out the front window and could just barely make out the fuzzy shapes of two, maybe three, small helicopters. They appeared to be high-performance Armed Aerial Scouts, the AAS-72X+s, ready to demonstrate their survivability. Each one carried heavy weaponry designed for strong payload capacity and endurance under harsh combat conditions, the kind we were about to face in the Stonyford region.

I couldn't see much behind my craft except solid blackness and the foglike substance surrounding us. It felt as if we were sitting inside some kind of black hole. The fog thickened so heavily that even with the landing lights and takeoff lights on high beam it was becoming difficult to see the runway.

While Tony checked the instrument panel, it suddenly occurred to me that none of us had tested the transmitting system since the power returned. We began switching on different instruments to see if anything would respond. The only thing we heard was loud bursts of static.

There was not even a single sound from the ADF, even though the fluorescent master switches showed that everything should have been working.

I stared intently out the front window and also the side pilot window, as if I were trying my best to see something in the far distance beyond the boys ranch. But again, the only thing I could see through the thickening fog was pure blackness.

I looked around aimlessly at my crew. They were staring back at me, trying to figure out my next step before we became airborne again. For some odd reason, I very reluctantly opened my side pilot's window. Carefully, I leaned my head slightly into the thick, moist fog. My heart was pounding as I hoped that at this moment I wouldn't see anything unexpected. Yet at the same time I hoped I might see something—or even hear something—that wasn't coming from the craft. I felt within me an anxious desire to destroy the enemy.

I knew the doors were locked tight and nothing could get inside this big bird without one of us opening them. Still, I felt an uneasy curiosity that seemed to cause my imagination to run slightly wilder than ever before. Something strange had happened, and whatever the entire crew had experienced had me wondering how such a thing could even take place during our journey on this now somewhat distressing plight.

Still staring outside the window and occasionally glancing back at my crew, who were watching me, I looked down at the instrument panel and then turned my attention back to the outer surface of the craft. I carefully studied the ground, searching the portions I could see from my vantage point, while refusing to give myself any reason to stick my head out the window again—even while wearing my helmet.

My curiosity had already pushed far enough. I quickly pulled my head back inside the window and thought about everyone's present state of confusion and possible hallucination. It made me feel that every piece of protective gear was absolutely necessary. Whatever it was we were up against was out to destroy us.

"Bullshit!" Tony yelled. "Not again."

Suddenly the surround sound system came on full blast, playing the song "Hotel California" by The Eagles. The next thing we knew, this bitch had once again become completely airborne, along with every single one of the helicopters. We were now in flight at an extremely low altitude, flying the fuck out of the boys ranch at full throttle and in the direction we'd intended.

I could feel the powerful force of the engine as it ground loudly with such intensity that large sparks could be seen spurting from it from all the friction. It was said that people from as far away as Stonyford and the surrounding communities, more than thirty miles away, could at times hear the engines during the quiet of night. The noise from all the helicopters sounded as though someone had ignited huge cannons and powerful explosives, mixed with the blast of shotguns and dynamite. The force of the sound was so powerful that nearby campers and hikers found themselves violently disrupted and tossed around like rag dolls, many suffering ruptured eardrums.

Mounted glass in homes and businesses, windows, and sculptures began shattering from the thunderous rumbling of the helicopter engines. Each echo sent immense waves bouncing off the massive walls of the surrounding hills and mountains. The repercussions of those waves struck back and forth from slope to slope and was witnessed by vacationers as something horrifying.

Passing certain areas and locations that I could remember

from years long ago, I could see ahead through slight clearings in the fog the havoc and destruction being caused by the deep grinding roar of our helicopters. I could also see parts of the high mountain slopes and rugged hilltops collapsing. Steep cliffs and sharp rocks began breaking apart under the violent waves of sound coming from the engines.

Strange to say, but it was during my observation of everything taking place throughout this part of the region that I realized I was actually viewing the entire event through my windshield.

We were under attack.

A sudden death attack with no warning. It was exactly the thing Satan would intend in his effort to liberate his followers.

Suddenly there was firing coming from everywhere. Everyone had started what I had ordered. Just seconds earlier, I had been thinking about the fog and how dark it was. But now the thick black sky and the dense gray layers of fog were lit up in flashes of yellowish red and dingy blue, mixed with hazel green and purple.

My craft seemed to allow me to once again take full control of the throttle and master switches. I glanced over at Tony and could see he was busy checking the instrument panel while searching for whatever it was he had dropped on the floor.

Meanwhile, Karen, Regina, and Sandra were watching the radar and the objects moving across the screen, which they knew were the creatures we had already been battling. But we all knew the present fight would be the most intense struggle since our arrival in this region. It was time to engage in the battle of all battles. A military engagement similar to the one that had taken place in heaven when Lucifer's unlawful reign had spread through manipulation.

While observing my crew, I also searched for certain landmarks that might guide us toward the town of Stonyford. But the thick fog prevented me from seeing anything below except the rough surfaces of mountains and hills; their deep ridges and slopes made even the thought of a rough landing nearly impossible.

Everything appeared to be in ruins, destroyed by these uninvited creatures from the bottomless pit, ruled by none other than the devil himself.

"Oh, God. Somebody help us," a voice came screaming over the radio. "Oh no. Please, somebody help us."

"Anybody copy that?" someone asked.

"Yeah, I'm almost sure everybody copied it," another voice said.

"Doc. You copy? This is Knucklehead," he said.

"I copy there, Knucklehead," I answered. "Go ahead."

"Think we got some problems with a few crews out there," he said.

"Copy that, Knucklehead," I told him.

"Hey, can anybody out there hear me?" another voice came over the radio without identifying himself. "Can anybody hear me? This is an S.O.S. We need help."

The fog was thick again, and the firepower continued. Whoever it was needing assistance must have failed to realize we were in the middle of a war. The enemy was trying its best to bring us down, and whoever was up here in all this fog wasn't even identifying himself or his crew.

"Anybody who can hear us," he cried out over the radio. "Please help us. We're being attacked by a vicious dog onboard our helicopter. The dog is clawing at us. Its nails are just about ripping everything apart. I got deep scratches all over me, and my copilot... the goddamn dog has just about clawed him to pieces."

"Hey, we can hear you," someone answered. "Do you copy?"

"Copy!" he said. "We need help. I can't see where to land."

"This is MacDonald of Lodi," MacDonald told the man. "I need you to identify yourself. Who are you?"

"David Berkowitz, the Son of Sam," the man said over the radio.

"That's bullshit!" someone yelled.

"Yeah, ain't no way that's gonna be happening again," someone else said. "Dude done gone crazy out here."

"Hey, Knucklehead, this is the Doc," I said over the radio. "Got a line on whoever that is?"

"That's affirmative, Doc," he responded. "Sounds like it's coming from one of the AAS-72X+s somewhere in the vicinity behind us."

"If that's the case," I told him, "what the fuck are they doing with a wild dog onboard their craft?"

"Hey, man," the person crying out for help said, apparently listening in on our conversation. "We was buzzing the ground down here when all of a sudden the dog came out of nowhere and jumped in acting like... I don't know... like it was scared or something. I mean, I didn't know a dog could jump that high. But it did."

"Hey, uh, Buddy. This is Pee-wee," he said. "Who are you, and what are you flying?"

"Hey, man, Pee-wee," the person started saying. "Dude, that wasn't me talking that crazy Son of Sam shit, man. I want you to know that."

"Hey, it's cool, man," Pee-wee told him. "I just wanna know who I'm talking to."

"Well, my name is Terry," he told Pee-wee.

"Terry what?" Pee-wee asked.

"Terry Hayes," he said. "I fly one of the AAS-72XXs."

"Uh, Terry," I interrupted, "just where is the dog? Is it still on board your helicopter?"

"Yeah, that's affirmative, Sir," he said in a military tone. "I have him in sight as we talk."

"And can you tell me where he's located in your craft, Terry?" I asked, thinking the dog might be down on the floor.

"It's in the rear seat where my gunner sits," he said. "Sir—"

"Damn," a voice said quietly over the radio.

"And tell me, Terry," I asked, "just where is your gunner? Where is the rest of your flight crew?"

"Sir, it's..." he began. "It's busy devouring them."

"I know he didn't just go there," Karen said in disbelief.

"Oh, fuck!" someone yelled over the radio. "Got some for real zombies out here in this fog trying to hitch a ride."

"Man, what the hell are you talking about? Zombies?" someone asked. "You gotta be joking."

"Hey, got 'em down here too," another voice yelled. "Blast them motherfuckers. Take 'em out, man. Kill all of them sons-of-bitches."

"Oh yeah, that's right," someone said in a distraught tone. "And all this time I thought I was insane."

"What?" the man who had yelled about killing them asked. "What did I say that you feel is wrong?"

"Hell, you and your crazed desire to suddenly kill some freakin already dead things like zombies."

"And?"

"Well, doesn't that sound a bit twisted?"

"I don't think it does. Not under the circumstance."

"By the way, just who are you anyway?"

"Verl Baker, baby," he said. "What? You thinking about us possibly going out on a date when all this is over?"

"Freakin' queer."

"Is someone going to help me over here?" Terry asked again. "Please, you guys, somebody gotta help me."

"Pee-wee, you copy?"

"Copy!"

"Uh, I need you or maybe the Cat to fall back and see if you can try to locate this Terry person and his AAS-72X+."

"Copy!"

"Hey, Lodi is on it," the Cat said.

"We're coming in with you, Lodi," a voice said over the radio.

"This ain't nothing but a party getting ready to jump off down here with the homies."

"Who is that?" Tony asked me.

"Yeah, who is that talking about a party?" Karen asked.

"Well, whoever it is," Regina said, "they is moving pretty fast on the radar."

"Hey, Doc. You copy?"

"Copy!" I answered. "Whassup?"

"Man, Sacro's radar got whoever's assisting Lodi moving at a high rate across the screen," he said. "That's entirely too fast to be one of us, don't you think?"

"Lodi, pull out of there as quick as you can," I yelled over the radio. "Pull out immediately."

"Man, what the fuck!" a voice shouted.

"They didn't make it," Regina said, staring at the radar screen. "They didn't make it, Murdock. Lodi didn't make it in time."

Suddenly there was a huge flash followed by an explosion coming from beneath the thick foglike substance covering the region.

"Any sign of Lodi?" I asked. "Did anybody's screen pick up what it was that exploded?"

"Uh, I can't say if it was a Chinook or an AAS-72 or what," Tony said, staring intently at the radar screen. "But whatever it was, the blast looked like it knocked one hell of a hole in one of those hills next to that fucked up road down there."

"Hey, Sacro. You copy? This is Lodi," a voice suddenly said.

"Ah, man. What the fuck," Tony said out loud.

"Man, that's Lodi right there," I said, looking around and then out my side window.

"That sure is," Karen said, shaking her head.

"He's on the radar," Regina said, pointing at the screen.

"This is Sacro," another voice came over the radio. "Goddammit, Lodi. Man, I copy you big time. Just where in the hell are you?"

"Hey, you guys," the Cat started saying. "We heard you talking and wondering if that blast was us, but man, the radio went all the way dead. We couldn't transmit anything. Not until just a few seconds ago. Whatever that blast was, it knocked just about everything out. I even think it threw our helicopter a few yards back. If it wasn't for these helmets, we'd probably be deaf by now."

"Anybody know where the blast came from?" I asked.

"Hey, I think it came from somewhere out there in front of us. Inside a dark cloud or something," another voice said over the radio. "That's where I saw a big ass fireball coming from right before it happened. You dig?"

"He's right," another voice said over the radio. "It came from somewhere out there in this fog. Better yet, I bet it came from in the direction of Snow Mountain."

"You guys talking, this is Pee-wee," he said. "Identify yourself."

"Oh, yeah," a voice answered. "This is Undra Lee, commanding flight pilot of the AAS-72X+ Squadron."

"And yeah, I am co-pilot Michael Simmons in flight with Commander Lee onboard one of the AAS-72X+s."

"How come you're just now bringing yourselves to our attention?" someone asked.

"We thought you already knew," a voice said.

"Hey, we been right here with you guys. You dig?" another voice added. "I been out here firing away at these monsters, trying my best to kill all of them with everything I got."

"Yeah, and our gunner been giving them hell with all the firing he's been putting out," one of the voices said firmly. "Seriously, I gotta give my man credit for his job."

"And who's your gunner?" someone asked.

"Hey, you can just call me Fatmac," the gunner said in a firm tone. "That's what my comrades call me when they need me to do something dirty."

"But what's your real name, Fatmac?" a voice asked.

"I'll tell you, but then I just might have to kill you," he said with a snicker.

"Hey, man, this is me, Malcolm, bro. Malcolm Jackson. And I was just kidding about having to kill you. But everybody do be calling me the Jackhammer."

"There, everything seems to be working properly," Karen said, raising up after checking the transmitting system. "I even checked the switches to the transponder. It's all good."

"Hey you guys," I said over the radio. "Don't forget, we're still under attack."

Just as I was about to tell Tony to take the control stick, a voice came on the radio yelling "incoming!" Then there was a huge flash of light that looked like thousands of sparks streaking across the black sky, illuminating it in different colors. Some smashed against a few of the helicopters' windshields, leaving long bright fiery trails behind them.

In the distance ahead, something caught my attention. It looked as if it were leaving a blazing path across the sky, trailing a bright red and yellow stream like burning wood sparks. For a moment it appeared as if something had malfunctioned and exploded into a burst of glittering fragments, reflecting its deadly deception across the darkness as if sent by Satan himself.

"Ah, man," Tony shouted. "What the—"

Again there was sudden gunfire from every helicopter as everyone started firing at anything they felt was a threat. We were now flying over the outer perimeter of the boys ranch, where the giant Chimeras were known to gather and migrate periodically from one part of the region to another. This was also the area of destruction and ruins where the old snake hunter's cabin once stood, along with the collapsed remains of the deadly snake enclosure.

The fog had once again grown thick. Our flight altitude seemed to have gone haywire around two hundred feet. The barometer gauge, which should have been measuring atmospheric pressure, was unresponsive to any changes. Our bearing was also unresponsive, along with the calibrated airspeed device.

Although ARSA is not required throughout this region, a pilot knows that radio contact certainly is. But for reasons unknown, our radios were going haywire as well. Even the helicopter's artificial horizon, the instrument that shows pitching and banking, was on the blink.

We were flying under extremely low visibility, trying to rely on radios and radar that were barely functioning. The visibility had become completely obscured by a thick black fog, accompanied by a dull heaviness in the air that made it feel like the oxygen itself was thinning. I knew that condition could lead to unconsciousness, so I immediately advised everyone to climb higher and increase speed in order to avoid blackouts.

We were at a critical point. A particular danger existed in this region that some pilots had long referred to as the intersection between heaven and hell. Flights across this part of the Stonyford region were usually restricted during heavy crosswinds, and my magnetic compass was showing disturbances throughout the area that suggested we might even collide with other aircraft.

Other instruments were also displaying readings that suggested we were somewhere other than the Stonyford region.

"Hey, Doc. You copy?" a voice asked over the radio.

"Copy!" I responded. "What's happening?"

"Man, my instrument gauges are fucked up big time," the voice said. "It's like I don't even know where the hell I am. I mean, I know we're here because I can see bright lights in this fog shit coming from other helicopters."

"Man, that's the same way we're doing it over here," another voice said. "My gunner still back there blasting the fuck out them hills, don't even know what he's wiping out."

"Hey, man," someone yelled over the radio. "Just make sure y'all keep 'em pointed at them mountains. Keep 'em pointed that way."

The black sky kept lighting up from the constant firing coming from each helicopter. My only guess was that we were still en-route to Stonyford. Every now and then there would be a violent jerk or sudden tug from something in the fog trying to grip onto my craft. Whatever it was would wrench and yank at us, sometimes violently, but the massive blades would strike it away and release its grip.

Still, we had to face the reality that not everyone would be fortunate enough to make it to Stonyford.

This is when I once again thought about Margaret and how she had spoken in the words of a fortuneteller. Everything she had predicted seemed to come to pass. I thought about how badly I desired success with Karen, the result of events from a past life that I had failed to fulfill. If only I could have some time with her. Private time, just the two of us, far away from the Stonyford region. Honestly, I didn't even care where we might be, just as long as we could be in each other's presence.

So much was going through my mind about her. Would this be the last time we would be near each other? Would this be the conclusion to the uncertainty of the relationship we once intended when I walked away from the adventurous romance of our marriage? I have no problem admitting that I had become overwhelmed by her affection. It had a way of captivating a man like a mystery novel.

The situation concerning Karen was becoming far too impractical for me to deal with sensibly. There was something about her that was unlike anyone else. Something natural and rich that a man would gladly put up with. But it was also obvious that Tony was not impressed with her at all. At times he could be very disrespectful toward her, even bold and obnoxious, though he himself could sometimes prove to be extremely obtuse.

The convoy of helicopters was still holding formation, circling the boys ranch in the dense fog that had everyone feeling disoriented. The fog continued to obscure all visibility.

Suddenly there was an eerie sound in the darkness, like foghorns blowing somewhere out in the distance. It sounded like a warning of danger lurking unseen, something moving quietly and waiting for the right moment to strike.

Although the fog was thick, I could still sense something hovering over us, something threatening that our radar could not detect. Someone even claimed to have seen a moth the size of an African rodent carrying a giant guenon monkey on its back, like a man riding a horse. The monkey was said to have a long tail swinging back and forth, and from that tail a long narrow needle-like object protruded outward.

Some of the crew even claimed the monkey wore something that looked like a decorated Netsuke, covered in small colorful carvings, and that it had Mukluks on its feet, the kind of Eskimo boots made from sealskin or reindeer hide that covered its long hind legs.

The monkey was holding a shiny gold-plated horn in its right hand as it sailed through the thick fog over the region, under the power of the huge wings of the moth. On its head it wore a round, tannish Japanese hat that leaned slightly backward on its shoulders, fastened by a thin, tanned strap around its neck.

It was said that the monkey had similarities resembling that of a pigmy piggybacking on the back of the giant Lepidopter moth.

Its eyes were piercing, partly closed and squinting in a slant, as if gazing through a sharp instrument that could puncture the strongest iron.

“What about that Terry guy?” Regina asked, wondering if we had forgotten he needed help. “He’s still out there, you know.”

"Damn!" I shouted. "That's right. Can you see him on the screen?"

"No," Regina answered. "I don't see anything."

"Here, let me check," Karen said.

"I know one thing," I said, staring into the fog. "We gotta get out of this pattern before we end up colliding with whatever aircraft is on the radar."

The dark sky kept lighting up from all the gunfire coming from every helicopter. Still, I had to keep reminding myself that not everyone was going to make it to Stonyford. But those of us who were fortunate, I hoped to see when we got there.

I could feel the power of the massive blades chopping through the thick fog, which now seemed to be thinning just a little. The fog still gripped the region with what felt like wrenching hands, yanking at our crafts violently. Fortunately, we were now in flight and no longer stranded on the ground. We were on our way to Stonyford.

Strange that at a time like this, no one thought about the fact that our crafts needed refueling. The last thing any of us needed was to make an emergency landing after such a dangerous departure from the boys ranch. That would have been a disaster waiting to happen. An emergency landing at this point in the mission would prove the inadequacy of any pilot under conditions like these.

Again I thought about how strange it was that while observing everything taking place around us, I suddenly realized that we were actually seeing it all from a much clearer range of visibility through the cockpit windows.

It was as if the fog would open for a moment and allow the crew to see what was happening around us. Then the entire region would become hazy again, as though a strange mist had fallen from the dark sky.

I thought about the darkness and how it now seemed to have

turned light again. Only minutes earlier none of us could see anything, yet now these sudden clearings would appear out of nowhere, giving everyone a brief chance to feel free from the fog.

"Anybody see what's crawling about down below?" someone asked over the radio.

"Yeah, I copy that," a voice answered. "Looks like a bunch of creepy little things, like ants or spiders."

"What's happening?" Karen asked, staring out one of the side windows.

"Yeah, what are you guys looking at?" Sandra said while trying to peer out my window.

"Isn't it too foggy out there to see anything?" Regina asked.

"Man, it's a whole bunch of them things down there crawling all over the place," Tony said, slightly removing his face mask. "I gotta take a better look before that big cloud of fog covers everything up again."

"Can you see them?" Karen asked, turning toward me.

"Yeah, I see some of them," I answered. "Except I don't think you guys are looking at ants. That looks like a gang of scorpionlike arachnids. They say those things are supposed to be nonvenomous, but these here look deadly."

Suddenly one of the huge colonies violently exploded, followed by heavy gunfire. The overwhelming power of the attack showed the crew's determination to destroy anything that might be a threat. When the firing stopped, not a single colony remained standing. The giant scorpionlike arachnids were scattered across the hill, every colony reduced to ruins as if it had been blasted apart with dynamite.

"Damn, man," Tony shouted. "What the fuck?"

"Ah, man," Regina said. "Now that was really messed up, Murdock. Y'all done killed everything down there, even the little ones."

After hearing Regina express her sympathy for the arachnids,

I found myself once again deep in thought, focusing on our surroundings. The sky had already returned to a deep black darkness, mixed with dense fog that had everyone in a slight state of fear and paranoia.

The fog once again became so thick that it slowed our craft to what felt like a crawl, regardless of the power from the throttle.

Karen and Tony kept their eyes on the instrument panel while Sandra and Regina watched the radar screen for anything moving in our direction.

As for me, I kept searching for landmarks, hoping to catch sight of the town of Stonyford somewhere in the distance ahead.

Suddenly, a loud explosion snapped me out of my concentration and back into the present reality. We were being fired upon. I knew it was time to use every bit of energy we had if we intended to make it out of this place. This part of the trip required everything we had. We had to break through the fog while firing back at whatever was hidden inside it waiting to ambush the crew.

"Holy shit!" someone yelled over the radio. "Man, get all them motherfuckers."

"Oh no you don't try getting away from me, you bastard," a woman shouted at something trying to hide in the fog.

"Damn, that sounded like that lady from the Montana Hi-Line," Tony said. "You know, up there around Shelby."

"I know one thing," Regina said about the woman from Montana. "I know she ain't playin' around with whatever it is she's after."

"Get that bitch lady," someone yelled over the radio. "That's it. That's it Miss Montana."

"Got 'em over here too," another voice shouted. "Poppa ain't takin no stuff up here you ugly looking creature. Gotcha!"

"Yeah motherfucker," someone yelled. "Just like you and yo daddy the devil revolted against heaven, I'm revolting against you, you filthy sons-of-bitches. Now take this you—"

"Yeah that's right," another voice shouted. "They call me the original rebel. I'm so goddamn rebellious against everything you stand for, Lucifer. I hate you, you devil. Die you bastard."

To my surprise, I happened to glance back toward Sandra and Regina and saw them sniffing a shiny white powdery substance which I immediately recognized as cocaine. They both knew how I felt about narcotics, especially on board this craft. But then I also thought about what we had been through and how such an anesthetic, even though illegal, seemed necessary after all the weird shit we had experienced since taking on this freakin' assignment.

Truthfully speaking, I probably wouldn't have cared if the crew had been smoking a pound of good weed. We were being attacked by monsters and creatures of an unknown species without any real classification. From what I understood, these things might even have been the result of the people in this region doing all that interbreeding with each other. I had no specific facts to support that idea, but the medical records for many of the residents around Stonyford described various diseases that had long affected people living throughout this region.

The fog wasn't about to let up as we proceeded desperately on our way to the town of Stonyford. Each explosion sent a huge fireball upward, lighting up the dark sky. At times we could hear frightening cries of torment from both crew members and unknown creatures alike being hit and wounded during the attack. Crew members were angry at the thought of what was threatening them during this mission.

The thick fog made it impossible for us to see where we were flying. Checking the instrument gauges proved extremely unfavorable, preventing the crew from taking advantage of the situation under the circumstances. But we knew our only option was to fly the fuck out of this terrible situation, even if it meant blasting the freakin' doors off the White House. This was a conflict with deadly contentions, placing the entire crew in a position weighed down by the forces of the devil himself.

The cocaine had now taken full effect, stimulating everyone, including myself, causing restless movement.

But I could see that my crew was in full control except for the few pieces of clothing thrown about on the floor of the helicopter. Karen, Regina, and Sandra were now wearing undergarments similar to skin-tight swimsuits made by Naughty Nylon, revealing panties I must admit were very naughty. Within minutes they were topless, exposing their full breasts boldly.

I could just imagine what was going on in the other helicopters.

My eyes became like those of a predatory eagle in a high place built for a king, carefully observing his flock.

CHAPTER SEVEN

WE'D BECOME ENGAGED WITH A DEADLY ENEMY of war who was trying its best to interlock onto our system. The song "Purple Haze" by Jimi Hendrix could be heard blaring aloud on the entertainment systems in the helicopters. Each helicopter had a gunner gripping a powerful .50-caliber machine gun and a Mark 18 grenade launcher mounted at his side. No, this wasn't the Vietnam War era, but it was happening in the United States of America, in a small community in the northwestern part of California, known as Stonyford, California.

This was the place where so many of its residents had become victims of the most atrocious events imaginable, savagely done under abominable conditions. This was not some ancient time. This was happening in the United States of America, and we were at war, engaged with a deadly enemy named Lucifer.

This war had become something like an emancipation, with this crew of freedom fighters desperately fighting for our civil rights. The crew was ready to die for freedom, even if it meant engaging in a fierce battle against the devil's army of fallen angels from the bottomless pit of hell. This would be recorded as the most intense battle ever known to man, second only to the one long ago when Lucifer attempted to overthrow the Kingdom of Heaven. It would be remembered as among the most violent and hostile struggles imaginable, possessing strength from unknown forces powerful enough to destroy the universe.

Should anyone survive after this, they would undoubtedly find that the elevation of the earth itself would reveal boundaries that would prove to be incomprehensibly wrong. The Stonyford region and all surrounding territories would appear like a floating death field, unsuitable for human habitation.

During the realization of this war, many of Stonyford's residents would be seen scrambling through the streets searching for shelter and protection, while some would be smashing the valuables of their neighbors. The region would be afflicted with madness. However foolish it might seem, none of these events would be proof of Armageddon itself.

The battle between the forces of good and evil had always existed as an unfinished stage in which Satan attempted to prove himself the singularity of modern salvation. Considering himself exceptional, he had fashioned a profile of himself as the greatest production of God's creation.

The advancement from the bottomless pit of hell was a series of progressive steps in which Satan's fallen angels were reforming themselves and moving forward jointly throughout the Stonyford region. Lucifer had once been perfect in heaven until iniquity was found in him, and he and those who followed him were cast into the bottomless pit of hell. Although Lucifer was called the light bearer, it is important to remember that he was never the light itself.

God is the one and only light of all creation.

The disorder throughout the region was only the beginning stage of a ripple through a physical existence higher than our present understanding. It is strange how the accuser has brought about a false confession, making the entire region appear guilty under his authority.

And his associate is Death.

What a misunderstanding about the ending of time. We should understand why it is important to recognize Lucifer's final reckoning over the Stonyford region, just as Christ claimed the Church. Yet many in this region still disagree with the Scriptures and the words of Jesus. Under the conditions present in Stonyford, none among those residing here would make it to heaven, even those who consider themselves Christians. Lucifer himself knows that only God can determine salvation. His grace belongs to heaven, and anyone who disagrees will have no real chance to understand the doctrine that reveals what God's grace truly means.

It is Lucifer's will that communicating with him be like an obedient child seeking his father. Such a pattern is known to Satan, a kind of trinity doctrine used to condemn those unwilling to follow him. Christians proclaim Jesus and teach about an afterlife beyond death, but Lucifer proclaims a doctrine of life with him.

Humans are taught about lawlessness, which introduces them to the evil of Lucifer's earthly vessel. Many people have gathered misconceptions about Lucifer over the years, false doctrines that symbolize how easily he accomplishes what he desires through his encounters with the Church.

And then you wonder what the purpose of making this point might be. Lucifer's success has shifted from an endless cycle to a manifestation of his existence. It is astonishing how the people of the Stonyford region are themselves helping to declare his arrival in natural form, revealing principles that only someone driven by a deadly obsession might pursue.

During this indefinite time the demonstration will set in motion abuse like a product fermented from venom. The devil will influence mankind throughout the region with deception. Those opposing his principles will find themselves mutilated in shocking ways. His tactics will resemble a meltdown of rage sweeping across an entire region for miles, ensnaring both beast and man alike.

The entire event will become fascinating in the way it forms delusions of identity that threaten even the Antichrist and every false prophet.

As described in the book of Revelation, this will become a time when rivals deceive and conquer while innocent believers suffer under conflict created by Satan himself.

Thousands of fallen angels will announce their presence, declaring the arrival of Satan's new earthly kingdom. In this kingdom all natural organisms will fall under his domination as though they are one body, with Satan acting as the pivot on which everyone depends. During this period there will be but one gender until Satan himself eventually creates a third gender through his unnatural power.

The appearance of this third gender will cause violent outrage among the people of the region. The structure of this third gender will provoke unlawful acts and malicious behavior that threaten the natural order. Such acts will spread abnormal forms and corrupt growth throughout the region.

Because of Stonyford, the manifestation of this third gender will resemble a transsexual identity revealing new gendered behavior. Such behavior will become widely practiced by the people of this region, even more than Satan himself might anticipate.

In this picture, there is no David to bring down Goliath. There is only one battle, not two like the battles David fought against the Philistines. In those battles, David first consulted God and won through God's power alone.

But in the present situation, Lucifer is the one whom the Stonyford region consults as their god. For this reason, the creation of the third gender has appeared, spreading immoral principles throughout the region as part of Satan's new earthly kingdom.

Because of Stonyford, this moral upheaval will threaten civilization and social development, violating civil liberties and freedoms while fallen angels deceive the people.

These fallen angels are described as having long rough whiskers on their upper lips, thick bristles growing wildly from their cheeks like angry animals. Their piercing eyes appear capable of cutting through anything like a dangerous instrument. Their teeth are dangerously sharp, shaped exactly as Satan intended.

This is the beginning stage of the strategy set in place for the Stonyford region. However, the gathering in Stonyford may appear, this celebration is about to change into a deadly whirlwind that could wipe the entire region off the map.

The attack will be violently arranged to achieve its desired effect.

It will become a painful ordeal for this small community, directed under false authority by priests and ministers organized under Satan's rule.

Among the first specifications in these systematic arrangements, the command to honor Satan will be the recognition of the third gender.

The entire emphasis will fall upon the great attack and strategy carried out by both the devil and God through forces gathering from the north, south, east, and west. It will be remembered as the greatest war ever known to mankind. The conquering of Stonyford by fallen angels will throw everything into violent confusion and turmoil.

CHAPTER EIGHT

"THAT'S IT, DIE HARD YOU FREAKING filthy piece of slime," a voice uttered.

The song "Emergency" by Tank blared through the entertainment system as each helicopter blasted its way through the thick fog like an out-of-control house party with fragments shattering into thousands of pieces all around us. This was a vigorous attack on Satan's fallen angels.

"Regina," I yelled out, not wanting to take my eyes off what was happening in front of the craft. "Keep an eye on the screen."

I glanced in Karen's direction. She had that certain look she had during our marriage. I guess you could say that moment became something special to me while I was positioning the craft for an attack on the enemy.

I couldn't help wondering during this observation of Karen whether she knew just how much I needed her beside me. Regardless of the past, my love for her had endured. I was wrong for walking away and not living up to my responsibility, but what is done is done. There's no way to turn back the hands of time. I have always loved this lady. I have never in my life desired to be loved by anyone more than Karen. She was the one who truly turned me out, and if anything, a trophy should have been awarded for the love we once shared.

How could I have allowed myself to walk away from such a yearning desire for her? How could I have been so foolish?

And here I was piloting this huge MH-53J Pave Low helicopter with the best group of Operation Journalist Squadron you could ever meet, now flying into deadly combat on a crucial mission with everything working against us. Through small clearings in the fog ahead, we could slightly see a Chinook helicopter flying in formation, firing at objects to our right and left. The Chinook's effectiveness for the mission was obvious.

The Cat and MacDonald navigated the Chinook perfectly well under such conditions as we watched them firing their weapons toward Stonyford. On each side of my craft I could vaguely see, in the distance, the figures of a few UH-72A Lakota helicopters bobbing in and out of the clouds.

The outlines of other crafts were faint. Our entire surrounding had become heavily dense, making flight uneasy and visibility unclear.

The weather condition was unknown under the circumstances. Our radar had become useless. We were unable to detect any point from the boys ranch to our present location. Still, throughout this entire mass of confusion, my mind remained fixed on Karen and her ability to capture my attention.

So very stunning, I thought to myself while staring at her.

Her hair, her eyes, her face and nose, and that extravagantly beautiful figure. I deeply regretted walking away from her when I knew she needed me. The thought was killing me slowly in more ways than one. I wondered how I could have been so damn stupid to allow myself to abandon what I had only just begun to embrace.

I had forsaken the very thing I had sworn never to desert, and it was killing me.

Talk about a goddess. This lady in my presence was a true diva.

Although she could show a temper, she was never self-centered, though she came from a family of wealth.

But it was me who proved dysfunctional. My problem today is that I have a hard time trying to understand myself. How could I have walked away from the prize of my life?

Suddenly my attention was interrupted by loud voices coming through the transmitter and the roaring sounds from the helicopter's engine.

"Man, Murdock," Tony began. "How you guys be doing this is something I don't think I could ever do. You feel me?"

"Like what?" I asked him.

"Man," he said, scratching his head and slipping one finger under the side of his helmet, "you know, like what we're going through. This is some crazy shit."

"Part of a journalist's job, isn't it?" Regina said, surprisingly. "Tell 'em, Doc."

"Yeah then," Tony said, sounding a little embarrassed. "Then tell me why yo' butt ain't grabbin' that gun and firin' it at them things out there."

"Cause nobody asks me to," she told him frantically. "That's why. Now what you gotta say about it?"

Regina's conversation didn't seem normal as usual. I could sense something was bothering her other than what we were already going through. And as painful as this mission had become with everything we'd experienced, it worried me that Satan might seize an opportunity like this, when emotions were running high, and try to take us out. The best thing for us to do was try to remain as calm as possible under such circumstances. Flying through this fog had not been part of our plan. I'm sure the entire crew was trying to figure out just how much of this fog had been put in place by Satan.

We were under heavy attack. Firing and loud explosions could be heard all around us as this MH-53J Pave Low traveled through this hellhole of death. That was when I realized how thankful I was that this craft was bulletproof, protecting not only the equipment but us as well. The MH-53J was also self-sealing, which made it even more admirable.

Thinking about everything that could go wrong was a horrible, especially with these helicopters constantly moving through the fog. We didn't realize how terribly close we really while circling high above such dangerous elements that threatened the entire crew.

Thank God for the GPS system and for what radio communication we still had, which felt like a kind of armor against the odds set before us by Satan. By the grace of God we were still on our way to assist whatever was happening in the town of Stonyford. But many members of this mission's crew had already been critically injured despite how carefully this operation had been planned. It had become a disaster, as complicated as trying to thread a needle in the dark. Everything had become a threat, even when there was no immediate sign of danger. Something could still be concealed somewhere, lurking and ready to move against the crew.

That was when I suddenly noticed two AH-64D Apache helicopters glowing brightly in the distance as they moved through the fog. The thought of what they were about to do was terrifying. Suddenly fire erupted from the two long, narrow black objects beneath the cockpit area of each helicopter.

They were firing from crafts designed to destroy.

Through the haze, which made everything appear blurred, I again found myself thinking about Regina. I couldn't help wondering how she had become so distraught when only a few minutes earlier she had been full of energy.

Firing continued all around us as we tried to familiarize ourselves with parts of the region we could still see. In most places the biggest problem we faced was the ability to communicate with the rest of the crew. That was when I thought about how many of the crafts on this mission had been decommissioned years earlier. Now they were back in operation, highly maneuverable, lethal, and retrofitted for an important mission.

I thought about how the Apaches carried very effective weapons capable of employing flechette rockets, along with the AGM-114 Hellfire missile. That might have been what they were firing, causing such destruction against the rugged mountains that surrounded the region.

During this part of the flight mission high above rough terrain, we began to experience collapse from the instrument gauges. Satan was obviously obstructing our progress.

"Everybody, just keep pressing forward," I yelled out over the radio. "I do believe the key thing for us to do is to keep moving forward. And by all means, keep firing, regardless of the thickness of the fog."

It was obvious that anyone trying to attempt a landing in this type of environment could only find themselves contributing to Satan's agenda and become a target. Therefore the focus was for us to make it to Stonyford with only what communication we had left onboard our crafts.

Thinking about what we'd already gone through since taking flight from the boys ranch, I found myself in deep thought about one of the other team members piloting an AAS-72X who, I wondered if we lost them behind us somewhere. The pilot ID'd himself as Terry Hayes. His affirmative that a strange dog had somehow ended up onboard his craft was as mysterious as anything I'd ever heard from a crew member.

But was it impossible?

That would all depend on who you are talking to.

The fierce battle raged on like that of a deep-seated hurricane. The entire crew had become like diabolical evil people. Only Satan's demons were able to comprehend the purpose for such behaviors.

Helicopters were hastily crisscrossing each other in flight. They moved in a sluggish manner, circling around as if in a wide area, and flying aimlessly throughout the thick fog, firing their weapons.

"Hey, Doc," a voice called out on the radio. "You copy?"

"Copy!" I responded while thinking about how good it felt hearing the voice from one of the crew members. And especially after everything that was happening during this journey to Stonyford. I have to admit feeling a bit selfish at times from the mere thought of so many casualties. "Good to hear your voice," I told the person on the other end. "Whassup?"

"Just wanted to know if anyone other than my crew noticed the clearing above us?" he said referring to something that looked like an event that was full of outer space allusions in position regarding a variety of dark matter clumped together. "Uh, I know you guys are probably snickering at me but—"

"Yeah," another voice added. "I'm sure that almost all of us are."

"Whoo!" someone else yelled out loud. "Man, what the fuck is this?"

"Looks like a bunch of radiation with long flashes of dark particles crashing into each other, and destroying everything in their wake," one of our crew members said. He had studied the cosmos and held a graduate degree in cosmology. "You guys see, what you're looking at should give you reason enough never to think of yourself as something special. I mean, just take a good look at what you're able to see out there. Nothing but the universe and all those other important matters floating around us everywhere."

What had happened was that the fog had cleared in one specific area of the region, as if allowing a distinct hole in the atmosphere for us to see through. Inspired by such a sight, the key observation seemed to be the galaxy itself and its mass of innumerable clusters of particles moving violently and destroying everything in their wake. It was astonishing to observe the galaxy in such a form, even though it was frustrating to witness the fate of struggling planets.

I could only guess that perhaps this was what God had intended as the beginning scenario to block the scheduled launch of Satan's rebirth and his plan to spread power and terror across the earth. His attempt to rehearse such preparation would become nothing more than a performance without an audience to memorialize it. When it came to the citizens of the Stonyford region, despite everything that was taking place during their so-called joyous festival, my team's mission was to bring an end to the evil events brought about by the will of Satan.

Satan had methodically manipulated nearly every human being throughout the region into agreeing to surrender their souls. To put the entire ordeal into perspective, the technique had been carried out in relation to every aspect that Satan believed would support his views and his coming inauguration.

It was distinctly mind-blowing to think about the fact that the residents of these communities could have resisted if they had chosen to, yet for reasons unknown they had now come together collectively to share in this event.

"Sandra's been hit," Karen whispered softly in my ear. "And Regina isn't saying anything about it because I think she's afraid you might put her back there in the storage area."

"What?" I suddenly shouted, trying not to be too loud. "She's been hit?"

"Yeah," she said. "But I can't see any blood."

"Damn," I uttered. "You tell Tony?"

"Not yet," Karen said. "I'll let him know right now."

"Yeah, and make sure you tell him to stay calm," I told her. "I'll figure out something."

"Something like what?" Karen asked.

"Are you sure, Karen?" I asked, hoping that maybe Sandra wasn't really hit.

"Well, put it this way," Karen said, clearly worried. "Her eyes are shut tight and won't open. She isn't breathing. And she's really stiff."

"What's Regina doing?" I asked.

"She's just sitting there like nothing's happening," Karen said. "You want me to tell her you want to talk to her?"

"No, that's all right," I told her. "Just tell Tony about it and then tell him to check and see what's wrong with her."

"I told you, she isn't moving or anything," Karen said again. "What I told you must not be believable or something."

"No, Karen," I said quickly in a softer tone. "It's not that I don't believe you. It's me. I'm the one having a hard time trying to understand what you just told me. I have nothing against what you said about her."

Before I could finish my sentence Karen had already turned toward Tony and was apparently telling him what had happened. A few seconds after Tony realized what she was saying, a violent explosion erupted not far ahead of us, rocking our craft like crazy.

"Anybody get a reading on what that was and where it came from?" I yelled over the radio.

After a moment of silence, a voice finally came over the radio. I thought I recognized it as MacDonald. He confirmed without hesitation that the explosion had struck one of our helicopters.

"From what I'm reading on my little device here, something just made a violent impact with one of the AH-64D Apache helicopters," he said.

"It came from inside this goddamn fog," someone cried loudly over the radio. "It's that goddamn fog. It's coming back to finish the job."

"I think this has got to be it," another voice said. "This is gonna be that final battle all them good Christian folks been talkin' about. Armageddon. I think we're about to witness the final battle between the forces of good and evil."

After hearing all that talk about devastation over the radio, I turned around just in time to see Regina trying her best to resuscitate Sandra.

"Thank God for the Crucifixion," a voice shouted over the radio. "I been tellin' y'all for years that Jesus Christ was gonna return one day, and just look. The skies have opened and the dead are rising."

"Man, you crazy," someone said. "Keep that bullshit up and you'll be the first to go with your crazy self, talkin' all that foolish nonsense."

The fog had returned, and we were once again heavily at war with every deadly element Satan chose to throw our way. The situation seemed to grow more intense. My concern was that with Sandra's death my crew aboard this helicopter might allow themselves to become blindsided by her passing, like a dangerous whirlwind.

I thought to myself how creepy it was for everything the crew had gone through to even be happening. But everything we were experiencing had already been written in the Bible. It speaks about the clash between good and evil and how it would unfold, sweeping away everything just like a storm. Terror would appear in every eye as part of the Devil's strategy to complete his mission across the earth. His agenda is to find the weakness within a person's soul and attack it at will, confidently trying to destroy him and everything about him.

This would be the strategy Satan would undoubtedly use to focus his quick and effective agenda as he tried to take control of the region.

We were using just about every weapon we had, but the power against us had become far stronger than expected. The fog covering the entire region prevented us from seeing anything beyond a certain distance. Just another of Satan's territorial strategies. That was when we began using some of our heaviest weapons, deploying several of our anti-aircraft missile batteries along with every other weapon.

There was no doubt the entire strategy of this event had been meticulously planned and was now being carried out by the Devil himself through his fallen angels. Fortunately our departure from the boys ranch had been made in time without any of the helicopters needing refueling. Our mission was to make it to the town of Stonyford without placing ourselves in an even worse position.

"Oh, fuck!" someone shouted over the radio. "I think we got something going on over here."

"Yeah, like what?" someone else asked.

"Holy shit, you guys," the voice yelled. "I don't believe it, but we really got an emergency jumpin' off in my craft."

"What's the emergency?" I asked. "What's happening?"

"Oh my God, man," the voice continued. "Something is in here messin' around with everything. But we can see what it's doin'."

"Whatever it is, it's invisible," another voice added. "We can't see it, but we know it's in here fuckin' things up on the instrument panel."

"I think I'm gonna have to make an emergency landing," the pilot yelled. "I gotta take her down. I'm losin' altitude fast. I have to take her down."

"Uh, MacDonald. You copy?" I called over the radio.

"Copy!" he quickly answered.

"The crew making an emergency landing, can you get a position on the location?" I asked him.

"Already on it and locked in," he said. "Got 'em. They're not too far underneath us, a little off to the left."

"Hey, that's another one of those AH-64D Apache helicopters.

I think I can find it."

"Who are you? And where are you?" someone asked the person who said he could find the downed helicopter.

"Already on the ground," the man said. "And just for the record, my name is Manning Bey. I'm one of the pilots who flies with the group of guys that went down for an emergency landing."

"Can you see 'em?" a voice asked Manning Bey.

"Too much fog," he said. "But I know they're down here somewhere."

All around us we could hear loud firing and explosions going off as if they were happening right on top of us. But this Manning Bey guy was determined to reach his friends no matter what consequences he had to face. His determination was exactly what this crew was all about.

"By my calculation, and if the facts are right, we should be pretty close to Stonyford," Karen said while staring at Regina.

"And where is Sandra?" Tony asked Karen. "You guys already moved her body to the storage area?"

"I ain't moved nothing," Karen told him, still staring at Regina. "She did that by herself."

"Strange how she could do something like that without us seeing her," I said curiously. "You sure Sandra didn't just fall to the side?"

"Hey, Regina, where is Sandra?" Tony suddenly asked.

After Regina realized that Sandra was no longer seated in the chair just a few feet from her, she immediately started yelling and screaming frantically.

"Where is she?" Regina cried out emotionally. "Oh no, where is she? Where is Sandra? What'd you do with her? Where is she, Karen? You went ahead and put her in the back, didn't you? After I told you not to. And you guys helped her, didn't you? I hate you for doing that."

There was nothing I could do except sit there in the pilot seat and continue trying my best to bring us out of a situation that could only be described as Satan's hellhole. I now understood why Regina's mood had changed so drastically. Whatever had happened to Sandra that took her life had pushed Regina into deep distress. It was almost as if she had gone temporarily insane.

And now the situation on board my craft had become even more troubling. But the rest of us knew how important it was to remain as calm as possible. It was the only way to keep the spirit of the devil from gaining access to our lives.

Suddenly another violent burst of gunfire shook our craft.

"Check this out, Karen," I said, staring at her as if there was more on my mind than what I was about to say. Then I realized what had caught my attention. She had put on some clothing without me noticing it. She was now wearing a colorful bra top and a pair of tight black capris, along with a fashionable pair of military-style calf boots by Step Up Comfort. They were bright metallic red with shiny gold-plated buckles and black zippers, with half-inch heels. This lady was now dressed to kill.

"Uh, I'll be setting this baby to fly at an altitude I know you can handle like ridin' a bicycle. You feel me?"

"Uh huh," she mumbled.

"Just like steering a car, except this ain't no car," I told her. "You gotta use these rudder pedals and things that look like handlebars to control this helicopter when steering it in the direction you want it to go. I mean fly. However you want it to move. Put it that way, Karen."

"What for?" she said, confused. "I ain't never flown no helicopter. What if this thing crashes or something? Then what?"

"Then I guess you can say we'll be joining Sandra a bit early," I told her seriously.

The thing I really loved about Karen was her tone when she spoke. There was just something smooth about it that flowed like sweet honey.

"You're serious about this?" Tony asked me.

"Damn straight," I answered. "I need you to help me while Karen takes a solo flight. We've got something on board back there in the cargo area of this craft, and whatever it is, it's hitchin' a free ride on this vessel without ever bein' granted our permission to do so. It's a federal crime against this mission. Plus, whatever it is, I do believe it got Sandra back there with it, and we, meanin' both you and Ree, are goin' after it. Understood?"

Tony couldn't bring himself to say anything that would go against our attack on the Devil's fallen angels, but he also knew there was a chance this could mean the end of our survival. That had been a sensitive subject from the very beginning when we agreed to take on this mission. But when you really thought about it, we were all now very much in survival mode and capable of wiping out any suspicious target without definite proof of being attacked.

If the target moved in any offensive manner, then we blasted it to pieces nonstop.

I could sense Karen's control of the helicopter. She was determined to operate the craft under pressure while staying completely focused on everything around her.

"Ready to do this?" I asked Tony while watching him reach for a thick strap that hung not far from the co-pilot seat and carried a large amount of weaponry.

"Ready when you are," he answered, fastening the gear tight for the was a fierce battle with whatever it was that caused Sandra's death and taken her body. "Let's do this."

"Regina, you mind moving over here into the co-pilot's seat?" I asked her in a soft tone, trying not to cause too much alarm. I needed her to move so she wouldn't be in harm's way.

"Right here, Regina," Tony told her, pointing to the seat he had been sitting in.

"Now, on the count of three, flip that switch for the cargo door to open," I told Tony. "As soon as I push this door open, start firing. But whatever you do, make sure you don't hit Sandra's body."

I could tell how tense Tony was by the way he held the M-16. I could see a slight tremble in his arm. I knew he was just as curious as I was about the target on the other side of the door. I thought about what it, or something like it, had done to members of this team. I also thought about the MV-22 Osprey, the AH-64D Apache helicopters, the UH-72A Lakotas, and of course the attack on one of the helicopters from as far away as the Montana Hi-Line. Whatever these things meant to do, it was clear they intended to do some serious damage to us. They were out to destroy us and we knew it.

I nodded to Tony to flip the switch, and three was the only number I remember saying when loud gunfire started blasting from the weapons we held tightly against our shoulders.

I kicked the storage room door open as hard as I could, just a fraction of a second before Tony opened up with nearly everything he had. Because we were wearing helmets, the noise from our firing was muffled, though intense heat could be felt as if the craft had turned into an inferno.

Knowing he couldn't hear me, I raised one of my hands to signal him to stop firing. Finally, when everything went quiet, the only things visible were dense smoke and shell casings scattered across the floor.

"Cease firing for a minute, Tony," I told him. "Gotta see if we even hit anything."

I could hear him breathing fast and deep through his helmet mic as if he were hyperventilating.

"Man," Tony said, "whoever thought about this idea, I tell you, Doc, they had a fucked up perception thinkin' this was gonna be some simple in-and-out operation. My nerves are all shot to hell. And all that weird imaginary bullshit I used to picture in my mind when I was a kid, all that spooky stuff that used to scare me?

I honestly believe that shit is startin' to haunt me because it's really happenin'. Damn. I'm an adult now and all that shit is really up here in Stonyford happenin'."

"Just be cool, Tony," I said, trying to calm him down. "You're doin' all right and everything's gonna be just fine."

"I don't see anything," he said, sounding confused.

And he was right. We couldn't see anything. Whatever had taken Sandra wasn't anywhere in the storage area of the craft. I couldn't believe it. Nothing was there. We hadn't hit anything with all the firing we had just done.

But how could that be? I thought to myself. How could something get inside this helicopter, take Sandra's body, and then leave without us seeing it?

I began thinking about everything else that had taken place that we still couldn't understand. In the report there was mention of creatures. Invisible creatures hidden and lurking throughout the Stonyford region. These creatures were said to disappear only to reappear elsewhere, violently attacking as Margaret had described, crippling their victims, and then destroying them mentally and emotionally.

"Hey, Doc," a voice yelled over the radio. "What's happening?"

Hearing this voice ring loudly in my helmet jolted me back to the fact that we were still at war.

"You guys all right down there?"

Hearing that made me think about Karen still in the pilot's seat. She might have landed without us realizing it. Since it was her first time at the helm, and the helicopter's controls were set to something close to autopilot, I thought we had probably landed, or were very close to it.

"Whatever that was you guys were firing at, it's long gone, Doc."

I responded as quickly as I could and began questioning the

person on the radio.

"What did you see?" I asked. "What was it that you saw come out of my craft?"

"Yeah, I saw it, Doc," he said. "I think you lost a blanket, or maybe a rug or something."

"Where'd it go?" Tony asked him. "Where did it land?"

"I don't think it landed," someone else said while trying to describe what they saw. "It just floated like one of those paper airplanes. It kept floating into the fog until it couldn't be seen anymore. Just faded away like that."

"Anybody see anything carrying it?" I asked over the radio. "You know, like flying with it or—"

Silence, followed by a bit of static.

"Couldn't see anything else after it went into the fog," another voice said. "It was just up there floating like he said. I thought it was a piece of paper at first, but then I realized it was too big for that. So I figured it was a blanket you guys tossed out of your helicopter."

"What is it that's got y'all all stirred up?" someone else asked. "I mean, I ain't stupid enough not to know something ain't right about whatever that was floating in the air like that."

"Everybody just stay calm and let us try to figure this out," Tony said, taking charge of the moment. "Everyone start keeping an eye on your crew members. Count them and make sure you have the right number of people on board."

"Man, what's happening, Doc?" someone asked me. "One of them things out there tryin' to outright annihilate us from inside our helicopter?"

"This is the anniversary and inauguration date of Satan's return from the bottomless pit of hell," I told the man over the radio. "And I was told he's going to try once again to overthrow the kingdom of heaven, except this time it'll be right here on earth. I guess starting right here in the Stonyford region."

"So what's that got to do with us?" he questioned. "We been at war with these things ever since we got here. And our guys been around here dying like you would swat a fly. Our mission wasn't to come up here like a bunch of head-huntin' vigilantes, you know. Hell, I got a family waiting on me back home who depend on me to take care of 'em. I ain't a—"

There was a sudden outburst of an anguished scream of pain over the radio.

"Oh, no!" someone yelled. "Oh my God, no. Don't let this be happening to us."

"Jesus Christ!" someone else screamed over the radio. "It's going to kill us. It's ripping him to pieces."

"Kill it, somebody!" another voice screamed. "Kill it! Get it off me. It's killing me. Oh God, no. Don't let it—"

"What the hell's going on over there?" another voice shouted over the radio. "What's going on over there? Answer me, damn it!"

Whatever was happening in the helicopter, gunfire continued to ring out, lighting up the sky, as if the firing itself was some kind of violent spectacle. Everything within a certain radius around us seemed to burn in a wide circle. It looked as though heavy gaseous elements were exploding in bright flashes of red and yellow, burning the surface of nearly everything, including the boys ranch.

"Everybody listen up," I shouted over the radio. "Make sure to keep your helmets on. There could be dangerous gas in the atmosphere. Make sure your helmet covering is connected to your respirator. Check your filters."

"What if I already took my helmet off?" someone asked.

"Then put it back on as fast as you can," I told him. "That goes for any of you who did that. Put 'em back on if you wanna live."

"This is such a heartbreaking experience, Murdock," a woman's soft voice said sadly. "It's like something is trying its best to separate us from the rest of the world. This mission feels like we're about to make some huge sacrificial death just so those poor people down there in that town, Stonyford, can live."

"That's right, lady," someone said. "It's my willingness to do this."

"It's all of our willingness or we wouldn't be here," another voice added.

"Well, God knows what we're trying to do for those people. No matter how they've rebelled by refusing to hear his word, he still loves them enough to send us in to help them get out of this mess they're in," she said.

"I'm with you, ma'am," another voice said. "You can count on that."

Then a strange distress sound came through the radio. It sounded like someone trying to send an S.O.S. from some distant place and time. According to what our radar was indicating, the distress signal was coming from a location that had been destroyed earlier when other crew members fought creatures like the giant Chimeras, the huge Guenon monkeys, deadly Lemurs, and other vicious animals.

"You guys hear that?" a voice sounding like the Cat exclaimed.

"Copy that," someone replied. "I hear it too. Where's it coming from?"

"Don't know," the voice that sounded like the Cat said. "Tryin' to find out if I can."

"Hey, Doc. This is MacDonald. You guys hear anything strange on the radio, like a distress call or something?"

"That's affirmative, without any debate," I answered. "Just amazed where it's coming from and what our radar is indicating."

"I feel y'all on that," another woman's voice added. "Man, my radar's trying to tell me that whoever it is, they're from some remote time. Like real ancient history or something. Very old, but it can't be that old, because they're somewhere around us."

"There it goes again," said Pee-wee. "I wonder if one of us tries talking to it in code, will it answer?"

"Is that you, Pee-wee?" I asked.

"Oh, excuse me for not identifying myself," he said. "But that's a big affirmative. It be me."

"Hey, I think you'll do just fine making contact with the unknown," I said to Pee-wee. "I just ask that you be careful and keep in mind the fact that Ethan has obviously proved himself a part of Satan by doing his best to steer this mission into a course of tribulations."

"Well, it's as Margaret said in the documents referring to people who live in this region turning to a false redemption. This entire ordeal will be like a counterfeit bill during this period of persecution. Satan himself is anticipating the inclusion of the entire Stonyford region," a voice came over the radio sounding like the lady from the Hi-Line of Montana.

"Check that out, Doc," Tony suddenly said, once again moving into a defensive position while staring fixedly at an object he pointed to behind our craft. "Man, I swear, I think I just saw something that looked like a freakin' giant bug out there following us."

"What?" I asked him curiously. "What did you see?"

"Man, Murdock," he said again, "it was a big giant bug-looking thing, like a mosquito or something, but it had what looked like a human head on it, and it was following us just now."

"Hey, what the fuck!" a voice yelled over the radio. "You guys see that just fly past us?"

"Freakin' giant horsefly buzzing around my helicopter," one of the crew members shouted over the radio.

"Where'd it go?" another voice asked. "Where is it?"

Loud, continuous gunfire rang out once again from just about every direction. Giant mosquitoes and horseflies with human heads were buzzing around our helicopters as if they were scouting us, attempting to break up our formation, which we knew would allow them to isolate one of the crafts and destroy it.

I have to admit that a few crew members became disoriented. The strange buzzing and humming sounds from these creatures had an effect that felt almost like being tranquilized through hypnosis.

The loud buzzing seemed intended to place everyone into a deep trance. I must admit that, strange as it was, the experience itself was fascinating.

Realizing what the creatures were trying to do, I quickly reminded the crew to play a game by memorizing titles of favorite songs. This was meant to prevent falling into a hypnotic state caused by the constant buzzing sounds of the creatures circling our helicopters.

Then there was a huge explosion that sent a blast into the sky like fireworks. The fog lit up like a Christmas tree with thousands of blinking lights flying through the air and leaving long, trails behind them.

“What the fuck was that?” someone yelled. “The beginning of the freakin’ resurrection or something?”

CHAPTER NINE

"OH FOR HEAVEN'S SAKE," Blake shouted, kicking a small soda can into the air after noticing the huge, dark gray, dusty cloud advancing toward Stonyford. "What in Sam's name is that? Like I could use some more problems. And where the hell is my help when I need it? Somebody better start tellin' me just what the hell that thing is comin' this way."

"Looks like a thundercloud or something, Sheriff," one of the forest rangers said, puzzled. "Looks like a bunch of thunderbolts bouncin' around inside it, if you ask me."

"It's a thundercloud all right," one of Blake's deputies said. "Just listen to all that uproar and racket it's makin'. I think it's a bad one, Boss. We gotta hurry up and do something to help them people trapped underneath all them carnival rides."

"Yeah, and what about them poor teenagers who came down that hill on fire in that RV over there," another deputy said. "Somebody still has to find out what happened to them."

"You know," the forest ranger said, "we don't even know who they were in that thing burnin' up like that, but I think I got a good idea."

"Oh, goddammit," Blake shouted again. "Will y'all shut the fuck up and start doin' something instead of all this goddamn guessin'?"

"Well, I'm on it, Sheriff," one of his deputies said. "I'm just a bit confused about where I should start. I mean, gee, so much has gone on. I just don't know where to start."

"Well you can start by pullin' your head out your ass," Blake told him. "Then help these guys get their heads out of theirs too, if that'll do any good. Sorry sons-of-bitches."

Sirens from different emergency response teams could be heard in the distance, coming from all directions as they rushed toward Stonyford.

It was a catastrophic situation, and Blake knew it. But being stubborn, just like his dad, he believed he could still handle the situation and keep everything under control.

The truth was that it had become a serious disaster with many casualties throughout the northern region of California.

People were severely injured. Some were killed by something unknown. And others were simply disappearing.

The inauguration was scheduled to begin within the hour during the opening ceremony that was to feature a fireworks display. The gathering of so many people had drowned out the noise from the emergency response teams' requests blaring loudly over Blake's radio.

Various response teams were already on hand performing duties that normally would have belonged to the town's funeral director, a service that had not been prepared for an event like this.

"It looks like somebody done set off a hundred pounds of dynamite down there by the lake, Sheriff," one of the emergency response crew members told him. "Ain't in all my years on this job ever seen anything like it."

"Dynamite?" the sheriff asked, confused. "What in heaven's name are you talkin' about, young man?"

"I'm tellin' you, Sheriff," he said. "You got some serious problems on your hands. And them clouds up there headed this way look like a ball of fire if you really want the truth about it. That ain't no ordinary cloud. No exceptions about it. Whatever it is, that ain't your average cloud headed this way."

"Well, what's your guess on it?" the sheriff asked one of the forest rangers. "I'm sure you've seen things like this as long as you've worked for that outfit."

"I would agree with the fact that whatever that cloud is, it's not your ordinary cloud," the ranger said. "I mean, just look at that thing."

"Can't y'all hear all that racket going on up there in that thing?" one of the deputies asked. "You know what I think we got here?"

"Oh yeah, big shot," the sheriff said, leaning his head toward the deputy. "Why don't you just go ahead and tell us stupid people what you think we got coming this way. Go ahead, tell us."

"I think it's a freakin' volcano," he said firmly. "And all them explosion noises we're hearing that sound like a bunch of cannons going off at the same time—that's consistent with how volcanoes sound when they erupt. It's ejecting a lot of stuff from them mountains up there and lighting up the sky, making it look like something burning."

"Well, by golly there, young man. You should've gone and preached the gospel. I really think you'd make a good teacher," the sheriff told him. "In fact, I'm absolutely sure about it. Awful shame you wasted your brain on this volcano nonsense."

"What, you don't believe me?" the deputy asked, staring up at the cloud.

"Not that I don't believe you," the sheriff said. "I just think what you're saying is a bunch of bullshit."

While they were busy arguing, there was a sudden violent eruption from within the cloud. Something like a huge fireball burst outward.

Overflowing amounts of what looked like fireworks shot up into the dark sky. Long streaks of bright, colorful lightning flashed like thousands of meteorites burning across the atmosphere, advancing toward Stonyford, moving rapidly across the sky without stopping.

"Sheriff, I think we better get everybody to leave this area," one of the deputies suggested. "The sound of that thing is really boiling."

"You know," said the Sheriff. "This is one time that I have to agree with you. But just try and be calm about telling 'em, you know. Don't wanna be starting a rush that'll get all out of control. And Lord knows we don't want to be stirring anything up only to have it get out of hand."

"Yeah, I think I know what you mean, Sheriff," said the deputy. "What we don't need is to be provoking a riot."

"Goddamn right, boy," the Sheriff said. "Don't need a goddamn outbreak like that happening like that around here. We got enough problems as it is. By the way, you hear anybody screaming?"

Disrespectful laughter came from both the Sheriff and the deputy.

CHAPTER TEN

"I CAN'T SEE ANYTHING," Karen said, trying to stay calm. "But I think we're on the ground or something because—"

"On the ground?" I said, trying to hurry and get to the controls.

"I think it landed or something," she said again. "It doesn't feel like we're moving. I mean flying anymore."

"Tony, make sure that door's closed," I told him. "Let me see what's happening."

"See, you can't see anything," Karen said, pointing out the window.

"Karen," I suddenly said, staring at her helmet. "You have your night vision optics hooked up to your mask?"

"What?" she exclaimed. "Damn, wondering why I couldn't see where we were flying. I mean, it was only when all those bombs would be exploding that it would light up out there. Then I could see everything."

"Here, let me take the controls," I told her, allowing enough room for her to squeeze past me, though preventing the contact she eagerly desired during our passage.

"What?"

"Nothing!" was her only reply to what I did. "Nothing at all."

The helicopter was suspended, hovering in the air at a low altitude, as if within a few feet of the ground. But this was the mission for this big bird, and I knew the MH-53J Pave Low was like a piece of machinery with a mind of its own. The only thing it needed now were the instructions of its codes in which to communicate machine language like OnStar.

Thinking about all the things this craft could do, my mind for some mysterious reason shifted back to Karen, who was embracing Regina. This was the lady of my every dream on a mad-ass crazy journey just like the one she took with me on the train ride to the state of Oregon. I really felt for her as I did in the beginning when we first met, except this time I needed her far more than she could imagine.

Tony was busy tending to the huge .50-caliber machine gun mounted on the side of our craft. In fact, there was one on both sides.

But Tony's a damn good person in general, and Lord knows I respect him. I guess you could say he's the brother my mama didn't have by birth in the family. He trusts me just a little too much when it comes to Karen.

"Ah, man. What the hell was that?" Tony yelled out. "Do it again and I'll fuck you all the way up, motherfucker!"

"What'd you see?" I called out to Tony. "What was it?"

"I think it was that freakin monkey riding on that butterfly-looking moth thing again," he said. "Except this time it wasn't blowing that horn."

"Are you sure that's what it was?" I asked him.

"Yeah," he said seriously, gripping the machine gun even tighter while bracing his footing. "Next time I'mma just blast both of them bitches."

"Hey, we got a goddamn monkey riding around on his fuckin

pony out there," one of the crew members yelled over the radio.

"Blast that goddamn monkey," Tony said over the radio. "Send it my way and I'll do it!"

"Monkey!" someone else yelled out on the radio. "Where's it at?"

"That thing got a ponytail on it?" another voice asked.

"Y'all seeing more than just one monkey, you know," someone else said. "Cause the one I keep seeing got another one riding with it, hanging tight on the back of that moth with what looks like a shiny gold-plated horn in its hand, waving it around and pointing it at our helicopter."

"You guys just make sure to keep watch for unexpected explosions and eruptions from underneath us," I told everyone. "All of these explosions and stuff that looks like fireworks are being navigated, I believe, by those monkeys."

"Anybody got a position and location on that military AGM-114 bad-ass Hellfire missile?" someone asked over the radio.

"Just how the hell you lose a goddamn missile?" an unidentified voice asked. "Thing must not have been lethal."

"What kind of missile was it?" someone asked.

"Sidewinder," the person on the radio said. "An AIM-9 Sidewinder that was carried on a squadron AV-8B Harrier."

"What in the world are you doing carrying something like that onboard your helicopter?" I asked the person on the radio.

"It wasn't onboard my helicopter," the person said. "It was deployed by the Harrier from there in Stonyford as an attack on what the people in that town think is a violent volcano erupting and coming their way. What's happening is they're trying to find a way to change the direction it's going by using a lethal missile to make a deep ditch in the ground like a trench."

"That's a damn good way to make a radical change all right," someone added to the conversation. "Only thing is they don't seem to be aware of the fact that this ain't no goddamn volcano erupting up here in these mountains."

"Whoever is trying to find that missile," I said, "you need to let them know exactly what's happening up here before they end up starting something bigger than what they can deal with."

"What do I tell 'em?" the person on the radio asked. "Monkeys flying around up here on giant moths are attacking us and trying to start a monkey revolution to overthrow the government?"

"Ha, ha, ha," someone laughed over the radio. "Now that's good, my friend. A monkey revolution to overthrow the American government. Tell me something, buddy. Just where in the heck did you come from to be a part of this mission?"

"Incoming!" someone yelled over the radio as firing from below our flight altitude came crashing through the bottom of one of the helicopters, causing it to explode instantly upon impact with whatever had hit it.

"Damn!" Tony shouted. "I think it got 'em, Doc. I couldn't see the hit because of the fog, but from the looks of that explosion it had to hit one of our helicopters or something. That was another huge explosion somewhere down there."

"Anybody able to see what was hit?" I asked over the radio.

"We're trying to ID it, Doc," a voice said bitterly. "Whatever that incoming was, you can believe it hit something up here with us. Just can't see it because of all this fog."

"Tony, we're dropping down in altitude," I told him. "Blast anything that doesn't look friendly."

"I'm already on it," Tony said, swinging the .50-caliber machine gun to the center of the mount and locking it into position for immediate firing.

"I thought the hit was down below us somewhere from the way it lit up everything," Tony added. "I mean, that was huge."

"Just another part of his demonstration," I mumbled. "Compared to what drama we've already gone through, he's nothing but a real thief working furtively to take our lives."

"Uh, Doc," a voice said over the radio. "This is the pilot of an Apache helicopter. You copy?"

"Copy," I responded. "What's up?"

"Uh, how much further do you think it is to Stonyford?" he asked.

"At the blink of an eye," I told him. "Having problems?"

Suddenly there was an abrupt outburst of screaming, and it sounded as if someone was crying out for help over the radio. Tony quickly began trying to reset the position from which we were transmitting, but he had no success picking up the Apache pilot again.

"Can't find 'em," Tony said while continuing to push the persist button that enabled the self-operation system, which automatically searched for the position and location of the Apache helicopter. "Man, it doesn't seem like this shit is avoidable."

"Why don't you let Karen do that while you tend to that .50-caliber?"

"Think you can handle it, Karen?" Tony asked. "I mean, you already got your hands full, you know, like with taking care of Regina."

"She can go ahead and do it," Regina said unexpectedly, still squeezing her eyes shut tight. "I'm all right. She can do it for you."

Both Tony and I stared at each other, stunned by Regina saying that Karen could go ahead and operate the transmitter and that she was all right with it. I knew the ordeal was frustrating for the crew, but this was our mission as journalists. I considered this crew among the best journalist entrepreneurs in existence. They are a tremendous group of people to work with, whose skills and passion had become personal from the very beginning of this journey to Stonyford. I have, from the start, been deeply inspired by this crew, who seemed to have taken on an extremely deadly experience under such dangerous circumstances.

This mission had become somewhat like entertainment,

which was exactly what I needed during the whole experience, literally.

"Murdock. Uh, check this out, man," Tony said, trying to find his words. "Uh, that guy. You know, the pilot of that helicopter. Well, he was asking you about Stonyford. You know. And like how much further it was before—"

"Yeah, uh. I know what you're asking," I said, letting him know that I understood what was on his mind as far as how much more time it would be before we reached Stonyford.

"You told him at the blink of an eye," Tony said, curious.

"Yeah," I answered. "We're almost there, Tony. Just a little further and we'll be there, providing we make it."

"Hey, I'm not doubting you or anything," Tony said, assuring me that he wasn't doubting our distance from Stonyford. "I was just wondering how much longer we had to go, though—"

Suddenly there was another loud explosion on a large scale that I am more than sure shook the entire region, sending a huge fireball barreling upward a short distance in front of us. Through a slight clearing in the fog, burning fragments could be seen slamming hard into a few hills and mountainsides and then exploding on impact.

"Wow," I exclaimed with a loud exhale. "Talk about this becoming a full-scale war. I do believe this is about to be it!"

Machine-gun fire could be heard coming from just about everywhere, including Tony doing his thing and firing at will.

"Make sure you guys fasten your seat belts really tight," I told the crew again over the radio as I focused my attention on Karen. "Going to be one hell of a rough bumpy ride from here on out all the way to Stonyford. I really don't quite know just what it is that's happening or even what it means, but for strange reasons the temperature is even changing. It's getting hot out there. Just might be what's happening all over this place."

"Hey, Doc?" a voice came over the radio calling me. "You

copy? This is Pee-wee."

"Copy you, Pee-wee," I said. "What's up, man?"

"Hot all over this region. You feel me?" he said. "Everything really up in smoke. Burning like crazy out there."

Then, out of practically nowhere, through another clearing in the fog, a small four-seater airplane, possibly a 172, came flying past us in the opposite direction with its single engine roaring loudly before disappearing back into the thick fog. It could be seen for only a few seconds before vanishing, and then it abruptly exploded just above the rugged terrain below our flight path, bursting into flames.

"Looks like that thing was possibly on its way to the boys ranch," a voice said over the radio.

"I don't know," another voice replied. "As fast as it was moving, it looked like it was being chased or maybe just in a hurry to get where it was trying to go."

Heavy smoke continued to rise from below our crafts. It was like a bad fire had been ignited, causing the surrounding mountains to burn wildly out of control.

Just about everything was burning, and .50-caliber machine guns could be heard firing at will, hopefully destroying the intended targets that were attacking us.

Thick black smoke continued to rise upward, mixing heavily with the dense fog around us as flames burned rapidly out of control, sending huge balls of fire forcefully into the dark sky like fireworks igniting fires everywhere.

I found myself thinking about our casualties as well as those who were possibly hit, injured, and somewhere on the ground suffering without anyone there to help them. The fog made it almost impossible to spot those who were down with possibly damaged helicopters somewhere on the ground. I told the crew pilots to fly at a low altitude in search of downed helicopters and crew members who might still be alive.

Anything considered combustible onboard the downed helicopters caused them to explode upon impact.

I wondered if the mission had now become a disaster, even though we had launched what seemed like thousands of deadly missiles. These missiles were like lethal torpedoes, and although our gunfire was striking intended targets, crew members were dying at an alarming rate.

To my surprise, Tony was still blasting away, firing that .50-caliber machine gun at anything he felt was a threat to this mission. Watching him forced me to do some quick thinking about how wrong it was for me to feel the mission was a disaster. I guess my emotions were getting the best of me. But this was war, and war is war whether we like it or not. It's still war, and people are going to die.

I then turned my attention to Regina, who was just sitting there in the co-pilot's seat as though she were unconscious with her eyes squeezed shut. I thought about Sandra and realized how much she meant to Regina, which made me look toward the door leading to the storage area of my craft.

"Tony," I said quietly, not wanting to cause alarm while motioning my head toward the door. "Check it out."

"Got it," Tony whispered while unfastening the strap that held him secured inside the side sliding doorway of the helicopter where the machine gun was mounted. "Take this, Karen," he told her while strapping another of the deadly weapons against his body. "Push that button on my count."

Just as he called the number, Karen pushed the button activating the system that opened the rear door leading to the storage area of the helicopter.

"Nothing," Tony said over his helmet mic. "I don't see anything, Doc."

"All right then, Tony," I said. "Go ahead and secure the room."

"Okay," Tony said, staring out the back of the helicopter.

"What was it that you thought you heard back here?"

"I really don't know," I told him. "Just thought I heard something. But I guess it wasn't anything to worry about."

"Mind if I stay back here for a few minutes?" Tony asked. "I just want to check out a few things, though—"

"Hey. Suit yourself if that's the thing you want to do right now," I told him. "For whatever purpose you have. Just watch for unfriendly movement."

"I just want to check everything out from back here for a few minutes," he said.

"Karen, you got that?" I asked while shifting my attention to Regina again.

"Got what?" Karen asked.

"Anything that comes your way from out there," I said, nodding toward the outside of the helicopter.

"Yeah. I think so," she said. "What? I just start squeezing this here, right?"

"Uh, yeah," I said. "That's called the trigger, Karen."

"Where the bullets at?" she asked. "Think I need some more?"

"Not right now," I told her. "But check that box right there beside you to make sure."

"Right here?" she asked, pointing to the container on the floor.

"Yeah, that's it," I said. "How does it look?"

"It's almost empty," she said. "I mean—"

"Keep an eye on it," I told her. "I'll get Tony to hook up another one if you run out. Just let me know when you get too low."

Boom! Boom! Boom!

"Man!" Tony shouted. "What the fuck?"

"What's going on back there, Tony?" I yelled. "What's happening?"

"I don't know," he said. "But I thought I saw something. I don't know where it went. You guys didn't see it up front?"

"You see anything, Karen?" I asked.

"No," she said. "What was it?"

"Man, Tony," I said. "What'd you see?"

"Got something circling around and buzzing us again," someone said over the radio. "Looks like a freakin' monkey. Two of them on the move."

"Keep your finger on the trigger, Karen," I told her. "If you see anything I want you to start firing. You hear me?"

"I hear you," she said, sounding short of breath. "I'm having trouble with this helmet. No, wait. Okay, I think I got it working."

"You all right over there?" I asked, noticing her movement as she adjusted her helmet.

"I got it," she said, moving the machine gun around in circles. "I got this."

Boom! Boom! Boom!

Tony continued to blast away from the back of the helicopter. "Come on motherfucker, bring yo' ass up here again," we could hear him yelling to whatever it was he was shooting at. "Come on motherfucker, where y'all at?"

Suddenly, Karen started firing at something without hesitation. "Got it," she yelled. "Uh huh, that's right. That's what you get. Told you not to mess with me. Didn't I?"

Before I knew it, even Regina was yelling her dislike of the creatures attacking our crafts. "Get 'em, Karen," she yelled. "Get all of 'em, girl. Get 'em for me too, Karen."

Hearing all the blasting was when I began to maneuver the helicopter more rapidly in serious combat movement just as I had during our trip into this region. It was also then that someone switched the onboard entertainment system on, and the song "Thrill Is Gone" by B.B. King came over the speakers as we once again engaged in heavy battle, almost in slow motion.

"Yeah," a voice yelled over the radio. "Didn't think I could interlock onto yo' motherfuckin' ass, did you? You ugly bastard.

But yo' ass is toasted now, motherfucker. The thrill is really gone for yo' ass."

"I got one over here too," another voice yelled. "Oop! Oh well. I never said anything about loving you. No way, bitch!"

"Hey, Cat," I called over the radio. "You still out there?"

"You goddamn skippy, I am," the Cat answered. "Who dat there callin' me in the heat of the night?"

"Hey, Cat," I said. "This ain't nothin' but the Doc. What's up? Are you guys all right? Haven't heard from you in quite a while."

"Hell, my crew been out here in the dark blastin' monkeys or something from what I can see," he said, laughing. "How much further, Doc?"

"We be there," I told him, knowing it was what everybody was waiting for me to say. "Stonyford is a few seconds away. In fact, it's just below us. Just gotta get out this fog."

"What'd you say?" a woman's voice asked over the radio. "Don't look like no state of Montana down there to me. That looks more like that goddamn Stonyford."

"Yeah, and it's on fire or something," someone said. "Hey, Doc. They down there fighting too, or what?"

Realizing what the person on the radio had brought to the crew's attention, I found myself thinking about how Margaret had described the events that would take place in Stonyford, and how she had revealed such tenderness toward the people living throughout the region.

I remembered how she described being accused of the death of her sister, Wanda. Despite the tragedy, which had been so dramatic for such a young child, she was still held accountable for many of the tragic elements that had become morally significant and disastrous for the entire Stonyford region.

Her demeanor, as described by residents of the community, was unlike that of the perfect child who had been injured. For decades even her own family refused to reclaim her, which separated her from society and drove her into a kind of monstrous isolation created by her enemies, Lucifer's demons.

"Welcome to the beginning of Armageddon," I told the crew as we were about to appear over the town of Stonyford. "This is also the birthplace of the third gender, among other doctrines. Do I really need to reread the doctrine in question? This region will show you why we've come to Stonyford, the notorious town with its own theology from the Book of Revelation. The Rapture, in all perspective, will be revealed in interpretive timelines leading to Armageddon."

I could still hear Tony blasting away with the machine gun, as well as other gunners somewhere in the thick fog around us. At times I could hear Karen talking to whatever she was shooting at. She spoke to it as if she had become an enraged lunatic.

But thinking about it, I couldn't help wondering if the entire crew might be somewhat insane by now after everything we had gone through. And wherever Regina's mind was, it was clear that she was no longer really with us on this craft.

Suddenly there appeared what seemed like millions of bright colors forming lifelike images of people in front of the helicopter. Each of these beings had a strange beauty, like figures from dreams.

As a visionary myself, I could only describe the experience as images from the imagination, if guided in the right way.

But remembering my conversation with Margaret, I knew these sightings were none other than Satan using such images as part of a deception meant to entrap us.

His entreaty with the Stonyford region had been done to amuse himself through spectacle, enslaving those who had become fascinated with his demonstrations and placing himself on a throne through those who accepted his display.

"Tony, you copy me, man?"

"Copy!" he answered in a rough tone while firing the machine gun.

"Need you back up here with me," I told him. "Are the targets being elusive or what?"

"Elusive is an understatement, Doc," he said. "And the situation back here is only getting worse. You see all the twisted junk down there?"

Not knowing what he meant, I made a quick bank to my left in search of whatever he had seen below. To my surprise, what looked like a huge mass of twisted metal and burning debris lay scattered in ruins along the mountains and hillsides. Downed helicopters lay far from any smooth stretch of land where someone could attempt an emergency landing to assist the wounded.

I couldn't believe it. Here we were, just minutes from the town of Stonyford in the dead of night. The thick fog below us began to clear again, giving us a dreadful view of our downed crew members who had apparently been taken out by an unseen enemy, hostile forces acting under the devil.

"You see what I mean?" Tony shouted. "It's all over the place."

"Holy mother of Christ," a voice rang out. "Who in Heaven's name is responsible for this?"

"God! I praise you today," someone began praying over the radio. "We thank you that—"

"That's right, he's all powerful," another voice began.

"Jesus!" someone else shouted. "In your name, I do believe—"

Hearing the prayers rising to the Creator made me realize how devoted this crew could be during the ordeal of our journey. Most were believers in the Bible and trusted that Heaven awaited them beyond whatever might happen here. It was as if the greater the sacrifice, the greater the blessing from God.

"Blessed be Your name forever and ever," someone said.

As the words ended, something like a California condor sailed slowly over us. Unlike the condors normally found in the mountains of southern California, this bird was enormous. Its wings stretched nearly thirty feet across, and the body itself had to be at least twelve feet long. The head looked more like that of an eagle, and even from my distance it was clear that its size and strength made it a powerful, commanding presence.

As it passed closer, the eagle's head seemed almost like that of a lion or a wild mountain cat, perhaps even a cheetah, with long, sharp claws.

It sailed through the dark sky, lit by moonlight and the glow of burning trees and wrecked helicopters scattered across the mountains like the remains of a shipwreck. Yet the great bird simply drifted from side to side as if indifferent to the destruction below.

Suddenly, with great speed, a large group of bright, colorful giant dragonflies glided past us. Their wings were stretched out flat as they moved smoothly, almost as if floating over water, before descending and forming what looked like a circular flight pattern around the helicopters.

"Cease your firing," I yelled over the radio. "Cease fire. Nobody fire until we figure out what this is all about."

"What are you talking about?" a voice asked over the radio. "What you talking about? All them dragonflies or something?"

"Just cease fire for right now, you guys," I said again. "They don't seem to be any threat. Well, not that I can see."

"You mean they're not showing any hostility, don't you, Doc?" Tony shouted.

"Hey, it could be the method they're using before they, uh, you know, get ready to strike," someone said seriously. "Why take any chances when we can just keep firing?"

"You know what I think, Murdock?" another voice said over the radio. "I think they're using that subliminal crap to get to us, man. I mean, come on. Don't you think all these creatures around here think they're somehow superior to us right now, when we've invaded their territory? I know I would if it meant fighting for my country."

"Yeah," another voice added. "It's like this is their geographical area. It belongs to all the creatures in this part of the region. Without any authority, here we are invading it and wiping them out."

"You mean just like the government did, to a certain degree, when they took America from the native people who were already here?" someone said.

"Precisely!" I yelled over the radio. "So don't start getting sentimental about this conversation now, you bunch of mean, malicious, dishonorable cowards."

Everyone laughed.

"And here we are on the Devil's playground," another voice said. "This is his concealed crime against the people of Stonyford, stealing their souls."

Silence.

I found myself thinking again about how heartbreaking it must have been for Margaret to be pushed away during her most difficult times, not only by her neighbors but by her own family. She had been removed completely from the community and placed somewhere safe to be cared for by strangers.

The chance to love and be loved had been taken from her. Her family rejected her, and others turned away as well, separating her from the kind of childhood life that should never have ended so early. Yet her courage to survive the cruelty and hatred of a doomed community paved the way for a long and painful journey toward recovery.

The only thing I could do was think about the fact that she was a survivor and that we were here to write her story. Stonyford was doomed in every sense one could use to describe something malicious and dishonorable. Few things in my life had ever been so heartbreaking, and Margaret's story had become my central concern.

"All right, you guys," I said on the mic. "Time to descend and get ready for our arrival at Stonyford. Strengthen your hearts. Stay humble, and don't let distractions take your focus. Many dangers wait for us on this battlefield, and each of you may face personal risk. Just remember, never abandon the wounded. May God have mercy on your souls and comfort you during this trial. This mission isn't about restitution. We receive no compensation for loss, damage, or injury. So see this mission for what it is. The right thing to do. We're here to restore what we can: the condition of a town, and the strength of its people."

Everything around us seemed to be collapsing. As I stared out the cockpit windshield, I could see the dense fog beginning to clear in certain areas, though it was slowly moving toward Stonyford. I began checking the instrument panel, searching for any indication that it was time to begin landing.

Loud explosions and machine-gun fire filled the air again. Guided missiles streaked across the sky, slamming into the mountains with terrifying force. Thunderous blasts echoed across the region as violent bolts of lightning struck rocks and trees, followed by waves of shock and what looked like thousands of glowing fireflies shooting high into the dark sky from some highly combustible source.

Millions of small shining objects also appeared to be launching from something shaped like a massive vessel mounted on one of the mountains. The structure resembled a heavily armed battleship prepared for war. Its weapons looked like giant tube-shaped launchers, enormous bazooka-like rockets firing continuously.

"Ah, howdy there, neighbor," I said to the sight humorously, though I had never seen anything like it before. "Where'd you come from?"

To my surprise, there were hundreds—maybe thousands—of monkeys riding on moths circling high above.

"Hey, Doc," Tony called, sounding confused. "You hear me?"

"Yeah," I answered. "You all right back there?"

"Ah, Doc. You copy?" another voice said at the same time. "This is Knucklehead, man. You copy?"

"Let me check this out first, Tony," I told him. "Haven't heard from Knucklehead since ancient times."

"Doc, you copy?" he called again. "This is Knucklehead."

"Copy, man," I answered. "Haven't heard from you in a while. Whassup?"

"Hey, uh," he started saying, "man, Doc, I think we just lost one of the German BO-105 helicopters somewhere out here. You hear me?"

"Damn," I said. "Man, how many crew members?"

"Believe it was some of the folks from possibly the Montana Hi-Line up there in Sunburst, or maybe even Sweetgrass."

"Hey, are you sure that helicopter wasn't from up there in the Hayfork, California area? Or it may have come from Weaverville," someone said on the radio.

"Uh, I think maybe Eureka or McKinleyville," someone else said. "Them folks been dealing with the same thing we're having to deal with."

"Wasn't somebody saying something about a place called Garberville?"

"Who said that?" someone asked on the radio.

"I heard they got some serious problems up there in the Mount Shasta area somewhere near a town called Weed," another voice said on the radio.

"Like what?" a snickering voice said. "With a name like that, it's no wonder what they're up there doing, probably smoking it with Bigfoot."

"Man, fuck Bigfoot," someone said with machine-gun fire going on in the background. "I'm blasting his ass to pieces right now."

"The only thing you're blasting is a dick, motherfucker," another voice said. "You foolish sons-of-bitches need to start taking things more serious. People are dying around here, and you're just up here in your helicopter playing around like some real jackasses."

Just as the voice was about to make another point to the crew, a huge thunderbolt of lightning crashed through one of the helicopters. There was a sudden explosion, like an electrical charge lighting the area, followed by something like a brief rainstorm of body parts falling from the dark sky.

Blood spatter and flying masses of human debris smashed against each helicopter like thick red liquid.

I immediately turned toward Karen. She was doing everything she could to keep from losing her grip on the machine gun she held tightly in her hands. She kept firing at anything she thought was a threat. Tony, on the other hand, I could vaguely see through the fog, still blasting away. The only sound from his gun was a deep, sharp spluttering noise as the bullets were fired non-stop.

*

I once again wondered if this mission had spiraled out of control. But I knew the battle would only increase once we reached the town of Stonyford. Lucifer and his deadly spiritual reign were influencing the entire region, exercising evil power to prevail.

From the looks of things, everyone had good reason to sharpen their skills during this final performance that had now become something like the Apocalypse.

The entire scenario seemed like a dramatic progression of events, almost like a movie where residents of this region appeared as characters caught in something far larger than themselves.

Common sense itself would come into question during the

personal choices and viewpoints surrounding Stonyford's fate. As the scriptures warn, the accuser of the brethren twists truth into false doctrine, betraying those who believe him. In that deception it is as though Satan proclaims that whoever sides with God is doomed in his kingdom, for he claims the power to seize and destroy the souls of those who oppose him. Yet even then, some would attempt to retreat and repent openly to God, declaring Satan a liar, rejecting the claims he presents as truth to the entire region.

*

"All right, everybody," I said quickly on the radio. "The town of Stonyford is down below us. Please be extremely careful."

"You still need me back up there?" Tony asked.

The sight of Stonyford burning in front of me seemed explanation enough. The town appeared to be slipping beneath deeper and darker clouds of the same dense, fog-like substance drifting from the boys ranch. That was when I suddenly grabbed Regina by her arm.

"I know you're going through something after Sandra," I said. "But please, Regina, we need you here with us to complete this mission."

"Nothing wrong with me," Regina said, staring around the cockpit as if she were trying to understand where she was. "What's happening?"

"Just stay where you are for the moment, Tony," I said, watching Regina's behavior. "We're about to land somewhere around here among all this burning. Are you all right over there, Karen?"

"I'll discuss that with you later," she said, looking like she wanted to fire off another round at something.

"Death isn't anything except a mass of memories for our

convenience," I said over the mic. "Those memories were full of promises that can no longer be delivered."

"What's your point?" a voice asked over the radio.

CHAPTER ELEVEN

"LOOKS LIKE ZEUS IS REALY MAD," one of Blake's deputies said, referring to the violent thunderbolts shooting from the dense clouds drifting toward Stonyford. "Ain't never seen anything like this, Sheriff."

"Zeus?" the sheriff asked. "Just who the hell is that?"

"Well—," the deputy began.

"Hold up there," Blake said, facing him. "I know who it is. I was just wondering why you mentioned his name."

"Because of the way them clouds look with all the thunderbolts," the deputy said, pointing at the clouds. "You see, Sheriff, the old tales say that whenever Zeus got upset about something, thunderbolts shot out everywhere. Lightning would strike the earth, killing anyone who got in its way. That's how the old stories went. It was also used to scare sinners into believing in Jesus and repenting of their sins if they wanted to be forgiven."

"Would you believe that's what we need right here in Stonyford?" another deputy said.

"And what makes you say that?" Blake asked.

"Because people around here are saying Stonyford's destination is an eternal trip to hell," he replied. "I mean, think about it. Folks around here act like believers in the Holy Spirit, but we all know the truth. They're nothing but a bunch of goddamn hillbillies, some of the biggest hypocrites and bigots on the planet."

"And that's why this Zeus person is upset and angry?" Blake asked.

"Could be," the deputy said. "Could be."

"Man, oh man," another deputy said aloud, sounding like he understood what the town was facing. "This is going to be bad. Really bad."

"Hey, uh, Sheriff," someone called to Blake. "I think you need to get these people out of here before them clouds do it for you."

"You think it's going to be that serious?" Blake asked. "Might just be a lot of noise without any real punch."

"But we shouldn't take that chance, Sheriff," the man said, pointing toward a huge bolt of lightning flashing above the cloud. "Did any of y'all see that? Next it'll be right over us."

"Oh, mighty Zeus," someone exclaimed. "Another fork in the road."

"You know something, Sheriff?" one of his deputies began. "Sure is a lot of explosions going on up there. Kind of sounds like bombs going off. I mean, just listen. Whatever is happening up there, I tell you, it's violent as hell."

"Anybody thought about trying to contact the boys ranch to see if the clouds passed over them?" Blake asked. "They might be flooded out up there, and here we are with our fingers up our asses doing nothing but enjoying a goddamn firework display."

"I don't think that's any firework display, Sheriff," the deputy said, taking a sip from the Styrofoam cup in his right hand. "Sounds like something far more threatening than that."

"Oh yeah?" the sheriff said. "So just what are you suggesting?"

"Something evil," the deputy said. "There's something

strange about those clouds. I mean, just look at them. When was the last time you saw anything like that?"

"Can't say I ever have," the sheriff said, staring into the distance.

"Sheriff Blake," someone called out anxiously. "Got a minute?"

"Somebody keep an eye on those clouds, will you?" the sheriff said.

"Sheriff Blake, we're having serious problems all over this place," the man continued. "Just about every carnival ride seems to be malfunctioning. Nothing is working right, and all proper operation has failed. I checked just about everything, and the few guys who were with me did the same, and what we found was very disturbing."

"And just what did you find?" the sheriff asked.

"Well, it wasn't the normal structure we put in place," he said. "Something weird is happening around here."

"Anybody injured?" the sheriff asked. "You know, like—"

"That's an understatement, Sheriff," someone said. "We've got people down there seriously injured just about everywhere you look. Sinkholes have practically swallowed groups of people. And the dead—don't even go there. They're everywhere, too, Sheriff. Everywhere you look, bodies scattered throughout the fields."

"What about that old farm out there in the field?" the sheriff asked, pointing toward an old rusted building sitting alone in the dark. "Maybe those folks out there with all them lights can answer a few questions about why all this is happening."

"What are you talking about, Sheriff?" the man said. "Ain't nobody out there in that old farmhouse. And there sure ain't anybody out there doing any kind of renovating when everybody's over here at the carnival, or supposed to be."

In the far distance, screaming could be heard along with loud banging from carnival rides being lifted upright as some were partially dismantled to free people trapped beneath.

Scattered body parts looked as if they had been discarded among the ruins, like waste littering the roads that ran throughout Stonyford. Thick red blood could be seen gushing from beneath carnival rides as hundreds of people lay unconscious, as if deliberately staged on display for everyone to see.

"Well, somebody is out there in that old farmhouse doing something," the sheriff insisted. "Can't tell me I didn't see lights flashing from one of them goddamn windows."

"I'm telling you, Sheriff, ain't nobody supposed to be out there."

"And just how do you know that?"

"Because I was already out there earlier today and again this evening checking on things. Ain't nobody out there."

"Hey, I think I just saw something too," another deputy said, staring intently toward the old farmhouse. "And just look up there on top of that mountain behind it. I don't know if you can make out what that is up there, but it sure looks like it's moving around or doing something."

"Yeah, you're right," the sheriff said. "Can anybody make it out?"

"I'm trying, but it's too dark out here," one of the deputies said, sounding uncertain. "I can see something, but I can't make it out. Whatever it is, it sure is big. Like a freakin' gorilla or something."

"Don't tell me it's some goddamn Bigfoot creature you're looking at," the sheriff said. "I don't want to hear that. Hell, that's all we need, a Bigfoot running around scaring the hell out of everybody. Besides, those things are up in Humboldt County. There ain't anything for them down here in Stonyford."

"Well, I think I might have to agree with him, Sheriff," another deputy said. "And truthfully speaking, I ain't afraid to say I think there's more than just one of them up there."

"I think y'all better get your shotguns ready," a nearby voice yelled in a rough tone.

"Shotguns?" one of the deputies said, surprised. "I don't think I heard you right. Shotguns for what?"

"For all these Bigfoot-sized footprints y'all standing on," the voice said. "Just look at them. And if they ain't Bigfoot tracks, then you tell me what they are."

"Oh, goddamn it," the sheriff said. "Somebody get the word out around here that we got a few goddamn apes running loose. And make sure everybody knows they escaped from up north."

"But, Sheriff," one of the deputies said, "how do we know they escaped from up north? I mean, ain't you just a bit unsure?"

"Let me tell you something, young man," the sheriff said, pointing his flashlight at the ground. "Now you see them prints? They sure don't match up to mine. And I don't believe they belong to you, do they?"

"No, sir," said the deputy. "Certainly not mine."

"Well then," the sheriff said, rotating his flashlight in wide circles over the footprints, "I need you to go find me one of them, uh, you know, powerful night-scope binoculars. You think you can do that for me?"

"I'm on it," said the deputy.

"Good," the sheriff said. "I sure could use it as soon as possible."

"Hey, Sheriff," someone standing nearby said. "Uh, I think I might have an old rifle scope somewhere in my toolbox if you need it. My pickup is parked right over there by your car."

"Yeah, but how powerful is it?"

"Well, I'd guess powerful enough. It's a .22 rifle scope that my son once used during night hunting."

"That'll be fine if you can get it," said the sheriff. "I just want to see what that is up there acting like it's overlooking Stonyford."

"Yeah, but that's not the only one. Just look over on the other part of that mountain and you'll see some more looking like they're staring down here at us."

"Wow!" someone screamed out loud. "Man! What the fuck!"

"What's happening?" one of the deputies asked. "What'd you see?"

"That big thing up there," he exclaimed. "One of them flew away like a bird."

"Are you sure?" the deputy asked.

"Man, I ain't lying," he said. "It flew away. And there goes another."

"Hey, Sheriff Blake," the deputy yelled out, excited that he had seen at least one of the objects fly away. "I just saw one of them myself. The thing just took off heading out toward the lake."

Suddenly there was a loud, violent outburst from the area of the lake where a the people vacationing in the Stonyford region had become trapped beneath overturned carnival rides. Some of the people had been thrown from toppled machinery with such overwhelming force that they had been overtaken by fallen angels concealed throughout the town during the celebration. People were screaming loudly for help, while others lay helpless.

Certain carnival rides, such as the Rip Cord, had somehow ejected people at a terrifying speed, launching riders far beyond the ride's normal limits and killing some instantly. Others, such as those seeking an evening thrill on the Mega Water Slide into Stonyford Lake, found themselves mutilated by the spirits of fallen angels who had planted thousands of blades along the slide at an angle. Anyone descending the slide struck the blades immediately, leaving them shredded and unable to escape.

"Take a few of the guys on over there with you to the farm-house," the sheriff told one of the deputies. "I'mma go find out what everybody's talking about with all these goddamn carnival rides."

"Will do," said the deputy.

"Think you can get a car up there?" the sheriff asked.

"Got a jeep over here," another deputy said.

"Is it four-wheel drive?" the sheriff asked.

"Oh yeah," the deputy answered.

Loud explosions could still be heard coming from the huge, dark cloud as it lit up a portion of the ground where the sheriff and his men stood talking. With each blast, the entire area shook violently, sending clouds of dust drifting through the dark sky. The ground smouldered like burning amber.

"You guys all right?" the sheriff asked. "Are you guys all right?"

Silence.

CHAPTER TWELVE

SUDDENLY, THE HELICOPTERS began emerging from the lightning filled clouds, firing at anything we felt was a threat.

"Everybody watch the friendly in the distance just ahead of us," I yelled over the radio.

"Man, this thing is on us over here," MacDonald screamed over the radio. "Somebody get him off our back."

"I'm on him, Mac," Pee-wee said. "Just hold on, baby, bro."

"Got them over here too," I yelled over the radio. "You guys watch to your left. It's a slew of those things just waiting for us to come their way."

"Damn!" someone yelled over the radio. "You saying a slew? We need some good fortune. What about a fluke?"

"Got some of that too," I told him. "But in this situation we gotta fight for it."

"Well a fight it's gonna be, dammit," the person said. "Poppa ain't taking no shit!"

"Well, get that dirty motherfucker then, youngster," Tony yelled over the radio. "Ain't nothing like a go-get-'em kind of attitude."

Loud explosions were going off all around us. Everywhere we looked, huge fireballs sailed across the dark, rough mountain terrain before exploding.

"Damn!" Tony yelled over the radio. "Who shot that bad-ass motherfucker? Hit that bitch like a freakin' missile."

"Smashed that ass, didn't I?" someone said.

"Yeah, and the intended target exploded on contact," Tony told him.

"You see the diameter of that fuckin' whirlwind of destruction just after the hit?" he asked Tony. "Did you see it?"

"Goddamn skippy," Youngster said, laughing.

"Y'all see that flock of them headed this way?" Tony yelled.

"Yeah, I see them," a voice said. "Why? And whatcha gonna do about it?"

"I'mma smash dead into them," Youngster said, laughing loudly. "And it'll be accompanied by another deadly torpedo from that ugly-looking thundercloud above us."

"And just how you suppose to do something like that from here?" Tony asked.

"Just watch me," he said, snickering. "Just watch me."

Listening to these guys talk, I could sense the mission had become far more personal than I had expected. It was like these guys, in only a few hours, had developed some sort of deadly vendetta toward anything hostile. They were out for revenge, like killing machines.

The hype was on, and someone had plugged another one of my favorite old-school songs into the entertainment system for the entire crew to hear. It was "Payback" by James Brown.The extra-long version. This version seemed to drive the crew into a frenzy, blasting away like out-of-control maniacs.

Suddenly, a fast-moving object came into view from practically nowhere, and just as quickly, it disappeared.

"Anybody see what that was?" I yelled over the radio.

"Yeah, we saw it too," someone exclaimed.

"Yeah, we saw it too," Knucklehead said. "But anyone see where it went?"

"Headed to the boys ranch," someone said. "They was really moving."

"They?" I asked. "They who?"

"Whoever it was flying that MQ-8C Fire Scout," the person said.

"Fire Scout!" I yelled out loud in disbelief. "Man, that's a an unmanned helicopter. Someone must be around here fooling with its auto control or something. Wonder why it went that way?"

"Hey, Doc,"Pee-wee called out on the radio. "You copy?"

"Copy," I answered. "Whassup?"

"Man. This is Pee-wee," he said.

"Yeah," I said. "Whassup, Pee-wee?"

"Man, got an incoming headed my way."

I then heard hundreds of rounds of gunfire going off as Pee-wee and his crew began firing.

While all the firing continued, I could not help wondering why the MQ-8C was being used in the Stonyford region. This particular craft was new and could only be deployed at an altitude of around 500 feet. And although this craft had approximately twice the capability of the MQ-8B, I was having a hard time understanding its purpose for being in this area, just as I was also wondering who was operating it.

And then, just as the MQ-8C sped swiftly past us, so did another craft in the same direction. Except it was not an MQ-8C. This was an emergency helicopter used during evacuations. It was the ambulance of the air, like the AUSA's.

"Damn!" Tony shouted out loud in a long, slurring voice. "Man, I wonder just where they're headed, cause they sho ain't playing around getting there."

"Yeah, I hear you," I mumbled nervously while maneuvering

this MH-53J through the clearing of the cloud and downward in a swift motion like that of an elevator falling to the first floor. "Cease fire. We're here. Cease fire."

This was when, for reasons unknown, Karen started firing aimlessly at something unseen by the rest of the crew.

"Hold up, Karen," I shouted. "What's happening? What are you firing at?"

"I don't know," she said, staring around outside the helicopter and gripping the machine gun. "I thought I saw something coming up here at us when we was going down. It had wings. Big wings flapping like a big bird or something. It was coming right at me."

"You sure?" I asked her. "I didn't see anything and I'm right here."

"I know what I saw," she insisted. "And it was a big bird or maybe a bat or something. I saw it, Mr. Murdock! I know what I saw, and I ain't lying."

While we were busy talking and trying to figure out why she suddenly started firing the machine gun just as we were about to land, there was an explosion not far ahead of us. It seemed to have come from the location where we could see thousands of different colors of flashing lights. The dense fog had cleared enough for us to land in a field where we could see a large gathering of people standing and waving bright lights in our direction.

"Hey, Doc. This is Pee-wee," he said. "You copy?"

"Copy, Pee-wee," I answered. "What's happening?"

"Hey, man. Something isn't right about this," he said, sounding nervous. "People are running all over this place."

"Now don't go having a nervous breakdown on me now, Pee-wee," I said on the radio. "In fact, I don't need any of you doing anything like that. We've come this far, and you should know that what you see is exactly what you get. Don't let your emotions get the best of you. You ain't seen nothing yet."

"I think these people are trying to tell us where to land," Karen said, looking down while still gripping tightly onto the machine gun.

"You guys keep your helmets on and mics in place," I told the crew. "I want everybody to be extra cautious about this area. Especially this area, because this is the place where Margaret Johnson suffered the most during her childhood. Whatever happened to her never went away. The thing is still here."

"What thing?" Regina suddenly said, staring directly at me.

"Whatever it was that attacked her," I said to Regina in a low tone. "Whatever it was that attacked her, we're here to find it."

I then looked directly into Karen's eyes. She had turned to look at Regina, surprised to hear her finally speaking. Regina unfastened her seatbelt and pushed it from her shoulder, and stood up. Moving slowly, she headed toward the storage area door, which was ajar.

"Where you goin', girl?" Karen asked, still gripping the machine gun. "We getting ready to land in Stonyford."

Acting as if she were incoherent, Regina continued toward the storage area where Tony could be heard yelling in a vulgar tone toward the giant moth trailing closely behind us.

"Come on, motherfucker!" Tony shouted. "Oh! You want some of this, bitch? Huh? You want some of this? Then come get it. Oh, hell no. Don't be tryin' to retreat now, motherfucker. Where you think you goin'? Bring yo' ass back here!"

Whatever Tony was doing caused Karen to fire a few rounds from the hip, triggering a chain reaction. Several other gunners who otherwise might not have reacted began firing aimlessly.

"You think that was one of them giant chimera?" someone asked.

"Fuckin' A," she said in a hostile tone, swinging the machine gun across the rack.

I then began hovering the MH-53J high above the ground.

"Hey, you guys," a voice came over the radio in a distressed tone. "They're on us up here. They are killing us. We need some help up here. These things are on us. Killing us. Man, my crew's just about out of freakin' ammo up here."

"Everybody hang on tight," I yelled to my crew. "Gotta help those guys. You feel me?"

"I see ya, Doc," the Cat shouted over the radio after noticing my craft make a quick, sharp fifteen-degree bank to the left, climbing to five hundred feet. "I'mma coming, too," he said.

"Hey, man. Y'all ain't gonna just up and leave us like that," Pee-wee said. "You know we ain't playin' that. Might as well make some room for the Sacro up there."

"What's he flying, Doc?" Tony yelled.

"A Scout 72X+," he said after hearing Tony over the helmet mic. "Man, we gotta get these things off us."

"Just hang tight, my man," someone told the pilot flying the Scout. "I got a good visual on them. You're right, they're following you, trying to get up close and very personal."

"Can you take them out?" a voice asked.

"Goddamn things are smart," he said. "Got the Scout surrounded. Think if it wasn't for the blades rotating, they'd be carrying them off somewhere."

"Hey, this is the Doc," I told the person talking. "Got you in sight. Think we can take one apiece?"

"Hey there, Doc," he said in a low, smooth tone. "You know somethin'? I've been waiting for an opportunity to meet you. Been hearing so much about your mission and all that, and finally here we are."

"And who are you?" I asked.

"You gotta excuse my manners right about now," he said, sounding overly apologetic. "But they call me Big Rick. Big Rick Hickman. But you can just call me Big Rick, if you ain't got no problem with it. You feel me?"

"What's that you flying, Big Rick?" I asked him. "And where'd you come from? Because I really don't recall ever seeing you."

"In case you didn't know it there, Doc, me and my group of people found your team of fighters on our GPS targeting AP system and thought we'd join in on all the fun. You know, all that bullshit out of Stonyford that got this whole region stirred up. We was already down there in Stonyford during the festivites, and then right around the time of the events all hell broke loose. That's when me and my guys hightailed it to our Kiowa Warrior helicopters, only to find ourselves being attacked by guided missiles."

"Hey, Big Rick. This is Knucklehead," another voice said. "I am co-pilot of Sacro out of Sacramento. Man, just what the fuck are you tryin' to tell us?"

"I'm trying to tell you that the town of Stonyford is all fucked-up, if you know what I mean," Big Rick told him. "Something crazy and really weird is going on down there."

"Hey, you guys," someone yelled over the radio. "What about that Scout? They're waiting."

"We're on 'em," I told the person on the radio. "Got them in sight."

"Who are the people flying that Scout, Big Rick?" someone asked him.

"Don't know," Big Rick said. "But me and my co-pilot, Jon Boy, tryin' to get a closer look."

"You watch on your right," someone yelled out on the radio. "Got a for real monkey riding a goddamn moth or something coming your way."

"Man, who is that, Doc?" Tony asked me.

"I was wondering the same thing, Tony," I told him. "Whoever it is, I think they are somewhere up above us or something."

Suddenly there was a huge explosion somewhere in the distance above us that lit up the dark sky.

"You guys see that?" a voice rang out. "Jesus freakin' Christ. I think that was one of ours."

"Big Rick, that wasn't you, was it?" someone shouted on the radio.

"Hell no," Big Rick responded. "I was wondering if it was you?"

"Man, fuck no," the voice said.

"Then who was it?" asked Big Rick.

"Tony, you see who that was?" I asked him.

"Man, I couldn't recognize them," said Tony. "Maybe Karen —"

"It was one of them other helicopters," she quickly said, firing a round from the machine gun at something. "Damn, almost got that thing that was chasing them."

"Ah, man! What the fuck!" Tony shouted out loud. "Ah, man. I know you didn't just do that, Regina."

"Hey, Doc," someone called my name over the radio. "You just lose something?"

"What's happening back there, Tony?" I asked him, trying to take a quick glimpse behind me to see what upset him. "What's happening?"

"Tony, what's wrong with you?" Karen asked him.

The only thing we could hear was Tony screaming and yelling at Regina.

"What did she do?" I asked Karen, who was now trying her best to see past the door to the storage area of the helicopter. "Can you see anything?"

"I don't see nothin'," she shouted. "Not him or even her."

"Tony," I yelled into the helmet mic. "Man, you hear me?"

"Ah, man. Doc," he said. "Man. Damn. I hear you. It's Regina, man."

"What about Regina?" I nearly had to yell. "What's happening?"

"Man. That crazy fool just took a swan dive right off this

platform back here," he said, upset.

"What!" I yelled in disbelief. "She did what?"

"You said what?" Karen yelled, stunned. "She took a dive off the platform? What you mean she took a dive off the platform? That's fuckin' bullshit, Tony, and you know it."

"Hey, Doc. Man," the Cat called out on the radio. "Uh, you copy?"

"Yeah, I copy," I answered, knowing what he was about to say. "I think I already know what you're about to tell me. But go ahead anyway."

Instead of him talking, a woman's voice came on the radio saying, "Are you aware that you just lost one of your crew members back there? Well, in case you didn't know it, somebody just fell out the back of your helicopter. We couldn't see who it was, but they fell out."

*

Upon hearing the bad news, the entire crew immediately began trying to contact me all at once without even knowing anything about Regina's suicidal behavior. I would guess you can say she'd become a manifestation of wrath and received a form of a divine punishment, especially after the situation where Sandra is concerned. Still, what she'd done was unexpected. Regardless of her depression, she knew we were there for her no matter what.

"Yeah," I said on the radio. "We're fully aware of what happened. It was one of my crew members that you guys saw. Only thing is that she didn't just fall out. She apparently jumped, distraught from the loss of Sandra."

"Who? Sandra?" The woman said. "Oh, now I remember who you're talking about. She was that pretty little Asian gal, wasn't she? Such a loss, isn't it?"

Eventually, with the assistance of the crew and with the

losses we'd already suffered prior to the situation at hand, we knew it was important to gather all the strength we could to continue this mission. However uncomfortable the deaths of our crew members seemed to talk about, it was a reality we had to face. I knew the intelligence of this crew. I therefore had to make sure everyone stayed focused and capable of setting aside their personal opinions about this mission. Everyone knew that our trip to Stonyford was undoubtedly going to come at the cost of more lives.

Looking at the situation at hand, and at the execution of the infrastructure we had in place to identify intended targets through our GPS and other surveillance systems, we rejected suggestions to simply bury this town through our defense systems. The thought was unthinkable.

Our mission was to find a more dynamic way for the people of the Stonyford region to become free of Satan's regime and reign of terror, which by now had become a powerful influence spreading throughout the region.

There were no rules by which to control the behavior of Satan's followers. In some form they had consolidated themselves into his regime and had become remade in his likeness, with the capability to control the people of the Stonyford region through a manipulative operation. Those in Lucifer's likeness moved swiftly in an effort to encroach upon the rights of others, allowing them no means of escaping the rapture.

Thinking about the followers of Satan, I thought about Margaret and her labor of love in all its completeness. I thought of how it was such a privilege to gather what information I could while receiving such overflowing understanding from her. Her work was like that of the spoken gospel. Margaret was, and is, by all means a person of increasingly righteous blessing upon others. At her present age, I am saddened to think she will only be here for a time. And I must therefore carry the gift of Margaret's spirit with me during this journey, honoring her life just as the people of Stonyford are decorating their town for the inauguration and festivities for Satan.

*

"Tony, where do you think she might have landed?" I asked. "Wonder if we can find her."

"Man, Murdock," he said in a sorrowful tone. "All I can say is that she had to land somewhere back there, man."

"Didn't think that bitch would do anything like that," said Karen in a loud, dismal voice. "Shit really got me fucked up right about now. Regina was my girl. Y'all feel me?"

It wasn't hard to sense the mood of the crew. What we had gone through to this point had been an assault on everyone. We knew it was the work of the devil in his attempt to overthrow this mission. Except now an uprising was said to have started in communities as far away as the town of Maxwell, up through Redding, over to Hayfork, and back down to the towns of Garberville and Covelo.

I knew that trying to find Regina would be like trying to find a needle in a haystack. Just like Sandra, she had become the target of something more sinister than an ordinary kidnapping. Her vulnerability after the death of Sandra made her susceptible to greater danger because of her opposition to the principles of Satan.

"We goin' back?" asked Tony.

"Gotta," I answered.

"Ain't gotta ask me," Karen said. "That's my girl down there, wherever she at. That's my girl."

"Hey, man. Doc," someone said. "You copy?"

"Copy," I answered, making a quick, steep bank downward to my left. "I hear you. Go ahead. Whassup?"

"I think something picked her up before she hit the ground," he said.

"And how'd you know that?" a voice asked him.

"Yeah, just what makes you say something like that?" the soft voice of a woman asked him.

"Because just as soon as we saw her looking like she was floating down from up there," he said, "that's when I made a quick decision to try to rescue her. Well, that was until we heard about what had happened."

"You think she might have landed?" I asked. "Wonder if we can find her?"

"Did you see where she landed?" I asked.

"Man, I think it was about a good quarter of a mile back," he said.

"Watch it, you guys," someone yelled over the radio. "Got two of them coming your way."

"Big Rick," I called over the radio. "You copy?"

"Big Rick here," he said, with the sounds of gunfire in the background. "I'm here. What's happening?"

"Damn, man," I shouted. "What's going on? Is that you firing those rounds?"

"Man, bro," he exclaimed. "This shit is just like that crazy movie, *The Exorcist,* around here. Back there, you know, where you lost one of your crew members. Well, man, it sure looks like a bunch of dead people down there walking around like fuckin' zombies. That ain't no lie, Doc."

"What'd you see, Big Rick?" I asked, hoping he would tell me without getting too excited. "Tell me what you saw down there."

"Hey, man," John Boy said. "It was like a bunch of dead people walking around like reanimated corpses. They're everywhere, Doc. Everywhere you look, that's all you see. Zombies."

"Y'all sure you ain't got your hands on some of that weird shit to be seeing zombies?" someone said.

"What shit you talking about?" John Boy asked.

"Yeah, what you talking about?" Big Rick asked as well.

"That K-2 crap," the person said. "You should know that shit'll kill you sooner or later. Make you see things before you eventually end up going all the way off your rocker."

"Man, ain't nobody been smoking that shit, motherfucker," yelled Big Rick. "If anything, you're the one probably smoking it."

"Now don't go getting mad just because I pulled your ho card," he said to Big Rick. "That just goes to—"

"What you talking about, ho card?" John Boy screamed over the radio. "Bitch, you know who you talking to?"

"Hey, you guys," a voice sounding like MacDonald said over the radio. "I need you to hold up for a minute."

"For what?" Big Rick asked. "That motherfucker don't realize who he's messin' with."

"Hey, you guys. This is MacDonald," he said, identifying himself. "The person you're talking to, I don't think he's even part of this crew."

"Then who is it?" John Boy asked. "He's gotta be. You heard him."

"I did," said MacDonald. "But I think it's somebody down there on the ground. Whoever it is, he's trying to get you guys to respond so he can trap you."

"Punk'll get fucked up if anything," Big Rick said in an angry tone. "I ain't nobody to be played with."

Meanwhile, I was busy trying to locate Regina and the exact place where she landed. I could see Karen gripping the machine gun, ready to fire if anything threatened her. Tony, meanwhile, rolled his machine gun back and forth across the gun rack. That was just about all he could be heard doing. He was as ready as ever while searching in vain for any sign of Regina.

"She have to be down here somewhere," Tony exclaimed out loud. "Man, Doc, we can't leave without her. We can't."

From time to time, I could see Karen wiping her eyes. Regina's absence was a loss felt by the entire crew. Deep sadness caused by bereavement had, in more ways than one, become just another part of the mission. But the one thing we couldn't afford was to continue losing our precious crew members. The unfair treatment brought about by Satan was just another part of his attempt to humiliate us.

"Hey, you guys see all these weird-looking things like hummingbirds up here flying around our helicopter?" someone asked the crew on the radio.

"Hummingbirds?" a crew member said, astounded. "They fly in the dark?"

"Now isn't that strange," said Karen, still wiping her eyes at times. "Maybe that's a sign from Regina telling us she's all right."

Through it all, I continued to think about everything Margaret told me about the importance of God's law and the consequences we face under Satan's punishment. I had to see to it that the entire crew stayed focused, without the fear of judgment.

There is no mistake about it. For those who accepted such a relationship with Satan, there is no condemnation for their practice. But for those who refused, they were paying a high price.

Subsequently, regarding the consequences enforced upon these families who later found themselves following Satan's plan, their decision would inevitably be their own choosing, with absolute certainty. Being that we were all made in our Father's likeness to think, we develop such abilities from that image. However relevant the situation, some will undoubtedly desire the impulses to place great value on the things of darkness, only to end up confused.

"I think I'd prefer y'all to see big, beautiful butterflies flying all over the place after my death, with those bright, colorful wings spread wide for the world to see," a woman's voice said over the radio. "But when I really think about it, hummingbirds are beautiful, too. Providing they're from God's creation."

"Bravo for you, my dear lady," someone said over the radio.

"Bravo, and said with such brilliant style. I hate to say it, but I am looking forward to such a display. But only if you should die on this mission before me."

"Man, you got some weird people on this mission," Big Rick said. "Waiting on the next person to die just so he can see some goddamn butterflies flying around?"

"Hold up for a minute," Tony yelled out. "Thought I saw something down below us."

"What is it, Tony?" I asked, thinking maybe he had seen Regina. "You see something?"

"Naw," he said. "It wasn't anything."

Seconds turned into minutes, and the minutes began to feel like hours as we searched for Regina. Stonyford was now once again in the distance ahead of us, waiting for us to assist them in whatever it was they were dealing with.

Staring aimlessly around the craft and then out the front window into the dark sky, I manipulated the throttle system. I thrust the MH-53J Pave Low into a maneuver so dangerous that the powerful movement of the massive blades made enough noise that, by itself, it could inflict harm on anyone standing close by.

"Hey, Doc," Tony called out. "It looks like the fog is getting thick again."

"Yeah," Karen said. "It's getting thicker over here on this side, too."

"Looks like we got fog moving in again," someone said over the radio.

While we were busy observing everything and listening to gunfire coming from helicopters we could no longer see. Tony began firing his machine gun randomly. Karen started firing her gun in a pattern equal to that of Tony and the rest of the crew. The firing persisted as they searched for whatever it was they felt was out of the ordinary.

"Man, these goddamn things are all over the place," Pee-wee

shouted over the radio. "They're coming at us from just about everywhere."

"Man, what the fuck is this?" Big Rick exclaimed before an explosion was heard. "Damn!"

"Ah, man," Tony screamed. "Somebody just exploded back there. I hope it wasn't one of ours."

I then heard Karen swinging her machine gun across the rack quickly, firing in rapid bursts. Too quickly, in fact.

"What's happening, Karen?" I asked, not wanting her to lose focus. "You all right over there?"

The swiftness of her movements was enough for me to realize that a second more of firing at whatever she was aiming at could haul her completely off the craft and into the pitch-blackness of the night sky. I told myself to let her do her job while I used the hatchway compartment above and below me to keep watch for a safe place to land, as well as for anything threatening.

I hate the thought of reminiscing, but in our situation, recalling the past seems to have become a daily practice you just can't be without.

Suddenly, the realization of what was happening to the craft I was piloting, and scrambling to save, dawned on me as it dropped ever so low.

"Why am I about to panic?" I asked myself. "The rivers in Vietnam, I wasn't afraid to swim in them if need be. Plus, I can see a few boats down there."

And then, just as fast as my craft dropped, the next thing I remember is hearing a loud voice saying, "Hey, G.I., you soul brother number one. I your friend, G.I. number one." For a quick minute I wondered if I could see where my gunwale had landed. That is when I thought about the Bouncing Betty planted here in the jungles. When you step on one, it explodes and sprays shrapnel in every direction, shredding a leg instantly.

"G.I., soul brother number one," is what they called me. I'm sure they called many Black soldiers by that name. But anyway, Vietnam was home for well over six months. I can still see the blast of a grenade going off after the pin had been pulled, with men from within my Special Forces unit dropping like flies all around me. I think about my weapons of choice, which have always been a good .50-caliber machine gun, a Mark 18 grenade launcher, and enough ammo to finish the war. I think about how I seldom became emotional, and how my smile was gone despite the fact that my group made it home.

And now, here I am once again taking on this mission in Stonyford, in a spiritual war that seems to have taken its toll. None of these things used to bother me, but now enough is enough. It is time to get my guys home. We are all exhausted in enemy territory, where everyone is scrambling, despite Satan's claim that we will never emerge from this situation. Those threatening words are not what I sense to be the worst danger for my crew.

My eyes searched everywhere while I grabbed the arms of land mines, capable of destroying an entire squad. Under the circumstances, even my own squadron of soldiers was silent. Yet despite the horrific history of Stonyford's threat to mankind, the residents of this town were still trying their best to reclaim their farmland for the town.

As the firing raged on, with countless blasts of explosives hitting their targets, my eyes never left Karen. She desperately adjusted her helmet and hurled a fragmentation grenade toward something beyond the craft. It exploded on impact.

"Got it!" she yelled, the way a child might after winning a favorite game. "Got it!"

Tony, however I felt about his actions, was just firing, seemingly without end. I expected to see him come rushing into the cockpit for grenades. Under the circumstances, I was stunned by how he would occasionally mumble to himself in a vulgar tone. The quality and state of the crew individually, I guess anyone can say the use of such language, however vulgar, is exactly what it is, an expression used to summon greater strength and resolve toward the journey and mission of the crew.

"What is this, Doc?" Tony said. "Some type of a charismatic religion?"

"Just what are you talking about, Tony?" I asked him curiously. "What's happening?"

"It's like," he said loud enough for me to hear, "the devil is really trying to get everybody ready. You feel me, Doc? It's like he's checking to see how many of these people are in on this with him. Their loyalty or something. It's crazy."

"Yeah, I think I know what you mean," I told him.

"You guys really think all of them are going to be showing that kind of devotion to that piece of shit?" someone said on the radio. "Let's be a little more logical about this. You're all intelligent people. Why not admit the fact that the devil is this time intending to give God the boot?"

"How dare you say such a thing," a woman's voice quickly came over the radio. "What makes you say something like that? You should be ashamed of yourself. Don't you know you can be punished for that?"

"I'm going to leave that one alone," I said about the person's statement. "I'm already having a hard time as it is trying not to think the devil is trying to do something crazy."

"What? Like taking over?" a voice said.

"He's already doing that," someone said. "Just look there in front of us. If that isn't the devil's doing, then what is it?"

"The human cavity and chamber of every heart will begin to pump the blood of the devil," a very strange voice came over the radio. "I really do hope y'all are listening and paying attention. You should be using the helmet like you'd use a stethoscope. There are internal things you should be trying to zero in on."

"You know something there, whoever you are," another voice

came on the radio, saying. “All that mumble jumble crap is unimportant to me. And really, I just don’t—”

Suddenly there was the reappearance of an unthreatening individual on the side of one of the helicopters.

“What the hell is this?” A Black Hawk pilot screamed over the radio. “For God’s sakes, somebody answer me. There is somebody out there crawling around on my helicopter.”

“Hey, got a visual on the target,” someone told the pilot of the Black Hawk. “Looks like a snake or something.”

“Hold up, man,” someone else said, excited about what he was seeing. “I think my crew got a visual, too. And it ain’t no goddamn snake moving around on you guys’ helicopter like that thing’s moving.”

“Well, what is it?” the pilot of the Black Hawk asked, short of breath. “What is it, dammit!”

“It’s some type of creature or something,” he told the pilot.

“Man, what the hell you talking ’bout?” the pilot asked while firing erupted. “Answer me! Dammit, motherfucker. Answer me!”

“Whatever it is,” the person started, “it keep changing its form.”

By this time, after hearing what was said, I could see Karen moving the .50 caliber from side to side while reaching down for a few more cartridges. The cylinder on the machine gun continued spinning as if it would never stop.

“The lady done gone crazy with her pretty self,” I said to myself. “Trigger happy.”

I then lunged for my Remington 700 SPS Tactical Rifle in search for, I would guess, whoever it was trying to hitch a ride on one of our Medevac Black Hawk helicopters.

Since the loss of both Sandra and Regina, the temptation was to become an out-of-control killing machine. Everyone was on edge, ready to strike and destroy every intended target.

I could sense the crew was ready to unleash their anger on the enemy, without any mercy. Something had to be done to stop what was a holy war organized by the devil himself. From what could be seen, the entire location had been rearranged and fought over with madness poured out from the bottomless pit.seen enemy that knew how to manipulate the

"I got him over here," a voice cried out.

"We're on it, brother," said another voice. "Just hang in there."

"Man, get that motherfucker off me," another voice yelled. "Get him off me."

The engagements were forced on the crew's minds, a lingering effect of Margaret's attack. One that still lived in the memories of a community that blamed their problems on her. Bodies were everywhere, scattered about like rag dolls. The town of Stonyford was in ruins.

"Pee-wee, you copy?" I called out on the radio.

"Pee-wee, you copy?" I said again. I thought about Karen as she reached down to secure a few cartridges from the floor to insert into the machine gun. I wondered why she needed the cartridges instead of the fully loaded ammunition strap meant for the .50-caliber.

"We copy you," Pee-wee answered over the radio, his voice sounding disrupted.

"Hey, did I interrupt something?" I asked.

"Man, Doc," he began, "whatever it is we're fighting, they are flying all around us, everywhere, and duplicating themselves."

"How do you know that?" I asked him. "You see them doing it?"

"Man, you gotta check this out, Doc," he said. "These things come at us really fast, and the next thing you know, they split in half, making a twin or something identical to themselves."

"Shouldn't we be landing by now?" someone asked. "I mean, let's face it, you guys, my helicopter is getting really low on fuel."

"I think we're running out of ammunition over here, Doc."

"I'm almost on empty, too, Doc," another crew member said. "I gotta land this thing before we end up crashing into one of these mountains."

"Okay, I know you probably heard me say this a thousand times already, but I'm going to say it again and again if I have to," I told the crew. "Stonyford is down below us. Time to start descending. You guys see that clearing in the fog ahead of us? That's it."

"Man, it don't feel like this shit wanna let go or something," a voice came on the radio. "It's like something is trying to keep us up here. I got some heavy drag, like it's trying to pull me backward."

"Man, what the hell is that?" a voice cried out.

"What the hell is what?" another voice asked.

"Look to your right, up there on that hill, moving around."

"Too dark up there for me to make it out."

"I think I'mma fly in a little closer and find out."

"What is it that you guys are looking at?" I asked, curious.

"Hey, man. Whatever it is, I'mma light it up."

"Anybody get a clear view of the subject?" I asked, wondering what was causing all the disturbance among the crew.

"Don't look like no subject, Doc," someone said. "That's a big-ass giant monster up there looking like he's getting ready to come charging off that mountain."

"Hey, man," a voice rang out. "That's that ugly freakin' monster they call Grendel. You know, the one whose mother went smooth off a long time ago and slaughtered an entire village of warriors."

"Grendel?" another crew member shouted on the radio. "If I'm correct, didn't that monster end up getting killed?"

"Man, aren't you even listening to me?" the person talking said. "That is why the thing's momma went all the way off in the first place. One of them killed her ugly-ass son, and because of that, her revenge was on. So yeah, that ugly-looking thing you guys are looking at, it just might be another of Grendel's kinfolks."

"One?" somebody said, sounding confused on the radio. "That ain't just one. Man, that's more than just one of them things up there. I see a whole family of them ugly bastards."

"Hey, we need a medevac down here," someone yelled on the radio.

"Anybody get a reading on whoever that is?"

"Sounded like it come from one of them lightweight CBbs or something."

"What about down there on the ground? You know, like where them cars are parked."

"How many AH-64Ds are still with us?" I asked, not wanting to hear the word none.

Silence.

Surprisingly, someone finally said, "Still a few of us left. Maybe five, or possibly even six or seven."

"Why don't a few of you go on up there and check out whatever that is up there," I told them. "Think you have enough fuel for the run?"

"Not much. But we'll make it."

"All right then," I said. "The rest of you guys just follow me."

Just seconds after finishing my statement, a huge explosion seemed to rock the entire region, with heavy artillery blasting. I could see that both Karen and Tony were still wearing their respirators and were breathing normally without any problems.

Looking around as quickly as I possibly could, I could see nothing. I couldn't see anything that required me to react. But common sense told me that somewhere around me my crew was in some form of conflict with the enemy. That's when somebody yelled out over the radio, "Brace yourself, it's releasing something from its nose. I think it's radiation or something."

"Radiation!" I exclaimed. "Radiation from whose nose? Them

ugly-looking things you guys called grendels?"

"No!" a voice cried out on the radio. "It's a big-ass motherfuckin' thing that look just like a giant dragonfly flying around in the dark."

"Hey, there's a for real dragon up here, too," someone else said, sounding out of breath. "These monsters are all over this place just staring at us."

Hearing this was when I noticed one of the AH-64D helicopters fly directly into the past of a dragon. It exploded upon contact.

"Back off," I yelled out on the radio, hoping that the other AH-64D behind the one that exploded would hear me in time. "Back away from whatever those things are."

"We're already on them," said the pilot flying a CH-53E Super Stallion. "Got them in sight."

"I'm on 'em, too," said another pilot flying an AS-72X. "They ain't gone just outright think they can get away with murderin' us. Don't they know that a price gotta be paid for this?"

"You guys just might as well make room for us, too, in this battle," the pilot flying a UH-60G Pave Hawk said on the radio. "Ain't no party about to get started without us bein' involved. Y'all feel me?"

After hearing these guys making it known their mission, I then realized this war had become even more personal than I'd expected. We were now right over the town of Stonyford, and all hell was about to break loose.

This was indeed the beginning stage of Armageddon.

"How incredible is this going to be," one of the crew members said. "The scale is goin' to be huge, man. So many of the prophecies are about to come true. The devil is about to demonstrate his prophetic scenario to be seen by everyone."

"Man, you sound just like you're into the occult or somethin'."

"It's not me that you should be worried about, my brother. But really, you shouldn't be skeptical of what Satan has in store for you."

The firing continued as explosions from rocket launchers flew toward the ugly grendel-looking creatures and the family of fire-torching dragons.

"How you doing back there, Tony?" I asked, not realizing he was in a fight for his life, with one of the creatures that looked like a grendel chasing in behind our helicopter. "You all right back there?"

"Looks like your guy in back got his hands full, Doc," a voice came on the radio. "One of them grendel creatures is really hot on your tail, looking like it's trying to grab him. But as soon as it lingers a bit, I'mma blast it to kingdom come."

"Do it," I told him while squeezing the throttle control.

Just as we finished our conversation, I noticed Karen staring at me with piercing eyes through her helmet, as if knowing she could penetrate my heart. It was then that I began thinking about years past, when I had been untruthful to her. I didn't commit adultery, but I made the big mistake of walking away only days after we were married.

I guess maybe that's another reason why I have taken on this mission. A means to relieve myself from the pain of losing a good thing.

"If I really wanted to, I could let this grendel-looking creature get to Tony," is what I said to myself. But Lord knows I'm a much better man than to do something like that to my buddy. No matter how much I regret the past, Karen's happiness is and shall always be my concern. Plus, Tony is my God-given brother. I would never bring harm to my brother. He is not the demon that I am wrestling with, who seems to be busy trying its best to immobilize me. My struggles are against an opponent who thrives on the vulnerability of others.

I then noticed a sudden flash of fire flaring outward from the side of the helicopter. I thought to myself how heavy the friction must have been to create such an atmospheric display.

"What the?" Tony shouted loudly as the grendel-looking monster exploded after being hit by gunfire from an AH-64D Apache helicopter.

"And how'd you like them apples?" the pilot of the Apache said. "Won't be doing that again."

I then noticed a very large CH-47 Chinook zoom past, which I recognized immediately as Lodi. "Whassup, Cat?" I called out on the radio.

"Who's that?" he asked, dropping down into a steep 15° bank to the left, then pulling back up into a wide horizon at a 30° bank to the right, then another to the left at a 45° bank, all the while blaring the song "Black Magic Woman" by Carlos Santana through his onboard entertainment system.

"It's me, Doc," I told him. "What's happening?"

Pow! Pow! Pow! came through the radio. Lodi could be seen touching down in a field just below us.

"Man, Doc," he said in a mumble. "We fucked something up out there somewhere. My guys tell me it was grendel's mother. I really don't know, but we got the hell out of that area as fast as we could."

By this time an AS-72X, followed by a UH-60 Black Hawk, sped past us and touched down near Lodi.

"Did any of y'all get a sighting on my hit?" asked Cat.

"Nothing but a goddamn big-ass giant chimera monster," someone said. "And if I'm not mistaken, the damn thing got up and ran away."

"That's bullshit," exclaimed Cat.

"No, I think he's ri—"

There was a burst of gunfire within a short distance of the helicopters. People could be seen running in every direction for cover. I searched for a place to land this MH-53J. It was still dark, but we had to bring this baby down in a field not too far away from everyone else. The massive size of the blades on the helicopters was what concerned me most. Any form of contact with such powerful rotation could prove fatal.

"You guys get ready," I told Karen and Tony. "We'll be landing in a few minutes somewhere in one of these fields if I can find the right place to bring this thing down without killing anybody on the ground."

While making a quick 45° left bank and then steepening into a good 60° right bank to allow more pressure on my rear wheels, I found myself in a holding position. I applied more throttle to prevent losing altitude during my final approach for touchdown, then maneuvered so that the artificial horizon was just on the line I needed. I then dipped slightly below the horizon at a 30° angle and held it there just seconds before landing.

I could see what looked like thousands of lights flashing in a circle. The lights fluttered in a foglike haze. The sight reminded me of Kansas, where large numbers of lightning bugs fill the night sky.

Thinking it might be a large swarm of small winged insects moving through the warm summer air, I then noticed a pair of bright lights followed by another pair closing in from the front of my craft. I immediately recognized them as four CH-47 Chinook helicopters. It was an amazing sight watching them touch down ahead of me in formation. Cat was piloting one of the Chinooks with MacDonald as co-pilot, and there was no mistaking it. Seeing helicopters of that size involved in the mission was no illusion.

I then noticed more bright lights flickering in the air. These came from a group of OH-58 Kiowa helicopters, followed by another group of AH-64 Apache helicopters circling the entire area of the Stonyford festivities.

What stood out about these helicopters was that each had illuminated letters on the side identifying them. But what troubled the crew most was the devil, who we believed the region needed protection from. The disturbance of fallen angels emerging from the bottomless pit involved the release of a large group of long-billed birds. These birds were humans in nature, selfish and predatory.

But on this occasion the storks could be seen eagerly feasting on humans.

"Now tell me this isn't a religious festival," said Tony, coming from the back of the helicopter with a Remington 700 tactical rifle slung across his back. "Man, Doc. Don't these people even know what's about to happen?"

Suddenly an alarm went off on the control panel. Everyone on the crew dreaded what was about to happen, but we all knew it was coming. To say we were frightened would be an understatement. Judgment day, at least as Satan had planned it, was not going to happen the way he expected.

"Man, I don't know what to think about this," I told Tony while looking at Karen, who had now slid the gunner's door closed and was checking her armpits and shoulders after the strenuous workout with the machine gun.

"What's that?" Tony asked, looking surprised. "Is that an alarm going off again?"

"Yep," I answered. "Now, where is our fuel?"

"Hey," one of the crew members yelled to someone standing not far from where we landed. "You guys got a tanker to come out here to help to refuel these helicopters?"

Unable to see the response of the person standing nearby where we landed, I noticed another group of Kiowa Warrior helicopters landing within a short perimeter. There were at least four of these Kiowa Warrior helicopters, each heavily armed.

Upon reaching the mountain where there were creatures in the likeness of grendel, perched. Grotesque in appearance, there could clearly be seen an uprising of these monstrous creatures surrounding what appeared to be an object resembling the Tower of Babel.

The tower was being built to reach the heavens.

This identical tower in the town of Stonyford has been said to be the same tower of Babel. Some are calling it the Twin Towers developed from the same ovum.

"I really wonder whose idea of such a perfect model this was?" Tony questioned.

"Yeah, quite similar to the one in the Bible," I responded.

"I think the truck is on its way to refill this thing," Karen said.

"Mm," I mumbled. "Must be a refinery close by."

"Wonder why all them planes are taking off?" said Tony. "They ain't playing around. They're really taking off fast."

"Hey, Doc. This is Pee-wee," he said on the radio. "You copy?"

"Copy, Pee-wee," I answered. "What's happening? You land yet?"

"Not yet," Pee-wee said. "Called myself keeping watch behind a few of the AH-64Ds when, to my surprise, it looked like a large number of them ugly-ass chimera-looking creatures tried to snatch a helicopter or two."

"Seriously?" I shouted. "Anybody hurt or injured?"

"Really don't know yet," Pee-wee said, sounding upset. "I really don't think so."

"Well, did they do any damage to any of the crew?"

"Nobody reported any damage."

"What's your fuel looking like?" I asked Pee-wee.

"Need some," he said. "Where are the refueling people? Or are we here to do it ourselves?"

"No," I told him. "That's the tanker on its way right there."

Suddenly, just as the tanker was about to head in our direction, we saw a huge fireball with thick black smoke and flames on both sides of the tanker, burning everything. The entire area was engulfed in flames that flowed across the surrounding road like a river of steaming molten lava from a violent volcanic eruption as the tanker exploded.

Luckily, fortune was on our side. The explosion of the tanker resulted only in the loss of the tanker itself. The driver, realizing the tanker's acceleration had malfunctioned and was pressing down by itself, had jumped clear before the tanker reached the entrance to the field where the helicopters were awaiting refueling.

"Everybody stay clear of this area," I yelled on the radio. "That tanker explosion wasn't no accident."

"Hey, Doc," someone called on the radio. "What'd you say? That wasn't no accident? Then what happened?"

"It was intentional, another of Satan's undesirable events meant to keep us away from the town of Stonyford," I said over the radio. "You guys keep watching out for the unexpected."

"So what you're saying is that nothing from now on is going to be unintentionally done to keep us away from this place," a voice said on the radio. "Am I right?"

"What, you need my signature?" I asked.

"Well, in case you didn't already know," he said, "I just happen to be accident-prone."

"Damn, man," someone said on the radio. "What you need to do is quit accumulating all that shit and start gathering something else more important for your miserable life. Got any devilish misdeeds you wanna tell us about?"

"Yeah, I got something for you," the person said on the radio.

"Well, come on with it," the voice told him. "What? Cat got your tongue?"

Silence.

By this time another tanker had pulled in from another entrance to the field and headed directly toward us. It was a fire truck carrying a large gas tanker on the back. An emergency crisis was underway, with units responding from surrounding communities.

I could see fire trucks dousing the failed tanker with a thick liquid. These were the same response teams that had just moments earlier assisted in rescuing people from overturned carnival rides. The celebration had been interrupted by the sudden malfunction. Although the effort seemed endless, medevac helicopters continued to pour in to evacuate the injured.

Occasionally, I could hear painful outbursts from the area of the carnival rides, where paramedics and physicians were treating the injured and preparing victims for transport to Willows Hospital. Hundreds of preschool children had attended the celebration with their parents. There was also mention of various pre-science students from several small-town communities who attended different high schools and colleges, and had themselves come to the celebration.

My eyes slowly drifted to the huge dark figure standing in the shadows high above the region overlooking Stonyford. From what I could see, many of the town's residents seemed to fail to pay any attention to this immense figure, as if deliberately ignoring it. I said to myself, "How could this be?" The town was on the verge of ruin and seemed destined to be destroyed utterly.

Suddenly there was a loud rumbling sound that could be heard, as if it were coming from the Snow Mountain area. But then I thought to myself, "How could this be? We'd just come from that area, and part of the flight crew was still approaching Stonyford from between the mountains and hills surrounding Snow Mountain. They would have told me by now about any widespread rumbling sounds." That was when I contacted one of the flight crew members to find out what was causing such an intense rumbling sound.

"Hey, Greeneye," I called out on the radio. "You copy?"

At first there was nothing but static. It sounded like loud speakers somewhere in the distance. These noises could be heard in every helicopter.

A rugged voice answered, "Copy. This is Greeneye. Who is that trying to contact me?"

"It's me, Greeneye," I told him, relieved to hear his voice. "Murdock!"

"Hey, man. What's happening?" he said, sounding as though he too was feeling the strain placed on his crew. Although there was an unbroken bond between us, there was still a chance for Satan to push the limits and strong-arm members of the crew. "Where you guys at?"

Determined to remain undetected while proving that his crew could battle the enemy without fear, the pounding of gunfire striking their targets was exactly what he intended to accomplish. High above them, the distorted figure reached downward in a deadly rage, grabbing a fistful of helicopters. The sight was like something from a fairy-tale story read in preschool, like "Jack and the Beanstalk," where a seed sprouted into the sky and reached the castle of a giant that everyone feared. Realizing how similar that story was to the event now unfolding, Greeneye cast aside his fears and doubts and began his attack, slaughtering as many of the giants as his crew could possibly kill.

The carnage was terrible and as savage as one could imagine. But the giants were said to be responsible for the butchering of many people throughout the region. Stonyford had become known as the slaughterhouse of the north. The fear of it was felt as far away as the Klamath Mountain region of California.

But was this truly the beginning of Armageddon, as written in the most important book of prophecy? Distinct doctrinal claims about the Stonyford region were filled with false, devilish insight, something one should be extremely skeptical of, since the least among them seemed to have a price on their heads.

"Most of us have already reached the town of Stonyford and have landed," I told him. "A few will re-fuel and then come back to help you guys out."

"Sounds good to me," said Greeneye. "We're just about out as well."

"It's messed up down here," said Tony. "You know what I mean?"

"I hear you," I mumbled.

"What's that tower-looking thing about?" Karen asked, staring curiously at the tower. "They got it all lit up in the dark."

"For everybody to see, I guess," I said. "Try not to let any of this stuff confuse you guys."

"I've been lost and confused ever since we got here," Tony said.

Although it was dark outside, we could see large groups of people in every area where floodlights were placed throughout the celebration. But the climax of the festivity was yet to come. From my conversation with Margaret, I knew the climax would be like that of someone opening a floodgate.

I felt a warm breeze circling around the field where we had landed that had the same similarities as what I experienced during our arrival.

"You guys feel the same thing I just felt circling around us?" Tony asked.

"Felt strange, didn't it?" I said, staring directly at him.

"What do you think it was?" he asked, looking out the window.

"I really don't know," I told him. "Let's get out of here and see what's going on out there. We gotta find out what's happening."

"You just gonna leave me?" Karen said. "I ain't staying here by myself."

"Nobody's leaving you," Tony told her.

"Yeah, nobody's leaving anybody," I added. "We're just going out here to see if we can find out what's happening."

Just as I finished my statement, a huge fireball shot upward into the sky. The eruption was so intense that the ground shook.

We could clearly hear huge rocks and boulders falling down the cliffs, crashing into anything that stood in the way.

"What the hell was that?" someone asked over the radio.

"Whatever it was, they're firing at it," someone else said.

"Murdock, this is Greeneye. You copy?"

"Yeah, Greeneye," I responded. "You all right?"

"I'm all right," he said, sounding excited. "You guys hear that?"

"Everybody heard it," I told him. "You see where it came from? Or if it was one of ours?"

"No, I really couldn't tell you," Greeneye said. "But one thing for sure, it didn't come from anywhere up here."

"You see anything over there, Karen?" I asked.

"You guys, check that out," Tony said, looking in the direction where a large group was running down one of the dark roads leading into Stonyford. "I wonder what that's all about?"

"They're running from where that explosion came from," Greeneye said in a rough-sounding voice. "Something is burning out of control down there from what I can see. Want me to fly over and get a better look?"

"We'll do it," Pee-wee said over the radio.

"That you, Pee-wee?" I asked.

"That be me," he responded without hesitation. "I understand from listening to the transmitter that there were lots of barrels with fuel in them that exploded over there somewhere near the supermarket."

"Anybody hurt?" I asked, hoping he'd say no.

"Sorry, Doc," he said with regret in his voice. "Sadly, casualties are all over the place. I mean, it's like a war zone."

"That's really fucked up, if you know what I mean," someone said on the radio. "They're already having enough problems as it is. Y'all feel me?"

"It's the Rougarous!" a voice yelled on the transmitter.

"They're the ones responsible. It's the Rougarous!"

"Just what the hell is that old-timer yelling about?" a voice sounding like Knucklehead asked. "Hope he isn't talking about any more critters. Got enough of them things already."

"Yeah, and especially with some of the people around this place saying something about seeing dead people looking like zombies walking around."

"Voo-doo!" a voice yelled over the transmitter. "I done already told y'all folks once, and I'mma tell ya again. It's voo-doo they is in that parade practicing. Just look at 'em. They is acting just like a bunch of them reanimated corpses."

"Old-timer, you just done went and got yourself paranoid," another voice said. "You need to quit drinking all that goddamn moonshine. It's running you crazy out here."

Whoever it was that we were listening to on the transmitter, were apparently so full of moonshine that they lost their ability to understand what was happening to Stonyford. Their intoxication had become completely intolerable.

"Doc," someone said on the radio. "Who are these people? Some big-shot Stonyford politicians? They need to be in AA, you ask me."

"Just some busy drunks messing around on the transmitter," I told him. "Don't let it bother you."

I noticed that the four CH-47 Chinook helicopters on the ground in front of us rose and headed for the area of the malfunctioning carnival rides. Following directly behind the Chinooks was the group of Kiowa helicopters and a few Apache helicopters.

The firing continued high on the nearby mountain where the large creatures moved about aimlessly. I could see bright flashes of light coming from the barrels of high-powered tactical rifles. I could also see a group of AH-64 Apache helicopters and UH-60 Black Hawk helicopters maneuvering throughout the dark sky and down between the steep mountain slopes with skill. The crews were fighting against the prince of darkness.

"We got 'em over here too," could be heard from the radio. "Go ahead and take 'em down. But be extra careful, these things are duplicating themselves."

"Sounds like the third gender," someone said.

"Yeah, but what's the category?" someone else asked.

"Goddammit!" a voice shouted. "Don't tell me these ugly-looking things we're fighting are nothing but a bunch of faggot-ass queers. I mean, just in what way are they duplicating themselves?"

"If you don't mind me saying," another voice added, "from what I'm hearing, these things are both masculine and feminine, meaning they're capable, with enough equipment, of selecting whatever sex classification they desire."

"Wonder where they get the chromosomes from?" another voice asked. "I mean, you know. Come on now, you guys. We're all adults here. I'm talking in terms of hereditary characteristics."

"Truthfully speaking," the Cat said, "there should be a genealogy record of these things'somewhere around here, like in the Stonyford Library. I'm sure somebody has information about their descent..."

"Yeah, well, maybe somebody can tell us how big a population of these ugly reproducing organisms there is around here," a voice said. "Do any of y'all know?"

"Incoming off to the right of this mountain!" someone screamed on the radio. "Hurry up and pull out of there!"

I continued surveying everything from the ground and noticed people standing within a short distance from us in a discussion unrelated to the present situation. The town's people seemed to be identifying helicopters as targets for Stonyford's predators. It appeared there was considerable effort being made to ensure that my fleet of helicopters was destroyed.

However, knowing of this planned attack, we were well organized and ready with a coordinated commission of weapons to oversee the situation that would soon unfold in the heart of Stonyford. We were ready to deliver deadly force against a community not prepared to deal with such a mission. With our technology in place for this event, my entire crew began consolidating our payloads for an all-out attack against the enemy.

"I think all them people running are panicked or something," Tony said. "I know I saw some of them glancing over here."

"Why the panic?" I said to myself. "All we're doing is landing because we wanna try helping them."

Just as I was about to unfasten my seatbelt, I noticed Karen lunging toward the M-60 mounted on one of the helicopter's side panelings.

"Lady, what the heck are you doing with that M-60?" I immediately questioned her. "Whassup?"

"Shoot," she said in a sluggish voice. "I told you, I'm not staying in this thing by myself!"

I have to admit her response was moving. The one thing she refused to do was remain stagnant, which I appreciated.

"Hey, Doc?" a voice called out on the radio. "You copy?"

"Copy, my man. What's happening?" I answered in awkward slang, which I must admit was embarrassing. "Just ignore my clumsiness. My coordination should have been a bit more skillful. So I do copy. What's happening?"

"Clumsiness?" the voice on the radio said, snickering. "Man, Doc. This is Greeneye again. My co-pilot is the one that's been clumsy. He's up in this thing looking like he got the chicken pox or something."

"What!" someone yelled on the radio. "Chicken pox? Don't you know that stuff is highly contagious?"

"Man, I ain't got no chicken pox," the co-pilot said firmly on the radio. "If anything, Greeneye the one got it and trying to make y'all think I got it."

"What's his co-pilot's name?" Tony asked me. "I really can't remember Greeneye ever mentioning his name. I mean..."

"Man, the dude's been flying around with some of the weirdest people on board his craft," I said to Tony humorously. "But really, it's been lots of bizarre things happening on this trip. Take, for instance, that other guy on board his craft that you can sometimes hear him addressing as Hollywood. Now that's really..."

"Yeah, I feel you on that one, Doc," Tony said. "But what about—"

"Wait a minute," Karen said. "I know you guys ain't talking about Mr. Jangle, are you?"

"Who?" Tony quickly asked.

"Mr. Jangle," she said again. "You know, Esau."

"Esau," I said quickly. "So that's really that guy they be calling Mr. Jangle? Man, you guys. He's a gangster."

"Who?" Tony asked. "Hollywood?"

"No, Tony," Karen said. "He's talking about Mr. Jangle."

"Who's this Mr. Jangle person you guys talking about?" Tony asked.

"The gangster," I answered.

"The gangster?" Tony questioned. "Then what about Mr. Jangle?"

"That's him," Karen said. "He's Esau, but they call him Mr. Jangle."

"He's a gangster," I added.

CHAPTER THIRTEEN

"SOMEBODY GET OVER THERE and tell 'em to hold up," said the Sheriff, referring to the fleet of helicopters moving rapidly around him. "We could use all the goddamn help we can get around here. And just where is that goddamn Jerome when I need him? For God's sake, don't everybody answer at the same time. Really don't feel like being overwhelmed with your bullshit."

"I think some of the helicopters just went over there, where I think you already know," said one of the deputies.

"No, I don't know, goddammit!" the Sheriff said in a hostile tone. "Just why don't you tell me, you stupid son of a bitch!"

"It's the carnival rides, sir," the deputy said. "That's where they went, traveling at a slow rate of speed and at a very low altitude."

"Got me feeling like I'm on some kind of goddamn exhibit here," said the Sheriff. "Except it's featuring the abnormal mental development brain of whoever it is that's controlling you guys."

"Think we need to get on over to where all those other helicopters are waiting, Sheriff," another of the deputies said. "Ain't much we can do right here, 'cause I think somebody done already identified the younglings that was driving that there motorhome camper."

"How many was in that thing?" the Sheriff asked.

"They couldn't find but only three," the deputy told him. "But that's about it for right now."

"That's about it for right now?" the Sheriff exclaimed. "What? Is you saying there could be more?"

"Well, from what people around here was sayin', I'd figure at least five or possibly somewhere around six more was supposed to be in that thing. I mean, that's what the speculation is," he told the Sheriff.

"Anybody find out where they was coming from before the fire?" the Sheriff asked. "You know, like just how in the hell that thing ended up catching on fire in the first place. Hell! They made it all the way down to this point, didn't they? So I'm sure somebody can find out just where it all started from."

"Hey, Sheriff," somebody suddenly spoke up. "Looks like they must have had a flat tire or something. You know what I'm saying? It was like seeing something from out of a movie or something. That thing come flying just like a bat out of hell from around that bend up there, heading straight for Stonyford. I just knew they was gonna slow down or something. But then they all of a sudden started picking up speed."

"Yeah, he's right," another person said. "It just started going faster and faster when—"

"When?" one of the deputies said. "When what? What was it you were about to say?"

"I know what he was about to say," someone said from far back in the crowd where it was hard to see in the darkness. "I know because I saw it too."

"What did you see?" another deputy asked. "What was it?"

"It was one of them things up on that hill," another voice shouted. "It looked just like them things you call Grendels. It was on that road, running behind the camper."

"Did you get a good look at it?" the deputy asked.

"No," the voice said. "It was too dark to see, but I did see it when it blew a big ball of fire, and then the camper started burning."

"You say it blew fire at the camper before it started burning?" the deputy asked.

"Yeah, that's right," the voice said. "Then it exploded or something. The back of the camper started burning up. Everybody was standing here watching it. Some of us thought about trying to block it before it made it down here, because we knew that once it did, it might start a bigger fire when it passed the underbrush."

Sounds like you know quite a bit about this area," the deputy said.

"Well, I do a lot of landscaping," he told the deputy. "And I think this part of the region is going to burn like hell unless we do something to stop these fires. But as far as whatever it is that's exploding, I'm lost."

"That's these helicopters around here shooting at them monsters we're being attacked by," someone said, sounding like an elderly man. "I ain't never been one to believe in monster tales, but let me tell ya something. I done seen it for myself, and that's enough proof for me to start believing. The devil done come home to set up shop. We is in trouble and ole Stonyford is doomed."

"Now why don't you just shut your mouth there, old-timer. Nobody wanna be listening to that foolishness you talking," the voice of an elderly woman told him. "You is just like that Old Testament in the Bible. You old and decrepit."

"Ain't none of that what you sayin' going on with me," he said to the elderly woman. "I'mma still in the Marines."

"Ah, just shut your mouth before I has to shut it for you," she told him in a harsh voice. "You ain't nothing but an old dwindled-up old man."

"And who gonna help ya?" he asked her, mumbling to himself.

"You ain't the only one in this here neck of these woods, Junior," she told him boldly, as if somewhat impudent.

"What?" he asked, demanding her attention. "You tryin' to sass me?"

"You can just take it the way you wanna," she said in a brazen tone. "You call that sassin'? Then it'll be sassin'."

"Ain't nobody gonna believe what you sayin', and the way you is talkin' to me, Molly," he told her, surprised by her boldness. "They ain't gonna believe me no way even if I did try tellin' 'em 'bout your manners."

"Suit yourself, old-timer," she told him, giggling to herself. "Just suit yourself, you old decrepit fool."

Suddenly a loud explosion shook the region. A commotion began, with an cry of people in agonizing pain. The sounds were intense, spreading throughout the large mass of the once joyous festivity. The celebration and feasting had now come to an abrupt standstill. The only thing that could be heard were the sounds of loud boats traveling about aimlessly on the Stonyford lake in different directions.

Loud engines roared from helicopters and airplanes speeding down the makeshift runway made for an emergency escape from the activities being performed by Satan's fallen angels. The entire festivity began an abnormal formation.

"Looks like they done just about got a handle on that gasoline tanker over there," one of the deputies said. "Good thing it didn't make its way out to where the helicopters are waiting. We'd have a mess on our hands, Sheriff."

"Tell me about it," said the sheriff. "Uh, why don't one of y'all boys hurry up and get over there where them folks are refueling them there, uh, helicopters, and tell 'em to don't go nowhere, and that I need to speak with 'em. You think one of y'all can do that for me?"

"No problem, Sheriff," one of the deputies said.

"Well don't you think you better hurry up?" Sheriff Blake said while pressing the small round button on the handheld radio in an attempt to contact my helicopter. "Can anybody hear me? This is Sheriff Blake. I'm the sheriff here in the town of Stonyford. Come back."

"Sure you on the right frequency, Sheriff?" asked one of the deputies.

"Hell, better be," said the Sheriff, checking his radio channels.

"Here, let me see if it's right," said the deputy. "Now try it."

"Thought I already had it on the channel I been hearing them on," said the Sheriff. "Can anybody hear me? Like the Scare Crow, or—"

"Try again, Sheriff," the deputy told him. "Keep trying. All this —"

"This is the Scare Crow," I answered. "I copy you. Whassup?"

Hearing someone answer him startled the Sheriff. He felt it was quite bizarre to have someone answer him when not even his own deputies seemed coherent enough to pay any attention to their sergeant. The seriousness of the Stonyford situation just didn't seem to register with the deputies. All that he could think about was their peculiar occasional mumbling like a group of habitually gossiping homosexuals.

"And, Lord knows, I haven't anything against a person's gender," the Sheriff said to himself. "Maybe I am just a bit paranoid or something."

"This is the Scare Crow," I responded. "Whoever it is trying to make contact with the Scare Crow, I copy you. Whassup?"

The Sheriff finally replied while glancing around, wondering just what helicopter could be the Scare Crow. "This is the person in charge of the situation here in Stonyford. I was in close proximity to you folks' helicopters that came over them mountains and landed down here. Being that I am the one having the authority, and being that I've heard so much about y'all's team, and seeing that you and I seem to be in close, maybe you could just point me in the right direction of your helicopter and I could then come on-board and introduce. Over!"

"Oh, yeah," I replied. "Can't wait to become acquainted. I have myself heard so much about you, Sheriff Blake. Let me see now, we're just a few feet away from you. Why don't we start from where that tanker is burning. Is that—"

"Where did y'all originate from?" asked the Sheriff. "I'm just trying to establish a pattern which will help me find a better way to insert these things in my head."

"I think it would be safe to say, from all around you, Sheriff," I told him. "We are a special force of journalists and pilots sent here to assist you."

"Where is the location of your helicopter?" the Sheriff asked firmly.

"Apparently you really don't know much about helicopters," I said, not wanting to confuse him. "Just head toward that old farmhouse sitting out not far from where you can see that burning mountain. Well, not quite that far. But you'll see the word 'Scare Crow' on the side of my craft."

"What kind of helicopter is it you're flying?" asked the Sheriff.

"Damn, this dude must really be stupid," I said to Tony. "It's what you call an MH-53J Pave Low."

"Oh yeah," the Sheriff said, sounding surprised. "Hell, that's one of them big ugly designs. That's one of them helicopters make you think you is having a delusion or something. Just how the hell y'all get something that big and ugly through them mountains up there?"

"How the hell we did it?" someone yelled on the radio. "Them mountains opened up wide just in the nick of time. They saw us coming, and here we are ready to bust some asses wide open."

"Oh yeah," the Sheriff said. "I do think I see you there, Scare Crow."

Thinking the Sheriff was this big huge guy that was around ten feet or more, I was surprised to see him standing at five-foot-nine or ten, with an outrageous potbelly underneath his tight-fitting jacket and shirt, resting over his belt. He wore an out of control black-and-white beard.

It was quite obvious that Blake wore polyester clothing exclusively. Everything seemed to stick to him. Or maybe he was just an untidy person. Blake's verbal attacks toward his deputies suggested a man who lashed out, even if he didn't realize it. The man wasn't any spring chicken. He seemed to be a key piece of the puzzle surrounding Stonyford. A serious matter was at hand, yet the only thing he seemed concerned about was his reputation.

By the time he reached the helicopter, I was standing just a bit from the doorway, ready to meet him.

"Oh yeah," he said, smiling broadly. "Bet you didn't think I'd find which one you are flying, did you?"

"It's obvious you knew," I told him, extending my hand to greet him.

"Yeah, sure you did," he said, grabbing my hand in a firm grip. "I was once very much afraid of such a huge helicopter like this one. But now I am coming onboard to fly with you."

"Are you sure you're ready?" I asked him. "I mean, there's no telling just what might happen once we're airborne. Things can get a bit rough."

"What the hell," said Blake. "Aren't these things carrying air bags?"

"You mean equipped with parachutes, don't you?" I said while observing this obnoxious individual who, from my understanding, had a repugnant reputation. He now carried on like a child at play.

"Yeah, well. You know what I mean," he said arrogantly,

causing a sense of discomfort onboard the craft.

"Who he think he is?" Karen whispered in a slight mumble.

Tony shrugged both shoulders after hearing Karen's comment and quietly mumbled to himself, "Yeah, whatever."

"You've flown on one of these before?" I asked Blake.

"Nothing like this one," he said, staring at the co-pilot's seat. "I'm wondering if I can talk this young man here into letting me have his seat if I am going to be flying with you."

"I think we can move one of our adjustable seats right here up front between my seat and the co-pilot seat for you so that you'll be able to have a good view," I told him. "Think that'll be all right?"

"Well, couldn't he just let me sit there?" Blake said. "And he can sit here."

"No, I really don't think so, Blake," I told him. "I need my co-pilot right here beside me."

"But you see," Blake began, reaching into his coat pocket and bringing out fat Cuban cigar. It was wrapped in plastic, with loose tobacco leaves scattered inside the roll. The package emitted a strong odor, offensive to a non-smoker. "Hope you don't mind."

Tony looked at me as I stared directly at both him and Karen.

"You know what," Karen spoke up with an immediate response to Blake's annoyance. "Yeah, we do mind. There's no smoking on board this helicopter."

"Oh, please excuse me for becoming such a nuisance," said Blake.

"Nuisance!" I quickly said. "Nobody said anything about you being a nuisance. It's just that smoking of any kind can be very irritating onboard any aircraft, especially when there are strange recurring events going on all around you. We are under attack by an enemy that you see only on television."

"Just what are you saying?" asked Blake. "I mean—"

"What I am saying is this," I said. "Since our arrival in this region, the presence of something has been busy announcing that it is here. We've seen things that really shouldn't even exist. We've seen things happening that only happen on television. And just look at Stonyford, it's burning to hell. And you are making no explanations of the situation."

"My men are on the job helping me figure this thing out," Blake said.

"From what I can see, your deputies are as confused as everyone around here," I told him. "Can't you see, Sheriff Blake? This is a critical moment for this region. How many of the people here have to die before you realize it's time to evacuate?"

"Tell me something," said Blake.

"Yeah, what's that?" I asked him.

"Is all this mumble-jumble because I want to sit in the co-pilot's seat?" he said with a slight grin on his face.

"Mmm," I mumbled. "You're grinning. But Blake, this isn't any grinning matter."

"The grin is just something I believe I inherited from my old man," Blake said, smiling broadly. "Just like this job, it's also a part of my inheritance from him."

"Well, no. This what you consider mumble-jumble isn't because of your not being able to sit in the co-pilot's seat," I told him. "That's where the co-pilot sits, and that's that. Period."

"Your dad was the sheriff of Stonyford?" Tony asked him.

"He was," said Blake. "But that was—"

"So you are Blake Jr.?" I asked curiously.

"Yeah, that's right," he said. "But nobody really recognize me as Jr. around here. They only see me as Sheriff Blake."

"All right then," I suddenly said, surprising even myself. "I guess it's time for us to take flight and get a better look at everything."

"Just grab those straps there, Sheriff Blake," Tony told him, pointing at the shoulder straps connected to the chair. "Just make sure you place 'em on tight, cause man, the Scare Crow ain't nothin to be playin with."

"Yeah, I heard a lot about this thing," said Blake. "It might be the one I heard, thinking I was hearing thunderstorms making all that racket between them mountains up there."

"It wasn't that bad, was it?" I asked the Sheriff proudly. "I didn't think anybody in this area could hear us coming."

"Oh, we could hear you all right," said Blake. "With all that pounding it was making, how could we not hear you? For a minute there, we just knew that you guys was responsible for that RV being on fire."

"RV?" Tony said. "What RV?"

"Oh, it's the one just over there a little ways from here that somehow caught fire just below where you guys come from," Blake told Tony. "Poor kids inside didn't have a chance."

"Kids?" Tony said once again, surprised from the thought of the RV that caught fire with kids inside. "Man, where'd you say that RV's at?"

"Well, it's not burning anymore," said Blake. "Just smoldering."

"What about the kids?" I asked him. "You didn't get 'em out in time?"

"They're still inside that thing," Blake said with his head down. "There wasn't anything anybody could do to help 'em."

"Damn!" I said, trying to remember if I saw the RV burning. "Man, I just don't remember ever seeing any RV on fire up there."

"Just another goddamn misfortune for Stonyford to have that RV catch fire like that," said Blake. "Goddamn kids shouldn't have gone off like a bunch of wild maniacs in the first place."

"Yeah, but what about all the carnival rides?" Tony asked Blake. "People must be here from everywhere. And I know for a fact that some of these people traveled from as far away as the east coast."

"Tell me about it," said Blake, rubbing his chin. "From what

I've been seeing, I believe the perception everybody is having about this town is that it's full of so much superstition that most of the people are only coming here because they think they just might end up getting that once-in-a-lifetime chance to probably end up seeing that goddamn Elvis Presley, or maybe even some weird momentary glimpse of Janis Joplin and Jimi Hendrix."

"You serious?" asked Tony. "You really think some of these people came here just to see them?"

"You better believe me, young man," Blake said to Tony. "It's something strange about this celebration ever since it got started. You know what I'm getting at?"

"What you think about it, Doc?" Tony asked me, catching me off guard as I was staring intently at Karen. "You listening?"

"Yeah," I quickly answered, not really knowing just what they were talking about. I could hear bits and pieces, but following whatever it was that Tony and Blake were discussing had me at a loss for words, my attention focused completely on Karen. All I could say was, "Yeah, it is about that time to take this thing up."

"Now that's strange," said Karen. "I could have sworn on a stack of Bibles that I thought the Doc already had it up."

"Now just where have you been?" Tony turned toward Karen. "We haven't gone anywhere yet. We've been on the ground ever since we got here. That's in case you didn't notice. We're still down here, Karen."

"Mmm," Karen again mumbled, this time to herself. "Not the Doc. He's still up."

I guess I was the only one who knew what Karen was referring to. To be truthful, she was right. I wanted her more than ever, but the thought and desire were just that, a thought and one hell of a desire. It was important that I keep my respect for Tony, as well as for the sake of their relationship. All I could do was remember she used to be my girl. Lord knows I miss being able to wrap my arms around her. I miss everything about this lady. Just how in the hell could I have been so foolish to lose her...

"You all right?" Tony asked, bringing me back to reality. "Man, what a dream you must be thinking about. You were deep into whatever it is that's on your mind."

"If only you knew," I told him while slyly glancing at Karen. "If only you knew."

"A serious person usually acts on their thoughts," Karen said while staring directly at me, one of her eyebrows arching upward. "I know that's what I would do when the opportunity presents itself."

"Oh, now she didn't go there," I thought to myself. "Oh, hell no."

"Lots of truck trailers parked out here," said Tony, referring to the trailers sitting side by side near where the helicopter landed in the field. "What are they used for?"

"Let me see," Blake said, looking toward the bright light connected to the helicopter used for searching areas at night. "That's one hell of a spotlight you have here. Think I could use something like this around here. Now let me see. Oh yeah, they're used as temporary ice morgue trailers. Being that Willows is so far away, they're using these things to store bodies until they can be transported elsewhere."

"With all the other bodies out there that haven't been found, are you worried about diseases spreading?" I asked Blake.

"That's disgusting to even think about," Karen said. "So gross."

"What you talking about, Karen?" Tony asked her after seeing how she was frowning. "What's happening?"

"Didn't you hear what he said about them trailers?" she asked Tony.

"Yeah, so?" he said, shrugging. "So what?"

"What?" Karen said, surprised at Tony's reaction. "Dead people are in them things."

"Yeah," said Tony, unmoved. "Dead people are everywhere."

"Well, don't y'all be expecting me to go anywhere near 'em," she said.

"Who said we're going to?" said Tony. "Not unless—"

"Obviously you're afraid of finding yourself being asked to go anywhere near those trailers, am I right?" I asked Karen.

"I'm just sayin'," Karen said, glancing out one of the helicopter's door windows. "Been far too much going on around here. Nothin' adding up."

"Like that ole Remington-looking rifle you got there beside you," Blake said, referring to the tactical rifle I placed next to my chair. "Things sure do look ugly."

While Blake was talking, we could again hear what sounded like heavy gunfire and dangerous artillery blasting from weapons of massive production that were seemingly coming from high above Stonyford.

"All right, everybody brace yourself," I quickly said, engaging a tremendous amount of thrusting power to the engine. "Let's take this baby up."

Within seconds we were once again airborne, flying in the dark sky like a nighthawk on a hunt.

"You don't feel in any way threatened by these ugly-looking creatures?" I asked Blake.

"I ain't seen 'em yet," said Blake. "I only been hearing about 'em."

"What, you mean to tell me you haven't even seen these things all this time they've been here killing people?" I questioned Blake.

"Ain't seen nothin'," Blake said, staring around aimlessly. "Just been listening to folks talking about 'em. But ain't never seen any of 'em."

Strange that I wasn't all that surprised to hear Blake say he'd never seen any of the creatures. His statement was somewhat hard to believe, especially when there was a multitude of chimera creatures and also grendel-looking monsters perched about the Tower of Babel. Such a sight could cause anyone to start quivering. But I refused to allow such obstacles reduce the momentum of our mission.

"What are you carrying there on your side?" I asked the Sheriff after noticing the small nine-millimeter fastened to his tight-fitting trousers.

"Oh, yeah," he quickly said. "Just something I carry. It's a nine-millimeter Smith & Wesson automatic. Something my wife got me for my birthday. Or was it Christmas?"

"Hey, Doc," a voice came on the radio calling me. "This is Pee-wee. You copy?"

"Hold up for a minute, Blake," I told him. "Let me get this. Copy!"

"Hey, man," he said in a whisper. "Check 'em out. Them things are sprawling around up here on their elbows."

"What's he talking about?" Blake asked, staring into the dark sky. "I can't see anything."

I then noticed both Karen and Tony frantically moving around as quickly as they could while looking through their night-vision lenses in an effort to get a better look at whatever it was that Pee-wee was talking about sprawling around on one of the nearby mountains.

"What is it?" asked Sheriff Blake, leaning forward as if to get a better view of the situation. "What is it that you guys are looking at?"

"Look right there in front of us," I told Blake while handing him a pair of night-vision lenses.

"Oh yeah, thank you," he said, placing the lenses next to his face to peer through. "These are some really nice binoculars you have here."

"Can you see anything?" I asked him.

"Wait a minute," Blake said, removing the binoculars. "Am I seeing this right?"

As the helicopter hovered in the air not far from where we could see the creatures spread awkwardly across the top of one of the many mountains surrounding the region, through our night-vision lenses we could see a few of them spraying a jet stream of vapor, like something discharged from a highly pressurized container when threatened.

What we were witnessing began to reveal why our weapons were at times futile during earlier confrontations, leaving the crew under deadly conditions.

"What in the—?" Blake mumbled to himself.

"You see that, Karen?" Tony asked her. "Man, these things are —"

"Hey, Knucklehead," MacDonald called out. "Hey there, buddy. You think you can take 'em down?"

It was apparent that the loud noise coming from the helicopters wasn't enough to faze the creatures. Instead, they continued their frenzy across the tops of the rugged mountains surrounding Stonyford.

"No problem," Knucklehead told MacDonald, quietly giggling to himself.

What they were about to do made me think about the situation we faced a few hours back when all hell broke loose. How many more of these crew members are we going to lose? This mission so far has failed to sustain so many members of this team, depriving them of ever again having the opportunity to be with their loved ones. Although most of the members of this team intended to pursue more than the accomplishment of becoming journalists and media professionals, most had backup plans they hoped to achieve by working together.

The Stonyford experience had become a pursuit driven by habit and necessity. However ingrained such habits might become during moments of crisis, this type of instinctive response belongs to environments where survival dominates, much like in the wild.

"Come on, baby, that's it," Knucklehead could be heard saying as though he were mumbling to himself. "That's it, turn your ugly-looking face to Papa."

Suddenly there was a loud explosion that caused a panic just as Knucklehead pulled the trigger on his assault rifle.

"Goddammit, where in the hell did that come from?" he shouted.

"That wasn't you?" MacDonald asked.

"Hell no," he said, surprised that someone had taken the shot intended for him.

"Then where'd it come from?" asked MacDonald.

"Hey, Doc," MacDonald called on the radio.

"Yeah, whassup?" I answered.

"Somebody just blew everything to pieces up here," he said. "You get a reading on that?"

"I really don't know," I told him. "But man, whoever it was just about blew us all up right along with whatever exploded."

Just about everywhere we looked we could see the smoldering remains of burning embers and melted plastic emitting dense into the dark sky. However, life could exist after such a violent explosion. We could barely see the large figures of creatures crawling around in the dark as though sniffing for signs of life.

"This shit is friggin' weird," Blake said. "Talk about something sickening. Well, this is it."

Suddenly we could hear what sounded like a loud rumbling coming from every direction.

"Everybody get ready," I yelled out over the radio. "It's time to take these motherfuckers down!"

"Man, I have to admit," Blake said. "I've noticed how you guys really move in a situation. No time for planning, but very meticulous about what it is you intend to do. And then you just do it."

"It can get very emotional up in here," I told Blake. "That's when you find yourself appreciating what time you've got left on earth. You know what I mean?"

"Oh, hell yeah," Blake responded. "I can just imagine what those poor people are going through down there. I just hope the entrances to this region are blocked off to prevent outsiders from being harmed."

"Yeah, but what are the guarantees that whatever you put in place won't fail?" I asked Blake. "I mean, just look at how we have been fighting these things with some of the most deadly weapons. It's like we're locked into an obsession, driven to destroy these things without emotion."

"Incoming on all sides," someone yelled out on the radio. "Here they come."

"What the heck is he talking about?" Blake asked, in a state of panic. "What's happening?"

I could see the frustration in both Tony and Karen's expressions. The thought of having to once again place themselves in position for a battle against the creatures was an absolute worry, driven by impulsive actions no one on this team could refuse. The suspicious killing of the Grendel creature was said to have caused the outbreak of the Ebola virus. But I then thought about the fact that such a statement could be just another of Satan's strategic tactics to influence the replication of his supposed authority through false prophecy.

Understanding the multitude of people being targeted through deception, put forth through disguises identified as the works of the devil, I knew that destroying these creatures was an enforcement rarely seen in such a conflict. But it would be the manifestation of the team's internal will to pull the trigger against these deadly creatures and carry out the coordinated effort to seek and destroy every one of the beasts.

"Come on, motherfucker," someone yelled over the radio

transmitter. "I got yo ass now, bitch!"

"Yeah, I tried to warn you, punk," another voice said. "I'mma real revolutionary from the past coming to get your ass."

"Cat, you copy?" I called out over the radio. "This is the Doc."

"Copy you, Doc," he answered immediately. "What's happening?"

"You guys all right?" I asked him.

"Well, we're not at all that inspired by these monster-looking things if that's what you're referring to," he said. "I mean, things could be a lot better, like being far away from here."

"Just think about it this way," a voice said. "We will most likely be famous once this is over. People will be reading about us all over the world."

"What? How something about your disappearance is still a mystery, seeing that you were never found?" someone said.

"Sounds like you're having a meltdown or something, saying I'll be a mystery because I'll never be found," the person said. "Remember, my friend, we're in this thing together."

We could once again hear multitudes of gunfire and the sounds of machine guns blasting away at the creatures high on top of the mountains. The dark sky lit up as each helicopter positioned itself for another full-scale war against creatures that looked like giant monsters moving through the blackness of the night.

But we were undeniably moving in an era where we had to protect the kingdom in which we lived. However, many times this mission repeated itself, we were ready to continue the fight in unfamiliar territory of the Stonyford region, where there seemed to be an overwhelming fear caused by Satan's fallen angels.

"Oh, Jesus," Blake mumbled. "Just look at 'em, they're all over the place."

"Hey, Pee-wee," someone called out over the radio. "Where are you?"

"Man, we're in what seems like an ongoing battle with a few

of these ugly-looking monsters over here on the other side of this mountain," Pee-wee said. "It's like looking into a mirror or some-thing. Every time we take one down, it's like two more appear."

"They're duplicating themselves," someone shouted. "We gotta find a way to stop this madness."

"Incoming! Incoming!" someone could be heard yelling loudly on the radio. "They're looking like dragons."

"What in the hell is that?" Sheriff Blake shouted after noticing a few giant moths flying around in the dark with monkeys riding on their backs.

"Thought you was aware of these things, Sheriff," I said. "We've been seeing these things ever since coming through those mountains. In fact, they were bugging the hell out of some of the crew."

"Goddamn things looking like the horsemen described in the Bible with all that shit they wearing," Blake said. "Hell, just look at 'em. Got me feeling like I'm seeing the four horsemen. You got the white horse, the conquering power, then the red horse bringing war and bloodshed. Then the black horse with all that black-shirt authority and control. And then the pale horse bringing death and everything else that follows."

"Damn," I said, congratulating Blake and acknowledging him for such an understanding of history. "Man, I'm really surprised that you actually know about the four horsemen."

"Well, didn't the Spirit testify these things being true?" he turned toward me asking. "And didn't the four horsemen end up being internalized in the primary pinnacle power in the present international order?"

"Monkey coming at you guys off to your left," someone yelled.

"Is it hostile?" a voice asked.

"Is it hostile?" someone else repeated, surprised that anyone would even ask. "It's a monkey, for Christ's sake. Take it out."

"Oh, no. Not the monkey," someone said over the radio,

sounding like they were crying in mock protest. "Please don't kill my monkey."

"Yeah, yeah, yeah," another voice said. "Goddamn monkey just might be like them goddamn rabbits."

"And how's that?" someone asked.

"Well, just think about it there, young man," the voice said. "Only real thing a rabbit's good for besides eating is procreation. Goddamn things always have millions of offspring."

"For your information," said the person asking the question, "I am not a young man, sir. I'm the lady here from the Montana Hi-Line of Sunburst and Sweetgrass."

"Oh, please excuse my manners, ma'am," the voice said apologetically. "Didn't quite recognize your voice, being that we are always having conversations with men."

"So what are you trying to say?" she asked. "I sound like a man?"

"And here we go," someone said.

"Stuck your foot in your mouth this time, didn't you, Seawood?" someone said over the radio, making it possible for everyone to know it was him talking.

"Thanks a lot, whoever you are," said Seawood. "Now the whole world knows it was me who mistook her voice for a man."

"Oh, quit your whining," someone told Seawood. "Take the punch like a man."

"Hey!" yelled Seawood on the radio. "Y'all the ones who've been using all that vulgar language around here. So you should be apologizing too."

"Man, fuck you, Seawood," someone yelled over the radio. "Down there sniffling like a bitch. Man, fuck you!"

Explosions and high-powered blasts continued throughout the dark sky above Stonyford, bringing an immense amount of devastation. The war against Satan's fallen angels intensified far beyond what anyone had anticipated, as each of the creatures continued duplicating themselves.

Karen started firing the machine gun, seemingly at random. From what we could see, she was shooting wildly in the direction of a target atop the mountain to our right. By this time Tony motioned to the sheriff to take position in the co-pilot seat, handing him an AK-47.

"What am I supposed to do with this?" Blake asked Tony. "We never used anything like this around here."

"You wanna live, don't you?" Tony asked, smiling.

CHAPTER FOURTEEN

THE LOUD NOISE FROM GUNS FIRING was more than enough to drive the average person completely nuts, let alone cause them to lose their hearing. That is why I strongly advocate the regular use of the headsets provided to us by military personnel. We were at war with Satan's army, who were themselves intending to take us all the way out of the game. This was the situation predicted by Margaret and possibly characterized as the beginning stage of Armageddon, carefully planned as the conflict of all conflicts.

The international order, according to Margaret, had been influenced by the spirit of Satan, who claimed to appear in person as part of his own doctrine, opposing God and refusing to accept Him as the one and only true God of the universe.

The Stonyford region had become inhabited by supernatural beings. However intelligent the human race considers itself, the intimidation and hostility of Satan's forces were clearly present. Periodically, situations set in motion by Satan and those who follow him would reveal themselves as monstrous efforts to destroy mankind.

Still, the rapture, as written in doctrine and interpreted by believers, remained a subject of debate for those who doubted it. Margaret had warned that such matters of prophecy and doctrine should be approached carefully and with understanding.

*

"Holy mother of God," the sheriff mumbled to himself. "I haven't seen anything like this in all my days on earth. Just look at this. Goddamn town done become like the book of Revelation or something."

"Talk about the book of Revelation," I said to the sheriff. "What we really need is some unmerited favor from God right about now. Seems like just about everything in the Bible is being confirmed, repeatedly."

"You really think the things up here on these mountains have the potential to take over?" Blake asked me while staring intently at the flashing sight of Karen's machine gun firing into the dark sky. "Oh boy, she is really trying to hit the mark, isn't she?"

"Precisely," I said, smiling to myself about Karen. "I really wouldn't quite know what to do without her on this mission with me."

"Sounds like you folks are all from the same branch of the military, the way I see you looking out for each other," Blake said.

"Sounds good," I told him. "But no. We're all from various parts of the US. Our social appearance is morally repulsive. Hey, that's how we ended up here in Stonyford."

"Yeah, well," the sheriff said, sounding as if he were beginning to have an attitude problem. "Uh, we could have dealt with the situation here in Stonyford with or without assistance from outsiders. I mean, it isn't like we don't have—"

"Wait a minute, Sheriff," I quickly said. "If by chance you're feeling that my team of journalists, who have devoted themselves to assisting on this mission, are here trying to take away however many minutes of fame you expect to receive, then such an illusion of belief is just as illogical as it is irrational. I am the one responsible for these people being here. I am also the person who contacted each individual and told them their assistance would be very much appreciated if they were to accompany me on this mission. They have often questioned me about this trip to Stonyford. So whatever it is that you are trying to insinuate is just another insult to this mission."

"Well, this thing was just supposed to be a celebration," Blake said.

"A celebration for who?" I asked him in a hostile tone. "Who was it that you set this celebration up for? Could it be for the devil and his fallen angels? Was it for their possible return? Like the inauguration to officially begin the ceremony that'll most likely end up being just like a wedding, where the residents of Stonyford welcome these ugly-ass unearthly creatures into their lives the way a bride welcomes her husband?"

"It was just supposed to be a celebration," Blake said again. "This was just something I was trying to do to bring the image of this town up a little so it wouldn't have to continue being blemished by whatever it was that happened to that little girl."

"You mean Margaret Johnson?" I said, helping him remember her name instead of referring to her only as a little girl.

"Yeah, that's who I'm talking about," he said, acting as if he really didn't want to mention her name. "That's a shame about what happened to the little girl."

"You know she isn't a little girl anymore, don't you?" I asked him.

"Well, come to think about it, I would imagine so," Blake said, somewhat embarrassed.

"Just thought you should know," I told him while making a sharp left bank, then dropping downward into a steep forty-five-degree bank to the right just in time for Karen to take out one of the creatures.

"Gal handling that goddamn machine gun like Rambo," Blake said with a huge smile on his face. "Wouldn't want to get into it with her. Hell no."

We could hear Tony in the back blasting away at something.

"Now just come at me again," he yelled at his target. "Yeah, that's right. I guess you must not have heard about me, mother-fucker!"

Gunfire could be heard coming from everywhere. The death toll was painful to think about, but the deployment of this mission was a more organized undertaking than anything the residents of Stonyford had faced. Most of them, regardless of their place in the community, had been unprepared for decisions that required them to help even their own blood relatives when those choices conflicted with their long-held religious beliefs.

As I continued searching the dark sky for potential creatures serving under Satan's elite command, bright lights from helicopters filled the skies over Stonyford. Thin, colorful traces of projectiles sped through the air in every direction, moving rapidly and illuminating a scene that looked almost unreal.

As aircraft sped down the makeshift runway and lifted into the air, I could see from high above the dark, dense shadows of what everyone had been describing as chimera monsters. Each of these creatures had wide, extended wings stretching nearly thirty feet across, with bodies shaped in grotesqueforms.

I then noticed three, possibly six, CH-47 Chinook helicopters attempting to take off from a nearby field where a huge double Ferris wheel lay tilted on its side after being toppled by one of the creatures. Each of the helicopters appeared to be carrying injured victims to local hospitals. Many of the wounded had been hurt not only by the carnival rides but also by snake bites and other species. In some cases, these creatures had become so widespread that certain counties had seen their populations reduced by the ability of the invasive species to adapt so quickly.

The Stonyford region had become a place heavily infested with snakes. The area was now overwhelmed with parasites carrying various viruses, breeding and spreading far beyond what had ever been expected.

Efforts to monitor and study these species had been devastating throughout the region. Scientists were trying to apply decades of knowledge and advanced biotechnology to control the outbreak and bring an end to the spread of these unknown creatures.

Circling around the Chinooks were what appeared to be attack helicopters. I soon recognized them as AH-64D Apaches. Each was heavily armed with ballistic missiles and cannon rounds capable of wiping out an entire village if the fleet found itself threatened by opposing forces.

I then noticed groups of potentially poisonous, disease-carrying lizards slithering their way into the many corpses scattered across the carnival grounds. Each of these reptiles was small, about the width of a baseball bat, yet their long tongues dripped thick saliva that they forced into the bodies they had chosen.

"Oh, no," Blake suddenly said, obviously worried by what he had seen on the ground below. "Please don't tell me you're actually going to try landing this thing down there. I mean, it's like this friggin place has gone batty tonight. And if you really think about it, there isn't even a full moon out tonight."

"Yeah, I think I know what you mean," I said, trying my best to avoid the word he expected to hear. "Things are a bit strange all over this place."

"Crazy, if you really wanna know the truth about it," Blake said in a disturbing tone. "I ain't never in all my years here in this town ever seen anything like what's been going on around here."

I guess when really thinking about it, I honestly believe the entire crew had by now become emotionally and mentally unsettled, as well as deeply troubled by the ongoing interference of the devil and his despicable group of fallen angels. They continued to disrupt just about everything on earth in spirit after the collapse of their attempt to overthrow heaven.

"This sight is really a disappointment to me," Blake said while staring out the window at the wounded lying helplessly on the ground. "I can't believe this is really happening."

We could easily see thousands of birds of prey flying throughout the dark sky with their short curved beaks and huge pointed wings spread outward like an overhead canopy. Each of these birds seemed to move with a calculated purpose, carefully circling and approaching whatever corpse they intended to claim.

"Hey, Doc. This is Tony. You copy?" Tony called from his mic.

"Copy," I answered. "What's up?"

Through all the loud gunfire, I was surprised it was even possible for me to hear Tony calling me, especially with his voice sounding almost like a whisper. I tried to glance back at him, but I could barely see past a few containers blocking my view. The door to the storage area was closed from what I could see. That was when I again found myself staring at Karen, who had locked onto something and was firing away. Whatever it was she was shooting at, it was impossible for her target to have any chance of survival. From what I could see, she was committing outright overkill on that target. Anyone witnessing it would consider it a one hundred percent certainty of destruction.

"Just in case you didn't know, something just grabbed an AH-64D as it was attempting to pull up," Tony said, sounding angry. "The only description I could get of the thing was that it looked just like a flying chimera monster or something."

"Man, what do you mean it grabbed it?" I asked him. "You sure?"

"No lie, Doc," he said, upset. "It's like it just glided through the sky, then snatched it and ran away."

"How the heck did it do that?" I said, really not wanting to believe what I was hearing. "Damn. Where'd it go?"

"Somewhere in the dark," he said, now sounding confused. "I really don't know."

"Boo-ya!" Karen yelled out loud. "Got me a Grendel monster."

"Wee-ha!" someone screamed with a cowboy accent. "Hey, y'all, here they come."

"Just what the hell is all the racket you making over there, Cowboy?" someone asked." "Just what you gotten yourself into now?"

Just as I thought, we had a real cowboy onboard this mission, and he went by the name of Cowboy. I'm really impressed by the thought of how this group of people have practically come out of nowhere in silence and dedicated themselves to this mission, most from as far away as the East Coast.

"I ain't got myself into nothin that I couldn't get myself out of, you know what I mean?" Cowboy said. "Just blasted the crap outta one of them there creatures. That's all."

"Well, did you get 'em?"

"Sent his ass straight back to wherever he came from," Cowboy said.

"Anybody know where that goddamn Seawood went to?" a voice asked on the radio.

"Yeah," someone said, snickering. "Last time I saw that fool, he was way back there somewhere chasing Snowflake."

"What'd you say?" I quickly asked. "Snowflake? Who, and what the hell is Snowflake?"

"Uh, is that you, Doc?" someone asked on the radio.

"Roger that," I said, slowly pulling back on the throttle to make a steep bank to my left.

"Snowflake is one of the young ladies piloting a glossy-looking AAS-72X+ Aerial Scout," Karen yelled out while firing the machine gun and occasionally looking at me. "I think they're from the Montana Hi-Line, somewhere up there in Shelby. But I do know a few of them are from a place nearby, Great Falls."

"That fool and his crew must be dreaming or something," a voice said. "Ain't no way he gonna get a piece of that."

"I heard that's why Seawood be having all them diseases," another crew member said. "He be catchin that stuff like a goddamn hailstorm."

"Everybody watch out for these giant-looking grasshoppers," someone yelled out on the radio.

"Man, you gotta be kidding me," a voice said. "They gonna leave all that soggy-looking green shit on my windshield."

I could then hear Tony in the back firing away at the grasshoppers somewhere behind us. Blake, on the other hand, seemed terrified by the sight of how these huge grasshoppers were busy eating up the town's livestock.

"What, hard to believe what you're seeing through that pair of night-vision binoculars?" I asked Blake.

"Can't believe what I'm seeing," Blake said.

"What you see is what's happening," I told him, occasionally staring down in the direction of the carnage caused by the grasshoppers.

"Incoming!" a voice rang out. "Giant grasshoppers just about everywhere you look and coming our way."

"Ah, man," someone said in shock. "Goddamn thing done wrapped its ugly self around another of our helicopters. Came out of nowhere and snatched it."

I wondered just how vulnerable each of these helicopters on this mission really was, considering the creatures threatening us were snatching them without hesitation. And considering ourselves professionals, our careers were, I guess you could say, pretty much coming to an end if we continued allowing these creatures to snatch our crew members.

"Man, fuck this shit," Tony yelled. "You ain't gonna keep snatching my family, motherfucker!"

The thought of what was happening to the crew made me realize an oversight I had to admit was mine, since I was the leader of this mission. I then ordered everyone to strike the enemy with everything they had.

"All right, you guys. It's once again that time," I told them. "Time to flip the script and make these faggots pay in a way they'd never expected. Let's destroy every one of them, including these freakin transvestite-looking creatures."

We could then hear static blaring loudly from the radio just as I finished declaring an all-out war on the enemy.

"You haven't fired a shot yet," I said to Blake. "Do you even know how to use that thing?"

"Oh, you talking to me?" he said, pressing his cheekbones together. "I was just—"

I'm more than sure the sheriff regretted his position as sheriff of Stonyford. He hadn't had any formal training or preparation for this part of the job. I couldn't see any real confidence in his expression except for a faint gleam of hope for the town's redemption, which he knew could come only from the man up above.

"You all right?" I asked him.

"I guess if I was one of them goddamn politicians sitting over there in one of them offices in Sacramento," he said in a somewhat irrational tone, "all my worries would be gone. I've learned not to ever underestimate those goddamn sons of bitches. You know what I mean?"

"Well, I really can't say that I disagree with you," I told him. "I mean, if that'll do any good. It's just overwhelming to think how your position as sheriff of Stonyford has placed you in something I'm glad I'm not dealing with."

"What, you wouldn't want to be in my position as sheriff?" he asked, staring directly at me. "You think I'm crazy or something?"

The only thing I could do was pause for a second or two, not wanting to answer his question too quickly. I also didn't want to sound rude. But I did answer, only to avoid certain topics that would lead to long, drawn-out discussions.

"No one has said anything about you being crazy," I said. "Quit trying to carry all the weight on your shoulders. You're not responsible for what's happening."

"Well, that makes me feel good to know that somebody agrees with me."

I watched him suddenly close his eyes tightly for a brief second, as if my words had given him some relief from all his worrying. I could sense he was deeply depressed about how Stonyford had become that peculiar country town considered the beginning stage of Satan's rise, just as some had feared.

"I wonder why nobody is communicating with each other," I mumbled out loud. "I really hate everyone being under these miserable conditions."

"Oh, my God," Blake suddenly blurted out. "Just look at that poor neighborhood down there. In spite of all the assistance around here, that police car just swerved so it wouldn't hit someone who was apparently trying to commit suicide."

It was my intention to drop down as quickly as possible in an effort to land, but my maneuverability was hindered by one of the Black Hawk medevac helicopters that happened to be pulling off an amazing steep bank downward, as if it intended to land in the same location I had chosen.

"Hey, I saw that," I said to the pilot flying the medevac helicopter.

"Oh, was that you I made that steep sharp curve around?" he asked while letting out a low snickering sound. "I'm sorry about that, but you know how it is there, Murdock. Had to make that loop to get down here."

"Yeah," I told him. "No problem."

"In case you didn't know, you guys are high-time celebrities back home."

"Is that right?" I said, suddenly realizing how this MH-53J Pave Low was accelerating across the dark sky and approaching an unbearable speed for any kind of touchdown. Before I knew it, the strength of the machine nearly had us disappearing behind the same mountains where other members of the crew had already used explosives to free themselves from disaster with the creatures.

"Are you still there, Doc?" the pilot of the medevac helicopter asked. "You guys ought to be landing by now."

"No, motherfucker," Tony suddenly yelled. "What we ought to be doing is kicking your ass."

"You self-centered ungrateful bastard!" a harsh voice said.

"Fuck you, motherfucker," Tony yelled again.

"I ought to blast your sorry ass to hell, you bitch," the voice said to Tony.

"Then start blasting, motherfucker," Tony said, furious.

"Really ain't worth my time, you bitch," the voice replied, laughing.

"Yeah, well, laugh when I get there," Tony said. "Laugh when I get there."

"I wonder just what the hell prompted that argument?" Blake said while adjusting his helmet.

"I don't know," I said, curious about the shouting match between Tony and the voice we thought had come from the medevac helicopter. "You having problems with the helmet, Blake?"

"It's this plastic covering," he said, pulling on the protective shield and leather strap, trying to tighten it around his chin. "Trying to get this thing to fit right."

"What's happening back there, Tony?" Karen asked him. "Can you hear me?"

"Yeah, I hear you," he answered, sounding disturbed. "I'm all right. Just thinking about that medevac helicopter making that crazy loop the way it did. Should have taken them out."

"Hold up," a voice suddenly said on the radio. "That wasn't any one of us on the medevac that you were arguing with."

"What?" Tony quickly asked. "Who is this?"

"I'm the pilot flying this thing," the voice said. "And it wasn't any of my crew members talking to you. We were listening too, and it wasn't anyone onboard the medevac that you were talking to."

"Then who was it if it wasn't you?" Tony asked.

"Damn if I know," the pilot of the medevac said, sounding confused. "I don't know."

"That sounds like it could be Ethan," I said, reaching for the throttle control.

"Hell yeah, Doc," Tony said through his helmet mic. "I bet that's who it was."

"I think that's who it is too," Karen said, firing a few rounds from the machine gun.

"So you think you got me all figured out, don't you?" the voice said on the radio and through the helmet speakers. "You'll never figure me out like I got you figured out. You hear me? Never."

"Hey, Doc. This is Seawood. You copy?"

"Copy you, Seawood," I answered. "What's up?"

"A big-ass crazy-looking dog just came out of nowhere and dove right into one of my crew member's helicopters."

"Damn, that's Ethan's dog," I quickly told him. "Tell your guy to land immediately. Don't waste any time. Do it now, before—"

"They're saying it just plummeted out of the sky while they were making a sharp bank and somehow landed in their helicopter, just missing the tail-end blades."

"Seawood, didn't you just hear what I said?" I asked, yelling. "That dog belongs to Ethan. It's the devil in the form of a dog getting ready to take your guys out."

Suddenly we could hear loud screaming over radio, followed

by a crashing noise, and then loud static.

"Man," Seawood yelled. "They just crashed and went down under the water."

"What water?" I asked. "Where are you?"

"They're somewhere over the lake," someone said. "That copter went in and sank really fast."

Seawood cried out on. "I just lost a few of my people, Doc. I think that dog had something to—"

"Anybody see where that helicopter went?" another voice asked.

"Hey there, buddy," someone said. "All we could see were lights blinking, and then it was gone. Just that quick."

"It went underwater just like the rest of them helicopters did," a woman's voice said, emotionally upset. "I couldn't believe what I was seeing out there."

"Hey!" someone started yelling. "I think it got another one up there by them mountains. Something is up there spinning like a goddamn UFO or something."

Strange but true. Just as all hell broke loose, the song "Eye of the Tiger" started blaring loudly through the transmitter. We could then hear loud whistles blowing as explosion after explosion signaled the attacks on the creatures scattered throughout the Stonyford region.

As the whistling sounds continued, we could see a burning platform with rapid movement circling around it. Later it was described as giant figures moving around the burning platform. Each of them held something in one hand that looked like a large brass horn, and each of the figures began to blow into it.

Thinking about what I was seeing, I thought about Margaret and how she had described, in important detail, the development of events like the ones unfolding now. Each seemed like part of a riddle Satan had set in motion. Remembering her warning against false false doctrines, I thought about the horns and what they might mean for Stonyford and the chilling events taking place across it. I then pressed the button on my control stick and set in motion the acceleration of the military-style .50 caliber machine gun mounted underneath the cockpit of the helicopter.

"Holy crap, man," Blake mumbled, shocked by the power of the helicopter's machine gun. "Outright devilish, isn't it?"

"Yeah, I suppose so," I said, staring intently out my side window. "We gotta hurry up and get out from between these mountains."

"Hey, Doc," a voice called out over the radio. "You got eight seconds to get out of there. Can't hold this switch indefinitely."

"Already out," I yelled, feeling the helicopter surge as we shot up and out from between the mountains.

"Oh, shit," Blake shouted while trying to reposition the AK-47 rifle. "Man, if it hadn't been for this seat belt, I'd probably have gone through one of these windows, or maybe even through the roof of this thing."

"Yeah, that could be right," I told him, smiling slightly. Knowing I couldn't stay between those mountains, I felt a certain satisfaction hearing the sheriff praise my quick move. It was like someone putting your favorite condiments on a meal. It felt good to hear that kind of admiration.

"You really know how to fly this thing," he said. "Maybe one day, when all this is behind us, you can teach me how to fly. I'd really like to learn your skills."

"You all right?" I asked Blake, noticing he was loosening his seat belt.

"Yeah," he said while still trying to unfasten the belt with one hand. "I think I done shit in my drawers when you made that quick move back there."

I then raised the MH-53J Pave Low higher, pushing the climb so we could shake off anything that might have latched onto the craft.

"These things look just like them Yeti creatures," someone said.

"You check out what they're doing?" another voice asked.

"No. What's that?"

"I think they're reversing themselves."

"What you mean?"

"Look over to your right, on top of that hill."

"Man. What the—"

"Hey, Doc. You copy that?"

"Copy, and on it," I said, watching the strange-looking creatures on top of one of the small hills turning around. "Looks like they're turning around just like he said."

"They're heading to the other side," someone said, sounding ready to start blasting. "Hey, I'mma drop a few grenades on 'em."

"Hold up," a voice sounding like MacDonald yelled. "Hold up before you do anything."

"Let him go ahead," someone else said, laughing. "We're thinking about adding a few sticks of dynamite along with your grenades."

"All right then," MacDonald said. "Let's do this so we can get the hell out of here."

"Is this where you guys came from?" Blake asked.

"A little further back," I told him. "That's when everything really started happening."

"What's the furthest you've ever been up here, you know, like when you were just a kid at the boys ranch?"

"I would say maybe at that small picnic area just a little ways past the boys ranch," I told him. "You know, where there is an airplane that I think crashed a long time ago."

"An airplane?" Blake said "What airplane?"

"Man," I said, tired of going into so many details about it. "It was just a small plane that I guess tried to land at the boys ranch, but instead ended up crashing near an old barn."

"And where was that?" he asked, curious.

"You know, up there by the boys ranch," I told him, hoping the questioning would come to an end.

"I'd sure wish I could see just what you're talking about up there," he said. "I'd really like to see it."

"We're not that far away from it," I told him. "But remember, Blake, it's still dark out, and—"

Before I knew it, we were en route to what seemed like another expedition back into the Stonyford mountains. I couldn't believe it, but it was happening. Although it carried deadly consequences, this was another mission with a purpose that had to be performed efficiently.

"Pee-wee, Cat, Knucklehead, and MacDonald," I suddenly called out on the radio. "You guys copy?"

"Who's that you're calling?" Blake asked while adjusting his seatbelt after returning from the bathroom.

"My guys, Sacro and Lodi," I told him, wishing he'd stayed in the back section of the craft. "Why?"

"Just wondering," he said, rubbing his hands together. "Now I see why you guys be flying these things."

"Oh, yeah," I said. "Is that right?"

"Oh hell yeah," he said, sounding impressed. "It's like you guys can go into different parts of the area without ever having to stop in any of the nearby towns you come across. With these things, all you have to do is keep flying right over 'em."

I then thought to myself just how foolish Blake really was. This guy was the sheriff of Stonyford, and yet he somehow seemed to lack even average intelligence.

"This is our profession," I told him. "What we do is in no way insubstantial. This crew has endured deadly attacks implemented by none other than the devil himself."

"It's hard to believe we're back here again," I could hear Tony saying. "Gotta repeat this shit all over again."

"Get a grip on yourself," someone said. "Better here than back in that town."

That's when I noticed flashing lights floating through the pitch-black sky alongside my craft, accompanying us back into the region where the devil's army began their terror. A light gray haze lingered in the air as if reluctant to evaporate.

"Thought you guys stayed with the action in Stonyford," I said, glad my team had joined us.

"Hey, Doc," Pee-wee said. "I copied you, but I guess you didn't hear me. I'm here with you, as usual."

"Roger that," I said while staring off to my right. "And where in the hell is Cat and MacDonald?"

"I think that's them over here on the right trying to light me up by shining that crazy-ass light on me," Karen said. "Keep that shit up and I'll have to aim my friend at you."

"Oh, no," someone said, laughing. "Please don't do anything like that. Lodi's on your side."

"Hey you guys, this is Knucklehead," he said. "Check out that area off to the right."

"Where is he talking about?" Blake asked, moving around in his seat.

"What the fuck is that?" someone said. "Just look at that."

"MacDonald," I called out. "This is Murdock. You copy?"

"Copy you, Doc," he said. "What's happening?"

"Need you to zero in on whatever it is down here," I told him.

"Roger that," he said. "Got a gentle breeze blowing up this way. You guys better pay attention to the atmosphere."

"It's a campground down there," Blake said. "That could possibly be a Buddhist meditation spot."

"Yeah, you could be right," I told Blake. "Especially with all the RVs and travel trailers down there. Looks something like a religious compound."

"Quite a few Winnebagos," Blake said. "And not the kind

you'd see at the fishing hole."

"Hey, Doc?" someone said on the radio. "You guys see what we see down there staring up at us?"

"Oh, yeah. I see it," Blake said, waving at the objects on the ground. "What the heck they doing down there?"

"Hold your positions," I said on the radio. "Don't nobody try landing. It got to be Ethan pulling this off."

"Ethan?" Blake said. "Just who the heck is Ethan?"

"The devil in disguise," I told him. "He should by now realize that we recognize his pattern."

"What pattern?" Blake asked. "What are you talking about?"

"The thing you were waving at on the ground," I told him.

"Oh, that," Blake said, sounding sympathetic. "That was just a little kid and his dog. He was waving. Maybe he needed our help or something."

"Wrong," a voice suddenly said. "We've been through this, and that kid wasn't trying to get nobody's attention. He's trying to take us out."

"Are you sure?" the sheriff asked, confused. "That was a little boy and his dog down there waving."

"That was Ethan," I told him. "The devil."

"I just can't see the devil trying to disguise himself like some little boy lost in the woods," Blake said firmly. "What you really need to do is turn this thing around and go back there to help that poor kid and his dog."

"I know you ain't talking to the Doc," Tony yelled. "Just keep being stupid and thinking that little boy won't take you out."

"Hell, I just knew you guys were a bunch of tough revolutionaries, unshakable by all that religious nonsense," Blake said in a slight mumble.

"Religious nonsense," Tony yelled. "Man, if only you knew."

"That's right. Religious nonsense," someone said, sounding offended. "You need to take his ass on back there, Doc, and drop him off so he can be with that little boy and his dog."

"Yeah, you're right," Blake exclaimed. "He can do just that, and I'll bet you me and that little kid can come walking outta here in no time. Better than what you're doin' for 'em."

"Looks like a few of the RVs exploded or something," Karen said, still gripping the machine gun. "I mean, just look at 'em."

"You sure about that little kid, Murdock?" Blake asked. "Wherever he and his dog went, 'cause now I don't even see 'em anymore."

"I know one thing for sure," Karen said. "All that blasting I've been doing hit the target. And I ain't got no problem busting loose on anything down on this campground. You guys feel me?"

"You ain't said nothin', Karen," Tony yelled while laughing. "That shit down there glistening like a bunch of stars looks like the reflection from all my blasting."

"Blake, when are you going to really use that AK-47?" Karen asked. "I ain't heard nothin' coming from that thing."

"I think he's scared," Tony said, snickering quietly.

"Doc," a voice called on the radio. "This is Cat. You copy?"

"Copy," I answered. "What's happening, Cat?"

"Hey, man. I just heard somebody on the transmitter saying they're having problems with the Verruck slide," Cat said, expressing concern. "It was something about people being sliced and cut up just like they did on the Mega slide where all those kids were seriously hurt."

"You just heard that on the transmitter?" I asked Cat.

"That's right," Cat said. "It's all kinds of shit going on."

"Hey you guys," a voice came over the radio. "We got some strange-looking things moving around down there at that campground."

"Hey, Cat," I said.

"Yeah," he answered.

"Try making contact with somebody about the situation going on," I told him. "Let me know what's happening."

"MacDonald's on it, Doc," he said emotionally. "Man, it's really bad, whatever is happening. Damn. Here it is, we just not too long ago left from Stonyford, and just that quick all kinds of shit is happening."

"It's like I already told you," I said, reminding him. "Try making contact and let 'em know that help is on the way."

"What's those things moving around down there?" Blake asked, leaning to one side with his head out the window. "They're moving around, and some of 'em are staring up here at us."

Just as I was about to tell Karen to zero in on whatever it was the sheriff was talking about, both Karen and Tony abruptly started blasting away. There was no question about it. They were using unrestricted power against whatever was on the ground with no intention of letting up.

When I turned my attention to the sheriff, who was trying to cover his ears, I couldn't help thinking about how badly he was disgracing himself. I wondered how a man in his position could become such a blemish on this mission. In truth, as the head sheriff of Stonyford, he had buried a fear inside himself that no one ever knew existed.

"Bloodshed all over this motherfucker," someone said. "Killing all these sorry-ass motherfuckers."

"Turned these motherfuckin' creeks into bloodstreams," Tony yelled.

"And we done just about got all these bloodsuckin' bitches," Karen said, laughing. "What? You want some of this too?"

I then thought about how bloodthirsty these creatures were, murderous things preying on the people of this region like parasites. Now they were trying to cling onto the members of my crew.

"Everybody listen up," I said, while hovering just above the campground. "We've all gone through this since arriving in this area. I'm sure you guys know this battle against these creatures is about to become even more deadly than before. Extremely lethal is a better way to put it. And it's going to be fatal to most of the people throughout half, if not all, of the northern region of California. This is going to be an intense battle, but as you know, it's our mission as professional journalists and media strategists to get the job done."

"Hey, Doc. This is Cat," he said. "You copy?"

"Copy," I answered. "What's up?"

"Are we staying up here for now?" he asked.

"Cat," I mumbled. "Truth is, it wasn't even my intention to end back up here. You feel me? The sheriff wanted to see something, and here we are back where we started from. So with that said, and hopefully with the strength to come out the other side of this ugly battle like a rose, I think it's time for you guys to tighten up your trousers and grip your bats, because it's time to start swinging."

"Yeah, like we ain't done this before," Karen said snobbishly.

"Where all y'all motherfuckers at anyway?" Tony said while swinging the .50 caliber across the gunwale. "Where all you funky monsters at?"

"Monster creatures," someone else called out. "Come out to play."

"Mmm," the sheriff mumbled. "Got these young men up here sounding like that Blooper stuff I remember watching on TV."

"Yeah, but," I said, staring directly at him. "Only thing about this game is that you die if you get caught sleepin'. You know what I mean?"

An all-out war between both good and evil was only minutes away from erupting high above the region overlooking the small town of Stonyford, California, while the song "Chase Me" by Con-Funk-Shun blared loudly on every transmitting system.

"What the!" the sheriff said at the sudden sight of the creatures reappearing on both sides of the helicopter. "Where the hell they coming from?"

"The campground," Karen shouted. "They're all over the place."

"Hey, Doc," a voice called out on the radio. "It's Pee-wee. You copy me over there?"

"Copy you, Pee-wee," I answered. "Whassup, bro?"

"According to the report about this place, we gotta use caution when approaching."

"That's what I intend to do," I told him. "But just what are you saying?"

"There's commotion going down there nearby where those RVs are all parked in a circle," he said. "I think they're waiting on us to land."

"Hey, you want me to start blasting on 'em?" Karen asked. "I got a damn good shot from here."

"Think you can penetrate one of 'em, Sheriff?" I asked, surprising him.

Blake waited a full thirty seconds before responding. "I really don't know about this, Doc," he said nervously.

"You all right?" I asked.

"I think I just saw something like one of them African monkeys riding something through the sky," he said, showing signs of embarrassment. "I think it was a Guenon monkey riding on the back of a giant butterfly that looked like a moth."

I knew he was right about what he saw, but knowing me, I had to question him as though I didn't believe it. "You did?" I asked. "But how could it be in all this blackness around this place? I mean, how could you even see anything like that as dark as it is?"

"Because of this thing," he said, pointing at the pair of night optics.

"Just thought I'd ask," I told him, smiling.

Suddenly a voice rang out over the transmitter saying something about the situation in Stonyford. "We need all the help we can get," the person screamed. "Everything's in complete disarray."

We could then hear distress calls coming from just about every radio and transmitting system.

"What in heaven's name is going on?" the sheriff asked. "It's like a goddamn hostile intrusion going on around here."

"Just the devil and all his stumbling blocks," I said. "Think he really trying to reverse God's creation."

"From what I'm hearing, Stonyford is being demolished," Karen yelled.

"Yeah, and in what unprecedented terms?" the sheriff asked. "This shit is just like a story you read in one of them goddamn novels. I ain't heard about any of this being controlled. From what I can see, every one of these creature-looking things is responsible for this turmoil. They're unrestrained, if you ask me. Unruly and definitely unequaled with all their madness, like a goddamn ground ready to give way at any moment."

*

To be completely truthful, I didn't understand anything Blake was saying, and I wasn't trying to be unkind.

There was no reason for me or anyone else to pretend sympathy for what was happening. Lucifer's attack on this region carried immoral purpose and deadly consequences of every kind. But I was just as certain as ever that the devil himself was behind what was unfolding.

Lucifer's behavior would prove contrary to natural law, something inhuman and relentless in its destruction. Unknowingly to the residents of this region, the entire operation had been designed under false pretenses and would, at the proper moment, expose itself in full without mercy.

Most people were going to suffer because of their failure to recognize the danger before them, their irrational behavior opening the door to the influence of Satan himself. Death would move through the region and claim the town of Stonyford as its own.

*

"Incoming!" a voice rang out on the transmitter. "Incoming!"

Every electronic system onboard the craft was now in full operation, sensors detecting something within striking distance of our helicopter. This was the moment when we either broke free from Satan's grip or fell deeper into it.

"Anybody copy this out there?"

"Anybody copy this?"

"Anybody out there?"

"Somebody, anybody, copy."

"Please copy."

"Somebody?"

"Copy?"

...

Acknowledgments

I am indeed grateful to those who so generously supported me under very difficult circumstances.

I particularly want to thank: Thomas J. Drennan, Theodore Redmond, Jr. (out of Topeka, Kansas) and the entire Redmond family, Dylan Turner, Cavan Brownlee, Raymond (Baandz) Rigazio, Jeffrey Baumann, and my generous friend, Joshua Lee Hayes Jr.

And finally, the staff at Word Out Books, who so graciously lifted me up.

About the Author

Bennie Ray Murdock is a fiction writer whose work explores horror through surreal, dreamlike narratives. His stories often blur the line between imagination and reality, placing him among the characters he creates.

Originally from the San Francisco Bay Area, Murdock has lived across the western United States. He currently resides in Kansas, where he continues to write.

Outside of writing, Murdock is a passionate aviation enthusiast. He fondly recalls flying aircraft such as the Cessna 150, 172, and 182, as well as a 1971 Aero Commander and a Piper Navajo Chieftain. His love of flight extends to helicopters and vintage warbirds, including the Bell 206B and the iconic 1945 P-51D Mustang.

He dedicates his work to the memory of his late wife, Vanessa, whose presence continues to inspire his creative journey.

www.ingramcontent.com/pod-product-compliance
Lightning Source LLC
LaVergne TN
LVHW030918080826
845145LV00013B/2946

9781947035683